"Lonzo, listen," the voice said. It was eerie and soft. "You're the only one I can talk to."

"Well, just hold it for the show," Gates said.

"I can't hold it. Lonzo . . . a conspiracy . . . a big one . . . killers," he said. "A Federal attorney named Lucius Darling. Kill everybody." His voice was coming quicker now, almost out of control. "You're the guy to uncover it. Only you. Make you a star again."

The man spoke again after pausing for a breath. "Nixon."

"What about Nixon?" Gates demanded.

"Nixon. A plot. Back in the seventies. Jericho Day. Jericho Day. Jer . . . "

All that Gates heard was a dial tone.

"Hello, hello, hello," Gates said. There was no answer . . .

WARREN MURPHY

JERICHO DAY

HarperPaperbacks

A Division of HarperCollinsPublishers

This is a work of fiction. The characters, incidents, and dialogues are products of the author's imagination and are not to be construed as real. Any resemblance to actual events or persons, living or dead, is entirely coincidental.

HarperPaperbacks *A Division of* HarperCollins*Publishers*
10 East 53rd Street, New York, N.Y. 10022

A hardcover edition of this book was published in 1989 by Diamond Books.

This book was published by arrangement with the author.

Cover illustration by Bernie Perrini

First HarperPaperbacks printing: March 1991

Printed in the United States of America

HarperPaperbacks and colophon are trademarks of HarperCollins*Publishers*

10 9 8 7 6 5 4 3 2 1

For Devin, Prince Philip,
Wrestle-man, St. George, Popeye,
Buckaroo, and Big Guy.
With love.

CHAPTER ★★★★★★ 1

The Near Future

MAYBE, OF EVERYTHING, HE HATED THE radio shows the most. He couldn't be sure, because he did not remember the past very well, but fifteen or twenty years ago the shows had seemed to be fun. At least, back then, everyone he talked to appeared to agree with him.

But now? Was there anybody anywhere who agreed with Lonzo Gates anymore?

Now the last phone caller: "Are we living in the same world?"

Just by hearing his voice, Lonzo Gates knew him. He had known him and hated him all his life. The caller was a rich kid. He had grown up eating Wheaties with skim milk. He kept his shoes shined. He had never had athlete's foot, a cavity, or acne. No hay fever. No nasal blockage. He had gone to a Catholic school. He was sleek, contented, and well fed. Gates knew him all right. He was *the enemy* and now he was saying, "Are we living in the same world?"

"I don't know. What world are *you* living in?" Lonzo Gates answered and smirked smugly at the woman engineer watching him from behind the plate glass of the radio control booth.

"I'm living in the real world," the caller snapped back. "Maybe you ought to visit it sometime."

He had the nerve to say that. And there it was, going out all over New York City and even into the suburbs, out there across the Hudson River and up north of the Tappan Zee Bridge, where ladies with blue hair kept plastic spoon rests as souvenirs of Atlantic City and had pictures of Jesus Christ with eyes that moved when you looked at them. And now those women were smirking at this clown who had the nerve to talk to Lonzo Gates like that.

Gates rubbed his bloodshot eyes. A small consolation, very small, was that nobody really listened to the show anymore, a little once-a-month radio call-in show on a New York station whose call letters nobody could remember.

In the old days, in the sixties, it was different. The show was on every week, and "Talking with Lonzo" was a smash hit, a cultural event. Everybody who counted tuned in. Lonzo was the counter-culture king of the United States. His column in *Mossback, The Magazine for Free Thinkers*, pioneered a new kind of journalism and was "must-read" around the world. Even the *New York Times* commented on his stuff back then. He saw a conspiracy in every

Washington chamberpot. He told the truth as he saw it and covered every story through his own personal vision. Sometimes his coverage was as big an event as the story he was covering. A whole world seemed to listen to him. President Jimmy Carter once called him "one of those uncensored voices whose continuing freedom is the greatest testament to our American way of life."

And now he, Lonzo Gates, great testament to the American way of life, was reduced to listening to this smug, sanctimonious little snot get shitty with him on the telephone.

Gates sipped treacly Southern Comfort liqueur from the styrofoam cup on the announcer's table, which was spread with papers, copies of his columns from the past, and tried desperately to think of something to say to this cretin who probably thought that America was just fine the way it was.

Before he could speak, though, the caller was talking again. Now he said, "You know, maybe all this conspiracy doo-doo was big back in the sixties when you were working, but it's crap today and we all know it. You can't have a conspiracy in the United States anymore because the mutts of the press are always chewing through everybody's garbage pail. There aren't any secrets left in the United States."

Lonzo Gates finally had something he could respond to. "The press?" he said and hooted like a wild man. He glanced at the engineer in the booth. She was looking away. Maybe he had hooted too loud. "The press?" he said again and did not hoot this time. "You think they really expose anything? They're in the pocket of the power structure. You think the *New York Times* cares about the truth? Or the *Washington Post*? Or CBS? With all those commercials and advertisements they run? Forget it. They only care about their bottom line. Profits, me bucko..." From time to time he talked like that; he thought it was fitting for a man who considered himself the grand old man of American journalism. "Profits are at the heart of everything. If somebody uncovered a CIA scheme to kill the chancellor of Canada and the people at Coca-Cola said 'kill the story,' it'd never see the light of day. And that's the truth."

He was going to cut the caller off now, feeling he had recovered just a little bit. But before Gates could snap off something quick and witty and dismissive, the caller said disgustedly, "Canada doesn't have a chancellor and there's just no point in talking to you anymore. You're a damned dinosaur."

Click!

Click? The little yuppie sonofabitch had had the nerve to hang up on him? Lonzo Gates? Who was once almost nominated for a Pulitzer Prize?

Gates looked at the telephone in his hand. He took another sip of the Southern Comfort from the plastic cup on the scarred wooden table, then glanced up and saw the engineer signaling wildly from the control booth. Ooops, dead air. Nobody liked it. The bane of radio land. Screw radio land. Screw this show. Why did he do this junk anyway?

Gates said, "And now that that redneck is off the telephone, we'll pause for a few commercials. Listen to them, folks, but don't believe them and don't buy anything you don't check out yourself. Don't pollute your own environment. We're 'Talking with Lonzo,' and we'll be right back as long as the liquor holds out."

He clicked off the microphone switch and looked at the booth, waiting for the engineer's signal that they were off the air.

Then he said, "Surly little prick." He knew his voice came over the speaker in the control booth and he waved the telephone receiver to let her know that he was talking about the last phone caller. The engineer shrugged. "Whatever happened to Americans?" Gates wondered aloud.

"Maybe they all grew up," the engineer said calmly in a light Southern accent.

"Grew up to be brain dead, you mean," Gates said. He sipped his drink again. Three minutes of commercials. Thank God. Three minutes in which he didn't have to listen to these goddamn Wall Street bankers explain how he was wrong and how America seemed to be working quite nicely. Didn't they know anything? Couldn't they see that the whole country was a living lie? Land of the free . . . What free? Who was free? Not anybody who worked for a living. They were the slaves of rich capitalist thugs who polluted the world and didn't care about anything except profits. Who was free? The blacks? They might just as well still be picking cotton. Women? Women were never free. There was just no equality for women, he thought, and glanced up to see the young engineer reaching high up over her head to make some adjustments on the radio board. She had a nice chest. That was the first thing he noticed when he came in today and saw her on duty for the first time. She didn't seem to know who he was and just kept staring at his hairline and he wanted to yell at her, "Not the hairline, the face! The face is famous." But she seemed fascinated by his hairline. Did she think he was too old? Did she know that in the old days he had to beat the girls away with a stick? Did she care? Did anybody care about anything important anymore?

It was all Richard Nixon's fault. That bastard had left office and America didn't have anybody to hate anymore, and Lonzo Gates was shrewd enough to know that his kind of journalism needed hate to survive. How could you hate Ford or Carter or Reagan or Bush or the new guy? Nobody hated pabulum. But you could hate Nixon. He lived to be hated. The evil, egg-sucking sonofabitch. Gates remembered one of his great columns in which he had suggested that Richard Nixon wasn't an American at all, but a clever Russian spy sent over here to prove, by his performance and person, that America's political system just could not work. Any system that could elect a Richard Nixon was doomed to failure.

Gates had based the Russian spy business on "Nixon's curious features. At one time I had thought them to be simian, but that never struck me as quite right. Then I realized the truth. Richard Nixon didn't remind me of an ape but of Leonid Brezhnev... the same eyebrows, the same evil eyes, the same lecher's mouth... to look at the two of them side-by-side is to suddenly have the truth revealed in a blinding Alamogordo flash of insight. The prick's a Red agent."

Gates looked at the small telephone console in front of him. It was the size of a loaf of bread and could handle eight calls at once. That was another thing. In the sixties and seventies, he had to have a person working with him to man the telephones because the calls had come in so heavily. The console then had looked like a Christmas tree, although that description had never really popped into his mind because he felt Christmas was a pagan commercial kind of thing that no thinking person would ever have any truck with. God neither. In his columns, Gates was always careful not to capitalize God... g-o-d... "small letters for a small concept."

These days, the telephone board was as dead as

a pet rock and lately, a lot of times, he had been forced to vamp through his hour-long show, reading from his old columns while waiting for somebody to call.

He glanced up at the control room. The engineer was sitting back down, smoothing her shirt over her nice breasts. Gates thought that he would like to help her smooth her shirt. He glanced at the clock. Another minute before coming back on the air to do another dismal thirty minutes of this crap. He sipped his Southern Comfort. A light flashed on the console. He flipped the button and lifted the telephone receiver to tell the caller to hold on until the show came back on the air.

"This is Lonzo. We'll be back on in a minute so hold your comments."

"Lonzo, listen," the voice said. It was eerie and soft, as if the man were whispering. "You're the only one I can talk to."

"Well, just hold it for the show. Only forty more seconds," Gates said.

"I can't hold it. Lonzo ... a conspiracy ... a big one ..." His voice was coming quicker now, almost out of control, as if the man were trying to get it all out before his breath passed from his chest. "You're the guy to uncover it. Only you. Make you a star again."

Again? Christ, did *everybody*, including this asthmatic old bastard, think he was washed up?

The man was still talking, faster now, his voice even softer. "Killers," he said. "A federal attorney named Lucius Darling. Kill everybody. Somebody should tell the story. You can."

Another nut. Didn't they ever stop?

But his ears perked up when the man spoke again after pausing a long time for breath. "Nixon."

"What about Nixon?" Gates demanded.

"Nixon. A plot. Back in the seventies. Jericho Day."

"What?"

"Jericho Day," the man repeated.

Gates looked at the clock again. Only a few seconds left. This sounded promising. "Listen," he said, "we're coming back on. Hold on for a second and then tell me about it on the air."

"Can't. Jericho Day. Jericho Day. Jer..."

Gates put the phone down on its side and when the engineer waved her arm, he flipped on the microphone switch.

"Back again. We're 'Talking with Lonzo' and we've got an interesting call for you. So stay right there and let's see what's going on out in the boonies." He picked up the telephone. "Okay, let's talk. You're 'Talking with Lonzo.'"

But all that he heard was a dial tone.

"Hello, hello, hello," Gates said weakly.

There was no answer.

CHAPTER ★★★★★★ 2

"WHAT DO YOU CALL THIS?"

"What do you mean what do I call it? I call it my column. The same column I've been writing for twenty years." The damned Philistines were running things and they had no sense of history. *Mossback*, in the sixties and seventies, had been a great magazine, first with everything—first with the exposé of the Warren Commission's report, first with the murder of Marilyn Monroe, first with the CIA's plans to wipe out New York City with poison gas in the event that Ed Koch got elected, first with the report on plans by America's police organizations to burn down black neighborhoods.

The scoops were never-ending. How Lee Harvey Oswald had been hired by the Teamsters to kill President Kennedy. How no bill could become law unless it were personally approved by Nelson Rockefeller. How John Lennon was murdered by the Israeli Mossad because he and Abbie Hoffman were planning to reunite the Beatles for a concert to raise money for the Palestinians.

But all those great stories had been published when *Mossback* was a go-go magazine and Lonzo Gates had been its biggest star. Now the damned magazine was in the hands of the accountants. Like this new twerp of an editor. Where did they get these people?

The editor was a short man with blow-dried hair. He wore a three-piece suit. Gates decided America had gone to hell as soon as editors started wearing three-piece suits. Lonzo had grown up in an age where editors, real editors, wore earth shoes and had little leather pouches on their belts to hold their stash. This bastard would think a pouch was to hold his change for the parking meter. Asshole.

The editor's watery blue eyes glanced around the room at the four assistant editors who were sitting around the table. All new. All in three-piece suits. All younger than Lonzo Gates. Who needed this crap?

The editor said, "I know it's the same column you've been writing for twenty years. That's the trouble with it. It's old." He looked around the room. "Just listen to this crap."

He cleared his throat and started to read from the papers in his hand.

"Dick, Dick, Dick, Dick, Dick. Dirty Dick, Dirty Dick, Dirty Dick. Richard the Turd, Richard the

Turd, Richard the Turd. Poor-no-more Richard. Poor-no-more Richard. Poor-no-more Richard. Dick, the Dirty." He paused. "And so on. Anyway, we get the idea. So what does this all mean?"

"What it means," Gates responded quickly, "is all the nicknames of Richard Nixon. I think it's a good column." He looked around at the other four editors, knowing he would get no support there, but hoping for it anyway. Not one of them had cracked even a smile during the reading; now not one of them would meet his eyes.

"I *know* that these are the nicknames for Richard Nixon," the editor said. "What I wonder is, why? Richard Nixon isn't the president of the United States anymore. What he is is some retired old bastard who lives in fucking New Jersey. Who cares about his fucking nicknames?"

Gates felt his face growing red. Christ, he could use a drink. In the old days he would have brought his Southern Comfort right in here, but this gang wouldn't understand. An awful thought chewed its way into his mind and he tried to push it away but it wouldn't go. He faced up to it. He was frightened of these men. Frightened of being fired.

"A lot of people care about Richard Nixon," Gates said.

The editor shook his head. Not a single hair moved from its original position. "Nobody but you," he said. "Not anymore." He tossed the five pages of

Gates's column onto the big conference table around which they were all seated. The pages scattered. Nobody bothered to gather them and put them in the proper order.

No. No. It wasn't possible, was it? Was it possible that they weren't going to use his column? For the first time in twenty-five years, they were going to publish an edition without a column by Lonzo Gates?

As if he were wired into Gates's head and heard the question there, the editor said, "We can't run this junk. Richard Nixon is old news. Nobody gives a rat's ass about him anymore." He paused and then tried a smile and said mock-plaintively, "Lonzo, Lonzo, Lonzo. What are we going to do with you?"

"Just run my column. That's all you have to do with me. That's what the readers want."

The editor looked at the four other men in the room. Gates did too. He'd bet that every one of them had gone to Wharton Business School. They all nodded at the editor who said, "Not so, Lonzo. Not so. We just got in the results of our new readers' survey. More people read our TV previews than read your column. It's not the sixties anymore."

He was making that up. Gates knew it. Horse dung. *More people read our TV previews than read your column.* What a lot of crap. Did he expect Gates to buy that? Lonzo felt like demanding to see the readers' survey but decided he was too tired to wade through a lot of numbers, even if it would prove his point that his column was still the cornerstone of *Mossback*.

"We have to have different stuff," the editor said. "Stuff that makes news. Stuff that gets people quoting your column again. Stuff that puts you back in the headlines. Lonzo Gates, crusading columnist for *Mossback* magazine, revealed today...stuff like that, Lonzo. Like you *used* to do. Stories that make news. Lonzo Gates, the great Gonzo journalist. Do you have anything like that in mind?"

This is serious, Gates thought with mounting panic. *These bastards are going to can my column and next they're going to can me.* He felt his palms grow wet and almost instantly, sweat began dripping from his armpits onto his sides. It felt cold. Cold as death. Cold as unemployment. Cold as wondering where your next meal would come from. Did these Wharton twerps know anything about that kind of cold?

What to tell these maniacs? Something. Something. He had to have something.

He smiled in what he hoped was a friendly, we're-all-on-the-same-team-fellas manner and said, "Well, I do have a story that I've been working on. Something that might be right in line with this new direction you're taking *Mossback* in."

The editor raised a finger and Gates thought, *They won't even give me that. They won't even let me save face.* And as he knew the man would, the editor said, "Not a new direction. The old direction but with new life and vitality."

Up yours with new vitality, Gates wanted to say. But instead he just nodded. "Well, as I said, I'm working on something like that."

"What is it?" the editor said.

"I can't tell you about it now," Gates said. "Not until I verify it from other places so my sources don't get handed up. But it's a story of a big government conspiracy."

"To do what?"

"Really, I can't tell you about it yet. It just wouldn't be right," Gates said. For good measure, he tossed in, "And it might be dangerous to some people."

"Okay," the editor said with a patronizing smile, so unnaturally filled with teeth that it resembled the senior class project at orthodontics school. "Protecting your sources. We can all understand that."

Gates just nodded. He could feel his heart pounding.

"When do you think you might have this piece in hand?" the editor asked.

"Just a couple more weeks."

"And does this story have a working name?"

"Yeah. You can call it Jericho Day."

The editor looked at his four clones sitting around the room. When he smiled, they smiled.

"Hey," the editor said. "Good stuff. Good title. You run with it, Lonzo." He gestured toward the pages of Gates's column still spread around the conference table. "And we'll just forget this column for this issue. It's not worthy of you."

You're not worthy of me. None of you are, Gates thought. But he only smiled as the editor nodded in a clear signal of dismissal.

Later, behind the locked door of his dirty office, Gates poured himself a drink from the bottle he kept in his bottom desk drawer.

It was all over, he realized. This week they had canned his column and he would not be far behind. The new *Mossback* wasn't interested in hard-hitting stuff anymore; these business school editors had wanted to turn it into a glitz magazine: "Michael J. Fox's Tragic Secret" . . . "Joan Collins—Never Too Late for Love."

Lonzo Gates didn't belong on a magazine like that. It was time to start looking for new work. He could buy a couple of weeks time by jerking them around with this Jericho Day business and maybe, by the time they had caught on, he would have landed on a payroll someplace else.

He retopped his drink.

Jericho Day. Maybe it really was something.

He remembered the man's voice on the telephone. He sounded afraid. Or in pain.

Why hadn't he held on to talk some more?

What the hell was Jericho Day?

CHAPTER ★★★★★★ 3

The Mid-1970s

Monday, October 17: The First Day

BACK HOME IN TROY, OHIO, LUCIUS DARL-
ing's position as an assistant attorney general of the
United States, Antitrust Division, rated him a seat
on the dais and an introduction at the annual dinner
of the Miami County Bar Association.

But in twelve years with the Justice Department
in Washington, D.C., that same position had rated
Darling exactly two closeup looks at an attorney
general of the United States. Both times, Darling had
been part of a group.

The last time had been in May 1967, when Darling's entire unit was called up to the fifth floor for
an announcement. The staff had been nervous.

"He can't abolish our division," another assistant AG had told Darling. "He'd have to find us
first."

This met with nervous laughter. They waited in the big room for a while and then the attorney general had entered through a side door, a gangling Texan who spoke in diminishing words as if he were going to be interrupted any second and would be grateful for it.

The AG had told them that their division would be expanded because "there is a growing need for it today."

"A great and grievous need," corrected an aide standing behind him.

The attorney general laughed graciously and easily, his right hand thrust boyishly into his jacket pocket. Like many tall men, he seemed to stoop.

"A great and grievous need," drawled the AG. "I didn't want you to read it in the *Washington Post* and have you say I never told you personally."

"The attorney general is putting this in a memo," interjected the aide.

"I'm just making the *Washington Post* honest," the AG said. "Their story today will say that I told you personally."

"We'll all swear to it," called out the assistant AG who had been nervous about their unit being abolished.

"Then thank you for coming," the AG had said. He had shaken everyone's hand, then had gone on to run unsuccessfully for the United States Senate.

Lucius Darling never saw him again.

The other AG he had met did successfully launch himself into the Senate. That was Robert Kennedy. Darling was young in the Justice Department, and being introduced to new AG Kennedy in the fifth-floor auditorium was like meeting a visiting politician.

"This is Lucius Darling," a Kennedy aide had said. "He's with antitrust and he's a comer."

"Glad to meet you, Darling. How do you like your job?" Kennedy had asked. He was short and wore elevator shoes and for all the talk about his toughness, he appeared vulnerable to a stiff wind.

"It's all right. I've been thinking of some changes."

"Good, good. Get 'em on paper and let's see them. I like changes. You've got to change even to stay the same."

Then Robert Kennedy was off to the next man down the line, then to his Senate seat, and ultimately to a bullet in a California hotel when a Palestinian outvoted California, Oregon, and Wisconsin with a .22-caliber pistol.

And now, five attorney generals and some dozen years later, Darling was going to meet the third attorney general of his life.

But this time was different. Darling had been summoned, individually, and he had ridden up the three floors in the elevator alone.

He sat in a brown leather chair inside the yellow-carpeted reception room on the fifth floor of the Justice Department building as the attractive blonde secretary looked up his name in a red leather appointment book.

Darling had developed the Washington habit of looking at people's appointment books and the Washington skill of reading upside down. He craned his neck slightly and saw his name and then nothing below it which, for the attorney general, probably meant golf this mild autumn day.

Darling knew this meeting was going to be short. He would be thanked for his work, get his hand shaken, and leave with only a notation in the secretary's book that Darling, Lucius, had on a certain day, at a certain time, met with the AG to implement his resignation which, like that news story some eight years earlier, had already been settled by government machinery. A formality.

Which suited him fine. His conscience was free of nagging because he had put in a dozen years at Justice, often ten hours a day, taking work home, giving up many weekends, even once giving up a week of his vacation. Screw 'em. Enough.

"The attorney general will see you now, Mr. Darling," said the secretary, and Lucius nodded a thank you that he had been told at one time was pleasant. He was a rugged thirty-nine years old, powerful enough in the chest and shoulders to make his six-feet-one seem almost average height until people got up close to him and realized how big he truly was. He had the sort of strong face, well softened by flesh, that could encourage some to attempt to deceive him. He had been told many times that he had a kind face and that his blue eyes matched his name.

Darling took to jokes about his name as an unbroken horse took to saddle. After a little bucking early in his life—"Actually I chose my last name just to see how many idiots would comment on it"— he came to accept it and to accept that other people, hearing the name for the first time, would be naturally tempted to comment. It also made it possible to tell which people didn't think before they spoke, and that was a good thing to be able to find out at the mere cost of having an unusual name.

The attorney general of the United States did not make a joke of Lucius Darling's name.

Darling was led through a Persian-rugged conference room that seemed to be choking on a wall-to-wall table. The secretary pushed open the end door, then walked away, leaving Darling standing there.

"C'mon in. Sit down. Let's get to business," said Attorney General James V. Walthrop, former senator from Ohio, former governor of Ohio, and one of the few who chose to end his career in the Justice Department instead of launching it from there. He had a face like a well-used hatchet and wore a light blue suit with a vest. His desk was like a mahogany playing field.

"You're an Ohio boy, too," said Walthrop as Darling entered.

"Yes, sir."

Walthrop rested his elbows on the desk, one hand atop the other. He looked squarely at Darling and did not refer to notes when he talked, something Darling always noticed. A man who sneaked glances at notes wanted you to believe he cared or that he knew more than he did. A man who referred openly to notes was more honest but was either unprepared or uninvolved. A man who knew details and looked you in the eye was a man who could make a decision because he knew what he was talking about.

It seemed curious to Darling, however, that a formality goodbye would warrant the attorney general bothering to look up Darling's birthplace.

"What do you think of the way the Justice Department works, Darling?"

"Which part, sir?" asked Darling, while wondering why Walthrop had a smaller office than some of his subordinates. "There's criminal and fraud and tax, not to mention antitrust. It's a big outfit, sir, as you know."

"Try the political trials, or the ones labeled political by the defendants after they've trespassed, advocated violent overthrow of the government, incited to riot, rioted, carried illegal arms, fled interstate to avoid arrest and then left the courtroom free, ready to sell their memoirs to some goddamn scandal sheet."

"Oh. Those."

"Those," said Walthrop icily.

"Sir, I don't think it's ethical for me for me to comment on a fellow attorney's competence."

"Ah, so you think we muffed them."

"I didn't say that, sir. Any such comment would imply a judgment on a fellow attorney's performance."

"Unless, of course, the bastards were innocent," Walthrop said.

"You've just convicted them, sir."

"So I have. That's partly because I have read the newspapers and seen television and frankly I don't see how you can fail to get a conviction on someone who commits a crime before fifty million people on television. Fifty million. Sonofabitch is standing in front of the cameras with a Kalishnikov automatic rifle. That's an illegal possession charge right there."

"Sir, you know you would have to prove that it was not an imitation weapon, that the weapon recovered was indeed the weapon he held, and that the weapon worked. With a firing pin filed off or something like that, it's not a weapon but a Hollywood prop."

Walthrop paused a moment. In the silence, Darling could hear the crackling of the fireplace and without turning around, he knew Walthrop was burning artificial logs of sawdust and paraffin. Another reason to go home. Back to real America, where people burned wood, real wood, in their fireplaces.

Darling could feel in his stomach the tension of the pause and reminded himself that this man staring at him would not be his boss by tomorrow.

"You're absolutely right," said Walthrop. "How long do you think it would take us to find out why we're having so much trouble with these cases? I could swear these things are open and shut for conviction, right up until the verdict. And then we blow it."

"I couldn't estimate, sir. First of all, what do you mean by 'these cases'? Do you mean college kids arrested for trashing some dormitory, or the Black Panther trials, or the Chicago Seven during the 1968 Democratic convention? What cases?"

"These headline-grabbing cases where we have them dead to rights and they walk out as national celebrities. The whole radical conspiracy."

"It's hardly a conspiracy, sir. It's right out in the open." He looked past Walthrop's right shoulder, through the tall windows that overlooked Constitution Avenue, and ventured a small smile. "It'd be the first conspiracy in history where you could get all the conspirators by buying subscriber lists to their revolutionary newsletters."

"And that too. Why aren't they in jail for ad-

vocating the violent overthrow of the American government? That's a crime. It even used to carry the
death penalty until our Supreme Court decided death
was cruel and unusual."

"I don't know, sir," said Darling. He felt uneasy
because the thought was occurring to him that the
attorney general of the United States was a loon. Not
that Walthrop's strong views were totally un-
founded. But why was he sharing them with someone who was leaving his department that day—an
assistant attorney general in antitrust whom he had
never met before?

"We end up with egg on our faces every time.
Not only losing cases, but losing them so badly even
the judges comment. You know we're going to lose
this Indian uprising case. I feel it in my stomach.
We're gonna lose it. That fucking judge out there is
against us, I know it. I can smell these things. There's
a conspiracy going on, Darling."

"Sir, you've been in Ohio politics. How many
real conspiracies get pulled off? You know five people can't keep a secret."

"Where'd you get that old wives' tale?"

"The Merchant Marine," Darling said.

"Then I'd give it some credence," said the attorney general. He flashed a smile. "I thought it was
some kind of idiocy you learned in law school."

"On a scale of one to ten, how many foulups
would you say are due to human stupidity, and how

many to subtle cunning analysis by a hostile force, politics or anything?" asked Darling.

"Nine for stupidity on the first foulup. But on the tenth and fifteenth, Lucius, I say fucking conspiracy. I say judges may have been reached. Juries may have been reached. Witnesses may have been reached in a grand design. You don't see it close up, trial by trial. But when you step back, as I have, and look at the big picture, you see a pattern. We're going to lose this Indian thing, mark my words. I don't like the noises the judge is making."

"By 'Indian thing,' you mean the charges involving the takeover at Wounded Elk, Montana?"

"Yeah. With that prick and his fucking Russian automatic rifle, or prop, that I fucking watched on national television when I was in the Senate. That one. The ones who were in full-scale firefights with federal marshals. The ones who desecrated an Indian church on federal-controlled land. That one. They're gonna walk, Lucius. They're gonna walk and the next day we'll see them on national television as heroes, with reporters feeding them questions like paid straight men."

"Well, I certainly wish you luck, sir," said Darling. He folded his hands on his lap.

"What do you mean by that?" asked Walthrop.

"I mean it has been a fruitful experience working in Justice and I appreciate your taking time to see me as I leave the department."

"What leaving? You *are* Lucius Darling?"

"Yes, sir."

"Then why are you leaving? Nobody tells me anything around here. You're one of eight I'm interviewing for a special project. You're not here to leave. What's going on? I'm not spending half a day with you just to pat your little ass for a job well done. What's going on?"

"On the tenth of September I submitted my resignation from the department, effective tomorrow. The termination form was received by your office and accepted by you, sir, with your signature."

"I sign a dozen resignations a week."

"So much for human error versus conspiracy," said Darling.

"My staff should have caught it. Why are you leaving?"

"To make money."

"You get thirty-one a year. You can go up to thirty-six. And your pension...you've got twelve years in toward your pension."

"Sir...with all due respect, sir, bullshit. That's not money."

"To be brutally frank, it's the most you've ever earned."

"That's correct. And I have outprepared and outthought and outskilled lawyers making three, four, five and ten times what I make. While I see other assistant AGs who do crossword puzzles, whose only significant achievement in life was passing the bar and who stopped thinking that very day, I see them make to the penny, the exact penny, what I make. I want to get paid for what I do. I like to sweat, but I want to sell my sweat, not give it away."

"Hmmm," murmured Walthrop and raised his hands into an arch where the fingertips touched. He looked over them at Darling. "Hmmm. Admirable," he said.

"Thank you," said Darling and waited to be dismissed.

"Very admirable. It's exactly the kind of man I'm looking for."

"I hope you find him, sir."

"I have," said Walthrop.

"If that's all, Mr. Walthrop, I'll leave now," said Darling.

"How's Frank Rumson? Ginny Daimler? Bob Brown?" Walthrop asked with a wry smile. Darling felt his stomach sinking inside his body. The attorney general was demonstrating just how well-connected he was back in Darling's hometown.

He forced himself to keep his voice level. "I only see Mr. Rumson and Mrs. Daimler at social events because I stay away from county politics. The Hatch Act, you know. Bob Brown is fine. In fact, he's taking me on as a partner next week."

Walthrop pressed the button on his intercom.

"Miss Napier, please get me Bob Brown in Troy.

Anywhere he's at. Thank you." Walthrop clicked off the speaker and looked at Darling. "If she were my second in command here, our foulup would never have happened. Glad it did though. It gave me a better chance to look you over. There is something about a man who wants to make a buck that I trust. Any sonofabitch who waves a flag, I find it powerful hard to believe that he's for real. Any sonofabitch who says he wants to help mankind, I find that hard to believe too. But greed, Mr. Darling, I believe in that."

"I'm not an easy person to push around, and I don't like what you're doing," Darling said evenly.

"Why should you?" Walthrop said with a shrug. "You know, Lucius... do they call you Luke?" Without waiting for an answer, he went on, "You know, Luke, it is greed and sex that keep mankind going. I believe that. Greed is just another way of expressing your desire for survival. I trust your greed."

"I don't think wanting to get paid fairly for my work classifies as greed," Darling said.

The intercom buzzed.

"Mr. Brown on the line," came a woman's voice through the small desk speaker. "The attorney general will speak to you now."

Walthrop winked at Darling. Into the little tan speaker box on the desk, he bellowed, "Hello, Bob. How you doing?"

"I was on the seventeenth green with the best

round of the year when they ran out of the clubhouse to get me."

Darling recognized Bob Brown's voice over the speaker.

"They must have run pretty fast, Bob," Walthrop said dryly.

"I was on the tenth near the clubhouse and I was doing lousy."

"I knew it. I couldn't see you leaving a good round, not even for an atomic war. How you been, Bob?"

"Fine. What do you want, Jim?"

"I need a favor."

"Name it."

"I need your new partner, Lucius Darling, for a little while longer."

"Jim, I'd like to help you but we are flowing out our own windows with work, and Darling is worth any five other men."

Darling felt good to hear that and he could not contain a smile, even though he knew Brown was probably just bargaining with Walthrop. If Bob had to trade something, naturally he was going to make it seem more valuable than it was.

"Which is why you were on the golf course," Walthrop said.

"I live to play golf. I work so that I can keep buying new clubs. I would rather play golf than eat or fornicate. I was just lining up my putt when I was told that the attorney general of the United States had to speak to me, emergency. I can see my foursome from here going on without me."

"Can I have Darling?"

"Does Luke know you're calling me?"

"Yes."

"What does he say?"

"He says no."

"Then there isn't all that much I can do," Brown said.

"If he's willing, would you be willing? For a fellow Buckeye?"

"No. But for a pal who never forgets a favor, yes."

"Then talk to your new partner. He's right here," Walthrop said and turned the tan speaker box toward Darling.

"We're talking on a loudspeaker, Bob," Darling said immediately.

"Well, then, we'll talk later. How's Kathy?"

"She's fine and anxious to go home. Washington is hard on women," said Darling.

"Except whores," interrupted Walthrop. "Here's a private line. Talk here." He handed a telephone to Darling, who watched him press a small lever on the tan speaker.

"We're on a private line now," Darling said. "Shoot." He saw Walthrop cup his face in his right hand, a bored look in his eyes.

"I'd appreciate it," Brown told Darling, "if you'd

give him what he needs. You know how big Walthrop is in this state, not to mention Washington. It'd be a hell of a boost for you, coming into the firm with a big favor owed by him. A big boost."

"It's hard to talk," said Darling. "What about the workload?"

Walthrop smiled briefly.

"We've got it, it's real, and we can use you bad," Brown said. "But it's nothing compared to being owed by Walthrop. If it isn't for too long, I'd consider it a personal favor if you'd do what he wants. Can you get away with an extra month?"

"Two weeks," Darling said.

"Starting today?"

"Right."

"Well, hell, that only costs us a week 'cause you weren't planning to start until next Monday anyway. Give it to him."

"Well, I don't see how I can say no," said Darling.

"Give my regards to the attorney general. See you in two weeks, Luke."

"See you, Bob."

"Tell him thank you," said James Walthrop.

"Yeah," said Darling disgustedly as he hung up. "Thank you."

"It'll be the best two weeks you ever invested, Luke," said Walthrop, rising to shake hands. "Find out what we're doing wrong in these political trials and what we should do right and what I'll owe you will be based on how good a set of guidelines you leave the department. And, of course, we've got to keep it secret."

"That's going to make it more difficult to get cooperation in the department," said Darling. "Who's going to talk to me about anything?"

"Well, then, just tell them you're doing a personnel study or something for me. But we can't go past that. The town'd go apeshit. Ever since Watergate nobody can confide in anybody. That Nixon . . . What an asshole. What an incredible asshole."

"No conspiracy to get him?" said Darling, smiling, and for the third time in his twelve-year career he was shaking the hand of an attorney general of the United States. "Two weeks," he said. "Two weeks, my report'll be on your desk."

"Fine," said Walthrop. "That'll be fine." But Darling wasn't listening. He was thinking of how to save his marriage.

Kathy Darling was stuffing half pages of the *Washington Post* into her grandmother's china when Luke nuzzled her behind the right ear, kissing a wispy strand of her light brown hair.

"Are the kids out?"

"Yes," she said.

"Are they coming back soon?"

"I don't know," she said. Her voice cracked.

Luke softly kissed her cheek and blew soft breezes at her eyelids.

"Have I ever told you I love you?" He cupped a breast.

"Yes. Many times."

"I love you, Kathy."

"I'm packing," she said.

"Screw it. Later."

"The moving men are coming tomorrow."

"We'll be done by then," he said.

"I mean I have to have everything ready by then, honey."

"One more time in our house," he said.

"This isn't our house. It's a rented place. Let's do it at home. Troy. That's home. That's an owned home. A rented house isn't a home."

"Where you and I are, honey, is always home."

Like a radar that has suddenly picked up an enemy ship from a cloud of aluminum chaff, Kathy Darling spun around. She was attractively plump with a hint of freckles on her perky face, moderately pretty in her youth and now growing beautiful with the years. A strong red flush filled her cheeks.

"We are leaving tomorrow, aren't we?"

"You're ninety percent right," said Darling.

"Give me the ten percent."

"The moving men will be here tomorrow. They will take our things home tomorrow. You and the boys will fly home tomorrow."

"The ten percent, Luke."

"I will meet you home in two weeks."

"Uhhh," grunted Kathy as if punched in the solar plexis. She threw herself away from her husband and with three sturdy paces toward the living room reached yelling range, where she spun and delivered.

"Jeeeezus Christ, Lucius Darling! Jeeeezus Christ . . ."

"I knew you were going to take it like this, Kath."

"You're damned well right I'm taking it like this. You could bet on it. What are you doing, mopping the floors for the department? Whose work are you making up for now? No. Not this time. No extra work this time. You're through with Justice. That was a promise."

"Now, Kath, be reasonable."

"Not with your reason, fucking lawyer."

"Kath. The kids."

"Fuck the kids. We have a commitment. You solemnly made it. You promised. You dedicated this to me, after twelve years, and I'm not giving it back. We're all going tomorrow."

"Would it make any difference if I told you it was a favor for Bob Brown? Would it?"

"What work are you doing for him here? What work?"

"It was a favor to him."

"Do I have to call him to find out?"

"Well," said Darling with a bit of acting guile he had picked up in courtrooms. "I don't think it would look right, you checking with my new partner even before I join the firm." *Call, call*, he wished.

"Bullshit. We've known Bob Brown forever. I'll ask Gwynn. She'll know. She knows everything that goes on in her husband's office."

"Now do you have to go calling Gwynn over something like this?" asked Darling plaintively. *Call, call.*

"Yes," said Kathy Darling triumphantly.

Luke sighed heavily. "All right," he mumbled. "Unless you've got some very strong reason for me not to."

"No, go ahead, dear. You won't be satisfied until you do. Go ahead."

Luke watched her dial on the yellow kitchen phone. She looked at him while she talked. There were many "uh-huhs" and finally an "All right, Gwynn. See you."

She hung up and was quiet, glancing at the sink and then down at the floor. Thinking. Finally, she looked up at Luke. He could see tears line her lower eyelids.

"Lawyer," she said softly, pronouncing the word with the precision of a loser explaining why.

And Lucius A. Darling, Esquire, felt like a warted toad.

Tuesday, October 18: The Second Day

After a night of very little sleep and of lovemaking that was curiously perfunctory for people parting, Lucius Darling arrived at his office early.

He turned on his small office television set, but kept the sound turned off. Then with two fingers, he personally typed a memo to Attorney General James Walthrop. In it, he outlined his needs and his goals.

Needs: five attorneys. Goals: 1) research and definition of political trials; 2) performance of judges and federal attorneys; 3) selection of juries; 4) unique aspects of political trials; 5) performance of defense attorneys.

"These," his memo concluded, "should cover the major potential factors involved in the government's failure to win such cases. Please indicate approval."

He signed the memo with a black ballpoint pen, sealed the light blue paper in a white envelope, marked it "Mr. Walthrop, Confidential," and carried it personally to Walthrop's office, where he gave it to the blonde receptionist.

Without waiting for the approval he knew would come, he asked his secretary, Miss McGirr, to select five attorneys to assist him in the project, and then went to the airport to see Kathy and his two sons off for Troy, Ohio.

When he returned to his office, he found an envelope from Walthrop on his desk. Inside was Darling's memo. Across the top, scrawled in red ink, was "Okay, J. V. W." At the bottom of Darling's list of five potential reasons for the government's poor performance in political trials, Walthrop had written, in the same red ink, a sixth.

"*Conspiracy*!" it read, including the exclamation point, and Darling laughed aloud, convinced now beyond doubt that he was working for a loony-toon.

He scheduled a meeting for the next day with the five attorneys Miss McGirr had selected, then turned off his television and went out and rented a hotel room, paying in advance.

For thirteen days.

CHAPTER ★★★★★★ 4

Wednesday, October 19: The Third Day

RONALD GILPERT, A NEWLY ENFRANCHISED lawyer who had joined the Justice Department at $15,000 a year to get courtroom experience, brought up an interesting point at the small meeting in Darling's office.

"We've really hit upon a good question here," Gilpert said. "Perhaps a government, a constitutional government with constitutional safeguards of individual liberty, cannot cope with a determined radical band. One of my professors at Georgetown contended we might need an altered standard for admissible evidence in light of the strains put on the old Anglo-Saxon based..."

Darling held up his hand, quieting the young man.

"Thursday. A week from tomorrow. That's the key," Darling said.

Gilpert's young smooth brow furrowed. The other four attorneys, equally young but slightly more experienced, smiled.

"I don't follow you, Mr. Darling," said Gilpert.

"Mr. Gilpert. Today is nineteen October. All of you will submit interim reports to me by next Tuesday and Wednesday. Clear the dates with Miss McGirr." Darling nodded to the woman, a prim middle-aged lady with short-cut hair and harlequin-style eyeglasses. "Unless there is a demurrer from me about your report, you will have its final version on my desk on Thursday, twenty-seven October. A week from tomorrow. Using your reports as a basis, I will complete my overall report on the following day and provide you each with a copy. If you have any corrections or criticism or comments, you will return same to me by noon, Sunday, thirty October. I will incorporate your recommendations, if I find them worthy, in my final report, which will be on Attorney General Walthrop's desk at noon, Monday, thirty-one October. At one-thirty on that date, I have a flight booked for the airport in Vandalia, just outside of Troy, Ohio, where at four P.M. the same day I will enter the law firm of McAdow, Brown and Darling."

"It seems to me we're a bit on the heavy side with the time frame priority," said Gilpert. "What if we don't have the project finalized within your time parameters?"

The other project members exchanged glances. Miss McGirr suppressed a smile. One lawyer later would say he could hear his cigarette smoke rising.

Darling looked past Gilpert's right shoulder to the bookshelf where the television was silently flickering pictures onto its screen. His voice was ice quiet.

"That's not possible, Mr. Gilpert," Darling said.

"Yes, sir," said Ronald Gilpert.

"Any other questions?" asked Darling.

Gilpert raised a hand.

"Yes, Mr. Gilpert."

"You have given out assignments to the staff here and mine is the definition of political trials and supportive research for the other staff members. Now, I happen to like research, but you have established Miss McGirr as the project coordinator. She is going to be the one who has the final decision on which cases are applicable and which cases are not. Such as a robbery where the defendant claims he is being politically persecuted. Maybe he is and maybe he isn't, but that is a sensitive decision and, in effect, you are putting in the hands of Miss McGirr, whom I happen to believe is a fine, legal secretary, a value judgment decision."

"Yes," said Darling. He glanced at his watch.

"In effect, Miss McGirr will be directing my work," Gilpert said.

"Precisely," said Darling.

"Oh," said Gilpert. "I didn't know you had...I mean, I was wondering whether you had intended ...uh, I see now. Right. I understand. Miss McGirr is coordinating. Got it."

The four other lawyers filled briefcases, tucked pencils into clipboards, and snuffed out cigarettes they did not want to carry lit from the office. But Gilpert had another question.

"What if we should stumble on some highly complicated substructure for the failure of Justice to successfully prosecute political trials?" he asked.

"You will find here, as in the rest of your career," said Darling, "that cases are lost because lawyers do not prepare them. I am not talking about prepare them brilliantly. I am not talking about keen insights into the esoterics of law. I am talking about the piece-by-tedious-piece of a good and thorough case. You will find, as I found when I was an assistant prosecutor in the Miami County Court in Ohio, that if you are thoroughly prepared, you will not lose a case. I hope I will not prejudice your work in advance by saying that I believe the government is not thoroughly prepared in these political cases, and we must find ways to correct that."

"What if the defendant is innocent?" asked Gilpert.

"Then you don't prosecute him."

"But it's possible to believe someone is guilty until you get into the courtroom and then find out otherwise," said Gilpert. Another lawyer nudged his ribs, signaling him to cut it off, but Gilpert ignored him.

Darling said, "Preparing a case means precisely that you are not surprised by witnesses and evidence. It means you are aware of everything in advance."

"That's impractical for every case," Gilpert said.

"Then I hope that if we ever meet as adversaries, you will have one of those cases where it is impractical."

"You never know until the jury's in," said Gilpert, his pale cheeks reddening.

At the door, Gilpert had yet another question.

"Mr. Darling, why do you keep the television on?"

"Mr. Gilpert, when I was a young lawyer in Justice, I once worked very late at night. I remember the date. It was twenty-two November, 1963, and I did research from eight in the morning until midnight. When I finally came out of the office, I found out that President Kennedy had been assassinated. I believe I was the only person in the United States who did not know of it. The next day I bought myself a television set for the office."

"And why is the sound always off?"

"Because I hate television," said Darling.

Outside the office, fellow staff members told Gilpert he had made a fool of himself. Gilpert responded that American jurisprudence was a field populated by boring, beaten men and that an attorney with a new idea and fresh approach could ride roughshod over the lack of creative opposition, just like Harold Albend did. He had defended the Chicago 12, the Panther 15, the recruiting booth rioters, and was now about to beat the pants off Justice in the Wounded Elk Indian uprising.

"I find myself on the opposite side of a man I admire," said Gilpert. "Albend is the way law is going in America. A people's law where courts can redress a new and broad range of grievances. I would, if you want to know the truth, I would prefer working for Harold Albend, who is tomorrow, rather than for our Lucius Darling, who is yesterday. If you want to know the truth."

To this, the other lawyers acknowledged that no, they really did not want to know the truth.

"Whether you know it or not, Harold Albend has brought a dynamism to a dying judicial process." Thus said Ronald Gilpert, twenty-four, a $15,000-a-year assistant U.S. attorney general, who was advised by Miss Mary Ellen McGirr that if he intended to be working late in the Justice library on his research that night, he should call the librarian to get clearance. "You have twenty-five minutes to call," she said. "Just tell her that you're working for Mr. Darling, and everything will be all right."

CHAPTER ***** 5

The Near Future

LONZO GATES WAS INFORMED THAT THE PER-
sonnel records of Justice Department employees
were not public documents and therefore, no matter
what he said, he would get no information on the
employment status, past or present, of one Lucius
Darling.

He had invoked the sacred name of the Freedom
of Information Act but was told it did not apply to
personnel records.

Then he had turned on his Voice of Sweet Reason
and said that he was just interested in doing a background story on a lot of Justice Department personnel and the only one he still needed to check on was
Lucius Darling.

"Now, it's not really that important to the story,
but I'd like to have it just to make sure that things
are well-rounded, you know. And this is going to be
a favorable story. It'd be a shame if it had a bad touch
to it because I had to report that the Justice Depart-

ment refused any information about one of its employees, Lucius Darling. I mean it would smack of coverup and...you know...give a sour note to a story that's going to be all favorable."

The information officer's response was brisk. "What did you say your name was?" she asked.

"Lonzo Gates."

"And you write for whom?"

"For *Mossback* Magazine."

"Well, I've heard of *Mossback*, Mr. Yates."

"Gates," he interjected.

"Gates. Yes. Mr. Gates. I'm not familiar with your work, and I really can't give out personnel information. Is there anything else I can help you with?"

"Yes. You can tell me why the Justice Department is involved in this massive coverup." Gates was almost shouting into the phone.

"Goodbye, Mr. Gates," the woman said.

"Bitch," Gates shouted as the phone clicked dead in his ear.

The Justice Department has really changed since Nixon's day, Gates thought. He got up from his desk and went to lock the door of his small, ratty office. In the old days, he could call the Justice Department and get put right through to the attorney general of the United States. True, they hated him and they hated the work he did for *Mossback*. But they were afraid of him, and so they kowtowed.

And now it had all degenerated to this . . . to some bitch in some low-level GS job who didn't even know his name. Christ, what the hell was going on in Washington, D.C. these days?

He opened his center desk drawer, after pounding on it for a moment to release the faulty lock, and pulled out a well-worn leather phonebook. Opening it to the first page, he prepared to go through the book alphabetically to see if there was a name or number of someone he could call, who might know something.

The first name was Harold Albend, the lawyer. He had had a string of battles with the feds in the late sixties and early seventies. He might just know who this Lucius Darling was. At least it was worth a try.

And at least Albend would remember his name.

Gates reached for the telephone and began to dial.

CHAPTER ✶✶✶✶✶✶ 6

The Mid-1970s

Thursday, October 20: The Fourth Day

LUCIUS DARLING GOT HIS FIRST CLOSEUP look at Harold Albend in the Billings, Montana, federal district court. Albend was chatting with several young female admirers in the visitors' seats behind the defendants' table. He rested on his left leg, his hip jauntily angled, his famous polka dot cravat nestling his gray goateed chin, his brown eyes rolling up into his head, his right hand plucking at his famous bushy eyebrows.

Albend was in his early fifties, the slope of a middle-aged belly being caught by a wide black leather belt centered with a large silver buckle that matched the buckles on his black patent leather Wellington boots. He wore a beige suit over a vermilion turtleneck, with a gleaming onyx pendant hanging down from his neck on a polished silver chain—all of it partially hidden, of course, by the famous polka dot cravat.

When Darling saw him, he did not bother to conceal from himself his envy. *I hope I can get away with that stuff at his age. Hell, I wish I could get away with it now.*

The young women, in their early twenties, smiled and giggled in their awe. Darling walked down the aisle of the crowded courtroom. The jury box was empty and the judge had removed himself to chambers. One defendant, Roland Watertree, his hair braided Indian-fashion, talked with a hard-faced woman in a tweed suit. The other defendant, Dennis Petty, dozed as—according to newspaper accounts— he had dozed through the entire trial.

The defense was on the right, prosecution on the left, but at first glance, the courtroom crowd, on both left and right sides of the aisle, were all pro-defense. There was a lot of Indian garb, a lot of beards. While that might be flimsy evidence to base an opinion on, it was enough for Darling this day.

Darling had read on the plane from Dulles Airport how the courtroom spectators had spent their time cheering the defense and booing the prosecution, and how Judge Andrews was constantly threatening to clear the courtroom. It was funny how courtroom decorum had changed. Back in Troy, at the Miami County Court, Darling as a prosecutor could usually count on gasps from the crowd to be in the prosecution's favor and he knew it could not help but affect the jury.

But this crowd, Darling saw, was orchestrated for the defense. Who knew what effect that might be having on the jury.

The federal prosecution team sat on the left, three men in conservative suits, looking like businessmen who had accidentally wandered into a college rally and decided to wait until it was over so they could get out without being crushed. They appeared isolated and alone.

"U.S. Attorney Roberts?" asked Darling.

A balding man in a gray vested suit and a face yet to see the lines of forty looked up, somewhat startled.

"I'm Luke Darling from Washington."

"Oh, sure. Sit down," said Roberts. He introduced two other assistant U.S. attorneys and, in the first spectator row behind them, two agents from the Federal Bureau of Investigation. Darling formally shook hands with all of them, then sat in a chair next to Roberts.

"This case has been a bitch," whispered Roberts. "A real bitch. Nothing's gone right. Maybe somebody in Washington can nitpick over some of my decisions, but we have had nothing but galloping grief from the first git-go."

"You're not on trial, Roberts," Darling said.

"No? How come I think I am then?"

"Didn't Miss McGirr explain the project to you?"

"Sure. A general overall report on how Justice is handling political trials," Roberts said.

"Right," Darling said. "So you're only a small part."

"I'm the biggest part there is today," Roberts said, unconvinced by Darling's open-faced attitude.

"Look, Roberts. I'm restricting our review to just four cases. I know you feel like the center of it now, but you're just one of the cases. We're looking for patterns, not people."

"Okay, then I'll tell you the pattern. Once they make it a political trial, we lose. You have the crime and you've got the bastards that did it, and then they try you for what's gone down for the last two hundred years. Where we lose is that we're not prosecuting them, they're prosecuting us."

"I've gotten that impression from initial surveys," Darling said, trying to reassure the man who seemed to be unnecessarily agitated. "How did Albend get the old Indian treaties in as admissible evidence?"

"That's simple. He didn't," Roberts said.

"But I read . . ."

"You read the testimony, but that was entered to show mitigating circumstances. It was nothing big in the trial itself, but the press made it a big thing. You'd think I was the first officer at the goddamn Wounded Elk massacre a hundred years ago from the way the newspapers covered that bullshit."

"Albend's pretty good, huh?" Darling asked.

"I wouldn't hire him to draw a will," said Roberts angrily. "I told you we had problems in this case."

"You're going to get all the transcripts to my office by Monday. Is that right?"

"Hey, this is a month-long trial and it's just ending. I don't know if we can get the transcripts in time."

"People do work on weekends," Darling said.

"Well, maybe you can get the court to get the stenographers to do it. I haven't been able to get salt from these people."

"The court's hostile?" asked Darling.

"Don't write that down," said Roberts quickly.

"Well, if the court is hostile, that's an important element."

"I don't want to look as if I'm bitching about the court," Roberts said.

"Then it's been impartial?"

"No. But I'm not blaming the court."

"I take it you think we've lost," Darling said.

"No, no. I don't think they'll get an acquittal."

"Then you won?" said Darling.

Roberts shook his head. "No. We're not getting a conviction either, I don't think."

"I don't understand."

"I told you, we were put on trial," Roberts said.

"Could you give me a fast review of this?" said Darling, turning around to see where a high-pitched giggle had come from. The gaggle of awed girls were looking up at Albend, who wore a triumphant smirk. The defense attorney looked to the prosecution's table and the girls giggled again, staring at Darling and Roberts.

"That's been going on since the beginning of the trial," Roberts said. "That's some nice-looking snatch they have as camp followers. Why is it the other side always has the good-lookers?"

"It's your imagination," said Darling. He made a note that courtroom atmosphere should become a topic in his final report. He probably should have caught that back in Washington, considered the emotional appeals of many of the cases. With a weak judge, an audience could affect a jury. It was the judge's job to keep juries free of contamination, either from news accounts or from a mob in the courtroom.

Eugene O'Connell, one of the five attorneys assigned to Darling, had been given the job of rating the judges, even though Darling knew what he would find. Some judges would be competent and some not. But there just might be a new element in the crowd atmosphere, and Darling would mention it to him.

The two-tiered jury box was empty, a rectangle of polished wood surrounding twelve seats. Most believed it to be the foundation of western jurisprudence. What was it Chesterton had said? Truly important things had to be left to twelve common men. Let the scientists play with the atom and engineers with bridges and skyscrapers, but leave matters of life and death and justice to twelve ordinary men.

It was more romantic than accurate, though, as any trial lawyer knew. Albend had been using a psychologist who claimed that he could tell how a person would react on a jury just by looking at him. In the three other major cases besides this one, Albend had used the new system and gotten three acquittals. Because of the jury makeup? Fred DeBaux was the attorney assigned to report on jury selection.

"All power to the people," said a man in a dungaree suit near Albend. Apparently, it was some sort of punchline because it prompted laughter. Darling thought about the Bolsheviks when they took over Russia. First they said, "Power to the People," then "All Power to the People," then "Power to the Soviets," then "All Power to the Soviets," and then there was only one political party left in Russia.

Max Rothblatt was working on that one: the mechanics of radical core groups in political trials. Seeing the people clustered around Albend, Darling wondered if their revolution was successful in America, how many of them would wind up in prison or hanging at the end of a rope. Revolutions were notoriously intolerant of their founders.

One of the FBI men handed Roberts a note. He glanced at it, crumpled the note to the floor, and turned away.

"This has been one doozy of a trial," he muttered.

"Something wrong?" Darling asked.

"Why do you ask?" Roberts said.

"You were...uh, sort of rude to the FBI man. Is there any friction here?"

"No. Fuck him."

"No friction?"

"Don't tell me FBI," Roberts said. "Just don't tell me FBI."

"Explain that to me," Darling said.

"You make your report, that's all. I know where you're coming from."

"No, you don't," Darling said.

"You're Washington. The bureau is Washington. You people pull the strings, and I'm going to be left out here with my bare duff to the four winds."

"We can talk about that. That's what my report's about. If you think Washington interference has hampered you, I'd like to know about it."

Before Roberts could answer, the court bailiff came to his table and said the jury members had requested dinner and were suspending their deliberations for the night. Roberts grunted. Darling suggested they dine together, but Roberts said he owed it to his wife to return home. Darling told him, "Bring your wife," and two hours later in a Billings steakhouse, Darling heard a young attorney's tale of woe.

The wife, a plumpish Midwestern girl with very exact lipstick and wisps of hair imprisoned in some sort of dried lacquer spray, provided a chorus of support for her husband, a good man betrayed by Easterners.

"I'm from Troy, Ohio, myself," defended Darling.

"Only someone from the East would think of Ohio as Midwest," said Nancy Roberts.

"Now, honey," said Roberts in almost a pleading fashion. Darling realized the attorney was worried about his wife baring family attitudes that never were meant to be made public. She ignored him.

"Well, it's true, damnit. Those people think we're just a bunch of hick cowboys out here."

"Nancy," said Roberts firmly.

"It's true," she said.

"Yes and no," said Darling. "There's prejudice and ignorance everywhere and if you know that, then you can use it. I have and I'm sure Bill has too. You make your accent a little twangier. You fumble a bit. You talk about the corn or the farming or the ranch, and then you take your opponent for his barn doors. But not all Easterners are that dumb."

"Well," said Nancy Roberts, unreconciled to the

possibility that some Easterners might not be prejudiced against her and her husband. She speared a white chunk of her crabmeat cocktail and rammed it into the red sauce. It disappeared into her mouth without a chew.

"So, why don't you just fill me in, Bill?" Darling said to Roberts. "Informally and unofficially. There will be another attorney talking to you officially and anything you want to say different to him is all right with me. I just want to find out what's going on."

Roberts began with the seizure of Wounded Elk by a tiny gang of Indian protesters, then the glaring media coverage that followed and led to negotiations with the group that had taken over the small Indian village. Then the breakdown of negotiations, the continuing of negotiations, the three firefights in which one of the Indians and two federal marshals were killed. The occupiers had been city Indians, and the local Indians had threatened to attack them and drive them from the village. The government waited as long as it could, then went in and finally got the protesters out. The federal grand jury handed down thirty-three counts of murder, conspiracy, civil disorder, burglary, and arson. Darling knew all those facts, having read a file on the case while flying to Billings, but he let Roberts talk, just to get the man in the habit of talking to him.

"This is off the record," Roberts said, "but what sane country would tolerate a revolutionary group taking over a town? What country in history wouldn't have gone right in there and blasted them the hell out with tanks? I mean, it was a damned revolution, a freaking war. And after they fight a war, Washington treats it like some minor civil disturbance, like a protest march. There's an incredible double standard here. They fight a war and we have to walk around with briefcases."

"And then they scream about oppression," said Nancy, dividing a roll in two and eating the first half plain, even while she was putting butter on the second half. "Oppression for them is when you won't let them mug you without fighting back."

"There are some who agree with you," said Darling, not committing himself, and he looked back to Roberts.

The legal problems, Roberts explained, began with the indictments. Every one of the occupying Indians was indicted. No one was left for witnesses.

"But you had a key witness," Darling said. "An eyewitness."

"Yeah, we'll get to that," Roberts said.

"That's your FBI for you," Nancy said through a mouthful of bread.

"Please," Roberts said to his wife. "You know when you have a good case for sure?" he asked Darling.

His wife interrupted. "When they call you a fascist pig," she said, and Darling smiled.

"Almost," Roberts said. "So we screwed up and didn't keep any of the occupying Indians for a witness. But even with having to use witnesses outside Wounded Elk, we still had a good case going. Even using federal marshals for witnesses. Albend and that twit with him were throwing fits. They were putting the country on trial, the judge on trial, the— excuse the expression—fucking ceiling on trial. Judge Andrews even had Albend locked up for a fucking weekend for disrupting the trial. He was going under. I could see it."

"Well, we both remember the old saying. If you have the facts on your side, yell about the facts. If you have the law on your side, yell about the law. If you have nothing on your side, yell about everything."

"Until Dempsey," said Nancy Roberts.

"Who's Dempsey?" Darling asked.

Just then the waiter came with their steaks and conversation stopped for a while as they ate. Then Darling asked Roberts again, "Who's Dempsey?"

But Roberts did not answer. Instead, he nodded toward the restaurant entrance where Harold Albend, a young woman on each arm, made his entrance into the steakhouse, receiving the stares and glances due a celebrity. They were seated at a table ten feet from Darling's. The women giggled and Albend held court. He had changed for dinner into a glaring purple Nehru suit, but the polka dot cravat was the same.

While Darling and Mr. and Mrs. Roberts finished their dinner, Darling heard Albend complaining about steakhouses in general. A steak was animal food, he said, as if that would be a big surprise to the two young women with him. But what could anyone expect out in the boondocks like Montana? There were no good restaurants anymore. Well, hold that. There was one in Cincinnati and another in San Francisco. But not one in New York City, except for steakhouses, and no one with any social conscience would eat steak anymore. Instead of steak, Albend ordered eight lobster cocktails with melted butter. And a bottle of cognac. He bemoaned the destruction of the West as a little island of protein in a sea of want and hunger and starvation.

Darling smiled and Roberts asked him, "What's funny?"

Darling nodded over his shoulder toward Albend's table. "That nonsense. All these loonies seem to think we find protein. Didn't anyone ever tell them that we grow it, we raise it, we work for it?"

"Good for you. It's ours and don't feel guilty about it and don't share it with anybody. That's what I say," said Nancy Roberts.

"Well, I think we ought to share it. We ought to fight starvation," Darling said.

"Why?"

"Because of who we are. If we didn't help, we just wouldn't be Americans anymore."

"We're becoming a mean country," she said. "And we dont don't have to be. We ought to give away every other meal. I'd do it." She was eating the crackers from the bread basket. "I would. As part of a diet. I'd do it. If others would. Why are you smiling, Mr. Darling?"

"Well, nobility on a full stomach is sort of easy."

"You don't think I would, do you?"

"Nancy," said Roberts angrily.

"He doesn't think I would. You'd let those niggers starve, wouldn't you, Washington bureaucrat?"

"Nancy," said Roberts again.

Darling unsuccessfully smothered a grin.

"You would," said Nancy Roberts and chugged the last clear alcohol of her martini. "Well, I wouldn't. I'd give this whole fucking restaurant to the niggers. Let 'em burn it down."

"Nancy," Roberts said again plaintively.

She ordered another martini, which Roberts immediately unordered, and she settled for cognac and coffee and cheesecake. She drank the cognac, ate the cheesecake, but left the coffee. On the way out, she blew a kiss to Albend and yelled, "Right on." In the elevator she expanded on her proposal to "give everything to the niggers." In the car she said she should have married some smart Jewish lawyer and lived in Las Vegas instead of "fucking Billings," said that the problem with the FBI was "mackerel-snappers like Calvin Dempsey," apologized to Darling in case he was a Catholic, then found out he wasn't and said the problem with food was the Roman Catholic Church. Had a very interesting point that would clear up everything. Started to deliver it and passed out.

Roberts put her on the back seat of his car and as he drove Darling to his hotel, got back to Calvin Dempsey.

"Dempsey's an FBI agent. He bugged one of the defendants' phones while the trial was in progress and the bugs were uncovered. And then he had two agents listen in on a conference in the judge's chambers while I was there. We heard something outside the door and Albend ran over to the door and yanked it open . . ." Roberts paused and Darling could see the younger man's jaw quivering. He breathed deeply before continuing.

"He snapped open the door to the judge's chambers in which I was sitting . . . I mean, we didn't need to have anybody listening in . . . he snapped open the door and two . . . two fucking goddamn FBI agents fell into the room. They were listening in. I was in the judge's chambers, and two agents like Fucking Laurel and Fucking Hardy fall all over themselves into the fucking room. The judge looks at me, and what am I going to say? They work for me. I'm Justice Department, so I get reamed by the judge. It was so bad that Albend had to come to my defense."

Roberts pulled into the driveway of Darling's hotel. Nancy Roberts still snored numbly in the back seat.

"Albend?" Darling said.

"Yes. He went into his thing on the system and that I was just a young lawyer and shouldn't be blamed for an entire department and that in his opinion I had, within limits, conducted myself rather fairly, considering the weak case I had."

"And what did Judge Andrews say?"

"He told Albend to shut the fuck up."

"Those words?"

"Yup."

"Boy, it doesn't sound like the FBI," Darling said. "They have more brains than that."

"That's not the worst. Dempsey comes up with an eyewitness mid-trial. Guy looked beautiful. Heard the defendants plotting the destruction of Wounded Elk, saw defendants firing on marshals. Had names, dates, could identify details. I thought, well, okay, we made a mistake in indicting everyone who took over Wounded Elk, instead of trading charges for eyewitness testimony. But I said, okay, the Lord has provided and here's our eyewitness. Bless Dempsey, he has redeemed himself. All right?"

Darling nodded.

"So I put on this perfect witness and he testifies and then he goes under the cross-examination and I discover in the courtroom—in the courtroom, mind you—that this eyewitness to Wounded Elk, to whom I shifted the whole emphasis of the case because he was so good, I found out he had a grievous flaw for any eyewitness."

"Yes?" said Darling.

"Yes. His eyes were in San Diego at the time. He watched it on television. A news show. He was a liar and Dempsey knew it . . . he couldn't have *not* known it . . . and he hung me out on a limb with him and watched me get cut off. After that, I did everything I could to make the thing a mistrial so I could start again without the help of Dempsey and his goddamn FBI."

"Wow," Darling said.

"Yeah. Wow," said Roberts, his voice dripping with disgust.

Friday, October 21: The Fifth Day

The jury came in the next morning with a verdict of not guilty on all counts. The government had not even proved civil disorder, an event which a television reporter commented had been witnessed by an estimated 285 million people around the world.

The judge had added comments for the Justice Department. Darling watched the television sketch artists make quick charcoal dashes across large white pads as Federal Judge William V. Andrews called the entire Justice Department "a sorry disreputable excuse for an alleged defender of the public interest and the constitution." He called their conduct "a spectacular failure of moral and legal ethics."

Outside the courtroom, Harold Albend posed for pictures, embraced by the two braided-hair defendants, and said that the people would always overrule a corrupt government.

A gray-haired woman in a black dress trimmed with white lace around the neck, a woman with majestic high cheekbones and black eyes and worn brown skin, sadly stood mumbling by a car at the curb. Darling heard her, and she said something that hurt him even more than Judge Andrews's angry tongue-lashing.

"They moved their bowels in the church my father and my brothers built. They tore out pages from our Bibles and wiped themselves with it. And now, they are heroes and all say they represent us. But we are many and they are few, and who will sing praises to God or clean the human waste from our House of God that we built? Who will do these things but us? Where is justice? Where is our justice? Where is the justice of the white man? Is there no justice but God's?"

A television crew pushed her aside, rushing by to get a good picture of Albend and the two defendants, Dennis Petty and Roland Watertree. Darling yelled at them to watch their step, but they were men who were used to being yelled at as they did their jobs.

"Where is justice?" chanted the old woman.

Darling phoned back to Washington that he wanted Calvin Dempsey of the FBI at his office at 9:00 A.M. Monday. Absolute imperative. Absolute.

"Get one of our five lawyers, McGirr. Have him call Dempsey. I don't want anybody less than an assistant attorney general on the phone with him. I want Dempsey, and I want him to bring everything he knows about Wounded Elk. I don't care if he's in Nome, Alaska, right now. I want him."

CHAPTER ★★★★★★ 7

Monday, October 24: The Eighth Day

RONALD GILPERT HAD AN INSIDE TALE OF FBI grossness for Luke Darling at 9:00 A.M. Monday, on the second floor of Justice. Darling, who had just spent his first weekend alone in Washington at a hotel whose burned luncheonette coffee substituted bitterness for richness, and who was now eating a fried egg sandwich on white bread with catsup and butter mixing and thus not liking the world very much, liked Ronald Gilpert even less.

This man, he thought, *is in the way of me going home to Kathy. If this man had a heart attack right now in front of my desk, I could have Miss McGirr take over his function very well in five seconds. Then I could send an interoffice memo that Ronald Gilpert had, at 9:02 A.M., suffered a heart attack in my office. I would send the memo for medical help next*

Friday. I could mail it . . . fourth-class. Darling knew
he would never act upon these delicious thoughts,
but they did sweeten the morning.

"I started with a simple phone call to Calvin
Dempsey. The Federal Bureau of Investigation took
ten minutes circuiting me around their offices.
When I did get him I found out I had gotten someone
else. I think it was some bureau in Billings, Montana.
They said he was there. Then they said he wasn't
there. Then they gave me a public relations officer,
although they don't call them that. The whole
damned bureau is a public relations outfit, if you ask
me. Then lo and behold I got Dempsey's secretary."

"And?" said Darling, who knew that if he were
to throttle young Gilpert there in the office it would
delay his homecoming by weeks.

"And she said he wasn't in but would return our
call."

"So that is how you got Calvin Dempsey to meet
me here today."

"That is how I didn't get Calvin Dempsey here
today," Gilpert said.

"All right. Go back to your assignment."

"I don't think we should let this gross breach of
common courtesy go unnoticed. Frankly, as an assistant United States attorney general, I was deeply
insulted. I won't stand for this."

Darling wiped the butter off his mouth with a
light blue interoffice memorandum sheet, the nap-

kin having been soaked to uselessness in the sandwich's transit. He inserted a yellow legal pad and three sharpened pencils into his gray work briefcase with the catch that needed fixing and headed for the door.

"I said, as an assistant attorney general, I won't stand for this!" Gilpert yelled as the door closed behind Darling.

Outside, Darling told Miss McGirr he was on his way to the FBI building to look for Calvin Dempsey. If Dempsey should call, tell him that Darling would be wandering around FBI until at least 10:30, whereupon he would return to Justice and that Darling must see Dempsey.

"Urgent. Immediate. Now," said Darling.

"What should I do about Ronny?" asked Miss McGirr, nodding her head toward the door of Darling's office.

"Murder him."

"Will you authorize that in writing?"

"Do it first and then we'll talk about authorization," said Darling.

"What the hell is going on? Will someone explain to me what's going on?" asked Gilpert, appearing at Darling's office door.

"Your research has to be updated," said Miss McGirr. "To include the Wounded Elk verdict."

"Where is he running to?" asked Gilpert, nodding toward the disappearing Darling.

"Work."

"I tell you, Miss McGirr, we are at a crossroads in the life of the American judicial system. And our attorney general, in his wisdom, has assigned the one man who will rush pell-mell down any path just to get the damned thing over with."

"Ronny, you've got work to do," said Miss McGirr softly.

"I am ashamed to be part of this project. I am ashamed that I have taken my law degree, my education and my mind—most of all my mind—and cast this whole lot with a man who thinks the main priority in our study of dissidents' trials is a stopwatch. I am ashamed."

"Ronny," said Miss McGirr, "are you talking or do you really mean that?"

"I mean everything I say," said Gilpert, trying to get the maximum possible hardness into his face.

"All right," said Miss McGirr. "Since you mean it, I'll explain to you how really thorough Mr. Darling is. You may not know it, but your work is already making judicial history. You've helped establish what a political trial is, by your cataloguing work."

"I have?" Gilpert queried, his face brightening.

"Yes. Our working definition of political trial is any case in which the defense can get admitted into evidence facts pertaining to social grievances. In other words, if a Black Panther should gun down a woman of the evening in a bar and he can get a court to accept that his views on society are pertinent, then it's a political trial. That's Luke's working definition. Your research has confirmed it."

"Well, I'll be . . . ," said Gilpert. "I didn't think Darling thought like that."

"Ronny, he's the best lawyer in Justice."

"So saith his secretary."

"So saith anyone who knoweth the law, son."

The new FBI building was on Halsey Street, the last project of the late J. Edgar Hoover. Darling could not help thinking that the shoddiness at Wounded Elk never would have occurred if Hoover still had been running the bureau. Contrary to stories that were becoming more fashionable, he knew Hoover did not spend his day plotting vendettas. He had spent his days making the bureau so thorough and incorruptible that his successes wound up looking like persecutions and vendettas. But it was just that the bureau was better prepared than anyone else. Calvin Dempsey would never have been allowed to pull those shenanigans in the Wounded Elk trial. Even if the U.S. attorney trying the case had wanted to blow it and had requested the unnecessary tapping of phones and the fake eyewitness and the spying on the judge, the bureau would have nudged him to his senses.

What Darling needed to know for his report to Walthrop was whether Special Agent Calvin Demp-

sey was a freak, or whether he represented some kind
of major breakdown in FBI efficiency. For this, the
first step had to be eyeball-to-eyeball with Dempsey.

Darling had heard that when organizations
moved into big new buildings, they often began to
die. It was some sort of French saying, he thought.
The French had a saying for everything.

The FBI had tried hard to make its new headquarters appear less grim and foreboding than usual.
The receptionist was personable and efficient and
informed Darling that Mr. Dempsey was assigned to
the Crime Records Division, which could be found
on the fifth floor.

Darling presented himself to a secretary in the
Crime Records Division and was advised, ever so
politely, that Mr. Dempsey was unavailable and
would Darling leave his name.

"Damnit, woman, I did not come over here to
leave my name. If I wanted to leave my name, I
would have had my secretary do it. Or a staff mem-
ber. I came here because leaving a name apparently
means nothing anymore in the bureau. Where is
Dempsey?"

The young, redhaired secretary seemed flustered.

"I don't know. Sir, we have a record of Mr. Gilpert calling for you last Friday. Mr. Dempsey will
respond. Sir."

"This is incredible," said Darling. "What has
happened to the bureau?"

The woman's green eyes blinked as her hands worked busily at themselves.

"Sir, you're not helping me."

"I'm not here to help you. You're here to help *me*. Where is Dempsey now?"

The redhead shrugged helplessly and said, "Please wait a moment, sir."

She rose and vanished into an inner office. As the minutes ticked by, Darling grew angrier. She had had enough time by now to make her phone call for instructions. Now she had had enough time to be called back by someone else. Now Lucius Darling was really going to raise hell. But the secretary prevented that by reappearing with a smile.

She handed him a yellow square of paper. He looked at the paper. It read "Lucius Darling for C. Dempsey."

"What is this?" asked Darling. "I need a pass to see Dempsey? How about shots? A smallpox booster?"

"I don't know, sir. You're confusing me. You've been incredibly rude and I don't respond to pressure that well. Please stop yelling."

"I'm not yelling, damnit," yelled Darling. But when he saw the girl wince, he lowered his voice. "Where am I supposed to go with this to see Mr. Dempsey?"

"Four hundred fourteen Barclay Street."

"Thank you," said Darling, feeling physically exhausted. He telephoned Miss McGirr at the office, told her that he was hopefully on Dempsey's trail, that the bureau was employing lunatics nowadays, and that he was off to 414 Barclay Street, wherever that was, where he fully expected to find Mr. Dempsey sitting nude in a corner with a lampshade over his head, sucking on an electrical cord, while a steam calliope wheezed "Columbia, the Gem of the Ocean."

"They're that bad nowadays?"

"Worse. My apologies to Gilpert. I assumed it was just his foulup that we couldn't get through to Dempsey."

"Ronny is really a lot more solid than he sounds, Luke," said Miss McGirr. "He's doing thorough work."

"Don't tell me about it. I don't want to lose my irrational, deep-seated hatred for him."

Darling hung up the pay phone and hailed a cab. Young Gilpert had just risen by light years in his estimation. McGirr could call them accurately.

Four-fourteen Barclay Street was a four-story warehouse building in a black neighborhood. There were few people on the street, but Darling could tell the ethnicity of the area by noting that there were no whites. Blacks walked around in white neighborhoods, but rarely was it the other way around.

The street smelled of urine. The building's doorbell was a loud alarm that rang someplace deep inside the structure. When it was not answered, Darling pounded on the door with his fist. He heard the semi-hollow *dack-dack* of his pounding on the sheet metal. The door felt greasy and he had an urge to wipe his knuckles, but he had nothing to wipe with. Someone with a neon green spray paint had left "Groo 122" as a testimonial to having successfully passed the door. Darling began banging on the door with his briefcase.

"Yeah?" came a male voice from inside.

"I've come to see Calvin Dempsey."

"No Calvin Dempsey here."

"Good," yelled Darling. "Now the AG can get the sonofabitch for desertion." He waved a goodbye to the closed door which suddenly parted a crack, then opened. Darling was somewhat surprised to see a man in clean white shirt and tie, pressed gray pants, and polished cordovans. He had expected a warehouse worker.

"Who are you?" asked the man.

"Lucius Darling, Justice Department."

"Do you have any identification?"

"Who are *you*?" Darling asked.

"Let's see your identification first," said the man. He appeared to be in his early forties, his hair parted straight, like a plumb line made of shiny scalp. His voice carried the authoritative boredom of an official. So did the thin mustache across his upper lip.

Darling flipped open his wallet to show identification.

"Is that all?"

"Oh . . . right." Darling showed the yellow memo slip the secretary had made back at FBI headquarters.

The man nodded and opened the door wider. Darling entered, wondering whether he would get the slip back.

Inside, the walls were clean and freshly painted. Fluorescent overhead lights made the long hallway seem like a brightly lit vehicular tunnel. Darling passed closed doors, following the man. None of the doors had numbers; all appeared to be gray metal with two dull brass locks that needed keys. The hall smelled musty, as if it rated only once-a-year cleaning. Darling could see scuff marks on the dull green linoleum floor.

"Dempsey has his office here, I take it," said Darling.

The man gave him a cold glance but was silent.

At that point, Darling vowed that the bureau, when his report was finished, was going to get a stinging memorandum on interdepartmental courtesy, with acerbic hints about the sanity of said Federal Bureau of Investigation. The man pressed a black plastic button set in a dull aluminum shield on the wall, beside what appeared to be a door. When the door slid into the wall at the right, Darling saw that it was an elevator. There were four buttons on an equally unpolished aluminum square in the elevator, which itself had the pungency of an old locker room.

The man pressed the third button. Probably a basement and three floors, Darling guessed.

The elevator started up smoothly and they rode in silence until the door opened to another hallway with unmarked locked doors. This hallway floor had fewer scuff marks but was equally unpolished. Three doors from the right, the man inserted a key into the top lock, and then another into the bottom lock, from a ring that had six keys. Theoretically, those six keys could handle thirty double-lock combinations. Just about the number of doors Darling estimated to be in the building.

The man reached inside the room and turned on a bright yellow overhead light. Darling saw eight upward-banked rows of hardbacked seats. Above the last row were three cutout squares in the wall. To his left was a white, glasslike screen, about eight feet by eight feet. Cigarette butts and dark burns covered the wooden floor. A fan hummed from a vent across the room.

"Is Agent Dempsey going to meet me here?" asked Darling. "You know my time is rather limited."

"This button," said the man, pointing to a small knob under the light switch, "gets you out. Just press it when you're through."

"All right, enough," snapped Darling. "Who are

you? Let's see your identification."

"Better take a seat before I shut the door."

"Listen... The bureau is going to hear about this. I have never experienced such rank discourtesy. I want to see Dempsey now. Now!"

But the man silently shut the door and the overhead yellow light went out, leaving Darling in blackness. He reached for the doorknob and turned it, but it would not open. He fumbled along the wall to where he remembered the exit button was. As his finger touched it, however, the movie screen at one end of the room lit up white and bright. He was going to press the button anyway, when the screen displayed a single word: "WHY?"

Then the screen filled with a shot of running, screaming demonstrators. The camera closed on a Viet Cong flag. Darling assumed it was the 1969 spring demonstration against the war in Vietnam.

"Ho, ho, Ho Chi Minh. Ho Chi Minh is gonna win," yelled the demonstrators.

"Why?" said a voice on the screen. The voice was metallic and echoed and hard to recognize. "Why?" said the mechanical voice again and the picture changed to a thoughtful-looking bearded man sitting in an easy chair. "How did this..." said the voice, and the bearded man spoke, softly and clearly:

"I think it's wrong that we are in Vietnam and I think we should vote against anyone who supports that war."

"...become this?" asked the mechanical voice-over, and the picture changed to a screaming mob advancing on the Pentagon.

"Or this?" said the voice, and Darling instantly recognized the students at Clark State University running into National Guard smoke.

"Or this?" and Darling saw the trunk of a body, the blood where its head had been still fresh in technicolor. The screen flashed white lettering: "WISCONSIN PROTEST BOMBING. Victim, a physicist who died, and years of his research destroyed."

Darling sat down in the nearest seat. That was no news film of a body. Television stations didn't run horror like that. He knew he had just seen a clip from a police film, and quickly he brought out a yellow lined legal pad and noted: 11:10 morning, third floor, 414 Barclay Street, Washington, D.C.

He wished McGirr were here so she could take her usual thorough notes. He decided quickly to take cursory self-reminder notes, then make more notes from them as soon as he got out of the room. He did not know what he was watching, but he felt something very important was happening. His mouth tasted brassy and the pen became wet with his own perspiration. Despite the vent with its noisy fan, the room needed air.

"Why?" asked the mechanical voice again, "did this..." and there was a full front shot of Thurgood Marshall, the Supreme Court justice who in his early years was a civil rights lawyer, talking about justice and equality, and then the picture changed to a young black man in a dashiki, his hair in an Afro, standing before a crowd of blacks ". . . become this?"

The young black spoke: "The white race is an evil putrescence that must be destroyed, must be burned from our black earth like the obscene invention it is."

Then the picture changed to that of a white arm, with the fleshy wrinkles of an older person. There were tattooed numbers on the inside of the arm, obviously the mark of a former inmate of a Nazi concentration camp. The camera moved back and Darling saw that the arm belonged to a woman whose face and chest had been ripped open with knives. Another police shot.

"And this," said the voice again and the screen showed a black woman with her face puffy from a beating, with blood oozing out of her left eye. Through split teeth, she said, "I was going to the store and I be hit and they take my purse. I be hit and they take my purse and the policemens never make no arrest."

A quick camera cut to an elderly white man speaking: "The police are just afraid to arrest anyone nowadays."

The camera panned back and at the man's feet, there was the blackened body of a little girl.

"RHONDA JOHNSON, 8, BURNED ALIVE WITH GASO-

LINE. DETROIT, 1974," flashed white letters on the screen.

And then the voice again.

"These are American cities at sunset," came the echoing words, and then there were still shots of empty streets. Shot after shot, empty block after empty block.

Voice over: "Where are the people?"

"Oh, you don't go out after dark." The voice was an elderly woman with a Southern accent.

"De street? Ah ain't goin' out on de street affa dark nohow." A black woman.

"One just does not travel anymore at night." Middle-aged white woman.

"They get you in daylight now." Young black woman, her face bleeding from a savage knife attack.

And then a montage of policemen's funerals and the voice-over saying: "Is it the policeman's fault?" Shots of grieving widows, both white and black. Police at attention, a crying black boy clutching his mother's skirt.

"How could this possibly come from *this*?" said the voice-over, and the screen flashed a picture of Martin Luther King at the Washington Monument. It was King's "I Have a Dream" speech, which Darling thought was the greatest speech he had ever heard. He listened to it again on this film and his heart jumped as it had the first day he heard it years before when there had been so much hope, when

America meant hope. And then, despite all the advances, the hope had turned to hate and bitterness.

It was after the civil rights bills had been passed, after people had stopped being lynched and were allowed the ordinary decency of drinking at whatever fountains they wished and sleeping at whatever hotels they wished and using whatever toilet facilities they wished, that the hate began. It was precisely when police no longer felt free to beat upon blacks that blacks had begun shooting at police. It was after people stopped being arrested for disorderly conduct that the Vietnam War protest had bloomed into real disruption.

Darling quickly returned his thoughts to the pages, making small notations.

"And how did this . . ." came the voice, and there was a film clip of Indians negotiating with a white man, apparently a government official, ". . . become this?"

And then Darling's heart leaped. There were scenes of Wounded Elk he had never seen before. Men shooting a cow, tearing up a Methodist church, and best of all, Roland Watertree, unmistakably Roland Watertree, Indian braids, sunglasses, and all. He was in a room with another man and a woman. They were sitting on the floor and the camera was angled from slightly above their heads. White lettering appeared on the screen: WOUNDED ELK, 1972.

The plump, dark-haired girl was speaking on the

film but her voice could not be heard.

Then Watertree spoke. "No, no, no. We're not here to make some deal with the Indian bureau. This isn't about a bunch of shabby reservation Indians. Indians have been dying since the white man set foot in this country. Come on. What kind of beads are we selling out for now?"

"They're willing to reopen the treaty hearing," the woman said.

"This isn't about treaty violations," Watertree said. "This isn't about some shabby Indian town. Loads of Indians are well off. I'm not here to make a bunch of reservation Indians a little bit happier for a few weeks or years or even for their whole [bleep-bleep] lives. I am here to stick it to the United States government in front of the world. We're here to mobilize support to overthrow that fat white capitalist power structure in Washington. What I want from this is bodies. Dead bodies. I want preferably United States marshals and if not United States marshals, the [bleep] Sioux. On television. Our mailing lists are already ten times bigger, and we've only been here a week. This is a revolution. It's against America. Don't talk to me about one tribe in one stinking little town."

Darling made quick notes, jotting down the time again so he could regain the frame. If Dempsey had this film clip at his disposal, he had had a conviction at Billings. Not only a conviction but a political devastation of Roland Watertree and his group. Here was a man issuing orders and establishing a motive for killing, plotting insurrection against the United States government. And if this were Dempsey's film, why in blue blazes did he recruit an unreliable witness and then push Justice into resting its case on that one man?

The image of the Indians faded. The metallic voice-over again.

"Why did this . . ." Again, Martin Luther King at the civil rights rally, ". . . become this?" Shots of armed black youths beating up a young black schoolboy. "And this?" . . . a shot of a former civil rights worker in front of a microphone saying, "I don't want God to get Whitey. He's mine."

"Why?" said the announcer, and there were the Clark State students running at the National Guard and the Guardsmen began firing.

"Beautiful. They shot how many?" And it was the face of Harold Albend. The face was in black and white and there was the polka dot cravat and he was grinning. "How many students did they shoot at Clark State? Beautiful. We've got them now." It was a grainy black and white picture and somehow it reminded Darling of the film of Roland Watertree, which was in color. Instantly, Darling knew why the films seemed similar. There was no movement to the camera, no cutting from angle to angle. Both cameras had been fixed in one location and undoubtedly were hidden.

Who concealed movie cameras? The FBI?

But if that loon Dempsey had access to this, why had he pressed for those idiotic solutions at Wounded Elk? Why hadn't the bureau informed Justice of these? And what were these films made for?

Darling felt closed in, almost trapped in the room. He wanted to get out, but he didn't want to leave these film strips. The next frame made his decision for him.

An attractive black woman, her Afro framing the screen, her face awash in joy, exclaimed in dull sonorous tones "the oppressive racist capitalist judicial system..." It was the face of Muriel Johnson, another of the four cases Darling's task force was studying.

The voice-over: "This is what guns registered in Muriel Johnson's name did to one of your judges."

The film cut to a photo of a judge in robes with a shotgun taped to his neck; a black prisoner held the trigger of the shotgun in one hand and a pistol in another. The film cut again to another still shot, and Darling almost threw up when he saw the picture of the judge's head mangled by the close shotgun blast. His jaw had been shot off and the roof of his mouth stood out eerily from the rest of his head. The picture ended at half a face.

Cut to a newspaper heading: "MURIEL JOHNSON FOUND INNOCENT."

Voice-over: "And this is what she said of the 'justice' that freed her..."

The woman's grinning face again. She spoke:

"Oppressive injustice that must be obliterated by the voice of the people. The people freed me. All power to the people."

"All power to the people" yelled a mob as the film cut to a group of students.

Darling noted two more fast cuts: one to the face of grinning Muriel Johnson, the other to the gruesome shot of the judge, and then a third to a grieving crowd around a graveside.

"Anyone ever hear of interstate flight to avoid arrest? It's a legal charge," said the metallic voice as the film cut to a newspaper headline that told about Muriel Johnson being arrested in New York City, this time without the theatrical Afro. It cut back to the earlier headline: "MURIEL JOHNSON FOUND INNOCENT."

Voice-over: "Anyone ever hear of a law against preaching the violent overthrow of the government?"

Film cut to Roland Watertree saying, "We're here to mobilize support to overthrow that fat white capitalist power structure in Washington, and we hope to do it with bullets."

Voice-over: "Anyone ever hear of incitement to riot?"

Then a still shot of the Clark State shooting.

Voice-over: "Let's look at these kids. Why are they charging National Guardsmen with guns? Why are they throwing rocks?"

More new white lettering: "CLARK STATE, AU-

GUST 18, TUESDAY, THE DAY BEFORE THE SHOOTING."
And then there was Harold Albend on film, haranguing a crowd of students, telling them to tear down the government, and then the next speaker, a black militant, yelling "Kill the pigs. Kill the pigs."

Voice-over: "And so these young college students went out..."

Scene of smoke and Guardsmen shooting.

"...and they tried to kill the pigs or whatever great thing they had been convinced they were doing. And four young people were killed."

Cut to Albend: "Four dead? Good."

Cut to black militant: "Whitey is mine."

And again the voice-over: "None of these people are in jail. None ever served a day for their crimes. But the children of Clark State are dead. And the people of the cities live in fear. And policemen die every day."

Darling witnessed fast changes of faces chanting, "Police brutality...Police brutality...Police brutality." He recognized Albend and the black militant and Muriel Johnson.

Voice-over: "When you say something long enough, people believe you. We've heard the Big Lie before." And then there was the still shot of the dead woman's tattooed arm. "That big liar put people into ovens. If you preach hate long enough, people are going to believe you. Even believe you enough to start throwing stones at soldiers with guns." The film cut to the Clark State mob.

"Poison," said the voice-over. "Poison."

And suddenly the screen went all white and Darling thought that the film was over.

But it was not. Faintly, as if far away, he heard on the film the sound of music. It was "America the Beautiful," and in the center of the film appeared a small dot, and then it grew and was distinguishable as an American flag, growing larger on the screen, as the music grew in volume.

And then the voice-over again:

"It was all poison," the metallic tones said. "And the courts never took care of it and the police were afraid. So could you blame me? With all the yelling you're probably hearing right now, think of who is the poisoner and who isn't. What are they yelling about? Who is your real enemy? Who did I—"

With a blinding blanket of sudden yellow, the lights were on in the screening room. Darling blinked to recover his sight.

"Hello, Lucius, have you seen Dempsey, sweetheart Lucius? Haven't seen you for a coon's age, Lollypop."

Someone was in the room, making fun of his name, and the man's voice was familiar.

CHAPTER ★★★★★ 8

The Near Future

"HAROLD, OLD BUDDY. HOW ARE YOU? IT'S Lonzo."

"Who?"

"Lonzo. Lonzo Gates." When there was no immediate response, Gates added quickly, "from *Mossback* Magazine."

"Oh, yes. How are you, Mr. Gates?"

"Don't be so formal. After all, we stood on many barricades together."

"Yes. Of course. What can I do for you?"

"I'm trying to run down a Justice Department attorney named Lucius Darling. I was wondering, you ever hear of him?"

There was a long pause over the phone before Harold Albend said, "This isn't some of this radical shit, is it, Mr. Gates?"

"No, but why do you ask?"

"Because that is not my life anymore. I'm a bond attorney. I work on Wall Street. It really doesn't do me or my firm any good to have the past constantly dredged up and a lot of irrelevancies reported in the popular press."

Gates wanted to shout at him, *Irrelevancies! You used to talk about overthrowing the government with guns, and now you call them irrelevancies! What was your price for selling out, Albend!* But instead he said, simply and untruthfully, "No dredging up here. Just trying to locate somebody. So do you know this Lucius Darling?"

"All right. This is off-the-record and you're not going to quote me. Understood?"

"Of course."

"The name doesn't ring a bell and it's not a name one would easily forget. Lucius Darling, you say?"

"Yup. A U.S. attorney."

"Wait . . . wait a minute, something's coming back." He hesitated, then said, "All right, back in the seventies, maybe 1974, there was some kind of Justice Department study to find out why they were losing political trials. Now that I think of it, I think somebody named Darling headed up the study. Yeah. Lucius Darling. I'm pretty sure that's who it was."

"They ever release that study?" Gates asked.

"Not that I know of," said Albend. "You know, I'd really rather not talk about all this."

"Okay, I can understand that," said Gates, who could not understand it at all. "Oh, one last thing. Does the name 'Jericho Day' mean anything to you?"

"I'm afraid not," Albend said.

Gates sighed. "Okay, then. Thank you for your time."

"You're very welcome, Mr. Gates," Harold Albend said before hanging up.

Gates was flabbergasted. The man was treating him as a stranger and he and Albend had spent years together on the barricades, fighting for a better America. They had fought together, partied together, drunk together, and late one night, in Albend's room, they had shared a co-ed. And now Albend called him Mr. Gates?

He drew an angry black line through Albend's name in his desk phone book. Someday he would do a column on all the people who had sold out the Movement and when he did, Harold Albend's name was sure to be at the top of the list. He got up to go to the magazine's morgue and check on back issues. If Albend's memory were right and Lucius Darling had been involved in a political trial study for the Justice Department, *Mossback* would have had a story on it. And that was a place to start looking for this goddamned Jericho Day, whatever it was.

CHAPTER ★★★★★★ 9

The Mid-1970s

Monday, October 24: The Eighth Day

LUCIUS DARLING BLINKED AND WHEN HE adjusted to the roomful of light saw a familiar face.

"Ramsey MacDonald? What are you doing here?"

"What are *you* doing here?" asked MacDonald.

"I'll be damned if I know," Darling said. He put his pad of notes into his briefcase and noticed that his writing hand was sweaty. "You're out of uniform."

MacDonald wore a gray suit with a striped regimental tie. Darling could not remember his wearing such a civilian suit since they had graduated Troy High School together and MacDonald had gone off to Annapolis and Korea and Darling off to the Merchant Marine, then college and law school.

In their earlier days in Washington, they had met

often but MacDonald had always been either loung-
ing in his backyard in slacks and sweater or wearing
his neat green Marine uniform with the colonel's
birds polished and his ribbons set out like a military
résumé for anyone who could read his chest.

"I heard from Troy that you and Kathy were
going home," said MacDonald.

"I got euchred into something," Darling said.
"Do you know what this place is?"

"You got me, Lucius sweetheart. I figured it
would be your cockamamie kind of thing. Passes,
unwashed hallways. Don't they ever clean this
place?"

"I just saw a film that blew my mind, Ram. Do
you know who runs this?"

"I would guess the FBI," MacDonald said. "Do
you know Dempsey?"

"I'm trying to meet him, but he's slippery as
fog," said Darling, looking at the door. It was slightly
open.

"Here. Watch this. Close the door," said Darling.
MacDonald, who had been about to sit down,
stepped back to the door and pushed. As soon as it
clicked shut, the lights went off and a big "Why?"
filled the screen and the narrator's metallic voice-
over began.

This time the lights went on and the picture
disappeared as MacDonald opened the door by pressing the button under the light switch.

"I've seen it," he said, apparently affected by the announcer's voice because his reflected a similar timber. Or was it that Washington made people lose their regional speech patterns? MacDonald had lost his Troy twang long ago.

"Do you know where I can get the original clips that were used for this film?" Darling asked.

"Why?"

"An assignment. I want to know what Dempsey's doing."

"You're not the only one," said MacDonald.

"So what are you doing here anyway?" Darling asked.

"I called an air force general a baboon at a party. Come on, I'll tell you about it over a cup of coffee."

The man who had let Darling into the building was nowhere around when they left, and they rode down in the elevator and let themselves out.

Outside, they had to walk six blocks before they could find a cab. As they walked and rode, MacDonald jawed about his problem. The last time Darling had seen him—more than two years before—he had been assigned as an aide to the general who served as White House chief of staff. It had been a great break. He would make general before fifty.

"I know, I know," Darling said. "How many times did I hear you say anyone can make general during a war but it takes talent to make it during peacetime?"

"I was on my way. And in all modesty, it would have been good for the country. I'm good at what I do. Every assignment, I've come out golden. Golden."

"So you're at the White House," Darling said. "So what happened?"

"Well, I got myself assigned to the National Security Council, working right out of the White House."

"Spy stuff?" Darling said.

"No, more like politics. You know, making sure that the White House view wasn't forgotten by the bureaucrats hiding in their offices out there in other departments. And then I was at this cocktail party, and you know I'm not a drinker..."

"I know."

"This red-faced air force general was. You know how they select for stars in the air force? Anyone who can hold a pencil without shaking. I mean it. In Vietnam, the air force was a disgrace. It's a wonder they even hit the country, let alone their targets. They run until they see a wisp of smoke, which might be antiaircraft fire, and then they unload wherever they are and rush back to invent details of scores. This is a fact. The only pinpoint bombing in Nam was navy air or marine air. The air force might just as well have mailed their loads. An air force target is anything that happens to be under their plane when the pilots chicken out. True."

"All right, I'll take the stars away from the air force," Darling said.

"I wanted to set the scene."

"So you told this general what you thought of his outfit and he didn't like it, right?" said Darling. The cab pulled up in front of the Mayflower Hotel.

"Have you had lunch?" asked MacDonald.

"I was going to do it in the office," said Darling. "I have an assignment to finish and then I'm getting out of this town."

"An hour make a difference?"

"A second makes a difference. You know how Kathy always was about going home," Darling said.

"I need your help, Luke."

"To eat lunch?"

"Partly. You're going to pick up the check because you're a rich lawyer."

"I'm *going to be* a rich lawyer when I get the hell out of Justice."

"Come on, the Rib Room has great roast beef."

Inside, MacDonald ordered shrimp cocktail, prime rib rare, salad with Roquefort, and Bavarian layer cake with chocolate and vanilla ice cream, and could the waitress get a little dab of whipped cream to top the dessert?

"You never put on weight, prick."

"I know. You can make so many enemies in this town by being able to eat anything you want and not gain. They could forgive you violent insurrection, but they never forgive you for staying trim on whipped cream and cake."

Darling ordered a chicken salad with black coffee. MacDonald asked if he were going to finish all the salad as two forkfuls remained on Darling's plate. MacDonald also ordered another basket of rolls, which he finished along with Darling's chicken salad.

Darling wondered if he could have a taste of MacDonald's ice cream.

"Order ice cream if you want ice cream."

"I just want a taste," Darling said.

"Order a taste."

"Forget it. You're incredible, Ram."

"Just a growing boy."

Through the meal, MacDonald unfolded a tale of military woe. So this general had been talking about Washington holding him back. He was talking about "significant tonnages" of bombs. MacDonald had merely pointed out that the tonnage dropped on North Vietnam exceeded the tonnage dropped in World War II, that bombing alone was an ineffective weapon. Against an industrial nation, airpower couldn't do it solo, let alone against a country like North Vietnam.

"Then their supply centers are fewer so we can knock them out," the general had said, ordering another drink.

MacDonald had pointed out, respectfully, he assured Darling, that the North Vietnamese supply centers were in Russia.

The general's response was that MacDonald was an insubordinate moron. The next day he was transferred.

"The guy didn't know anything about warfare, but he certainly knew Washington politics," said MacDonald. "He's got me in a trip. Get a load of this. I am now special advisor to the Joint Chiefs of Staff on possible military consequences of radical action. I report directly to that drunken flyboy."

"You're in over your head," said Darling.

"Yeah," said MacDonald. "You know how tricky this is. For one, I have no power to say who is a radical and who isn't. All I have to do is name some liberal organization and my ass is on some congressional carpet. And this sonofabitch general is pressing; he wants me to do surveillance work too."

MacDonald looked ready to cry onto his scraped-clean ice cream plate.

Darling asked, "How'd you run into Dempsey?"

"I used to bump into him once in a while when my job at the White House brought me over to Justice. So when I got this new assignment, first thing I did was take a couple of weeks furlough. Sort of to regroup, you know, and figure out what I was going to do. And I tried to reach Dempsey to ask him for help. It's funny how easy it is to locate people when you work at 1600 Pennsylvania Avenue and how hard it gets to be later. Anyway, it took me a week to locate him, and I was shipped down to that factory where I met you."

"And you still haven't seen Dempsey?"

MacDonald shook his head. "So now this general is on my ass and my first assignment is to get together an official report on radical infiltration of the armed services." He absentmindedly began chewing on a leftover piece of roll. "Luke, I need help. Legal and political savvy. I can weather this detail if I don't foul up. But I don't know the Black Panthers from the SDS. I'm a Marine, not a politician. All these guys sound like revolutionaries to me."

"Well, they are, but don't quote me," said Darling and he felt a little ashamed because in Washington, you didn't get yourself committed to calling anyone a revolutionary—not even if that's what they called themselves. It was a common code that you knew who the revolutionaries were but you never put it on paper. And here was Ram MacDonald, the big open-faced kid with the eagles on his shoulders, thrown right into this snakepit with its codes of what you knew and what you wrote and whom you could trust and whom you couldn't, and MacDonald was going to go down the political toilet.

And he didn't deserve it. He was a perfect Marine. He had learned his trade and done it honestly, and the country was lucky to have him. But in this job, well, he was like a tractor operator being sent in to do neurosurgery.

"Why can't I quote you?" asked MacDonald.

"Because you just don't go calling people revolutionaries on the record," Darling said.

"Some of these guys call themselves revolutionaries. I mean, if they call themselves revolutionaries, am I supposed to call them liars? I mean, what is it? What are the ground rules of this thing?"

"That's a big subject, Ram."

"That's just it. Could you put me in contact with someone who knows where the pitfalls are? I thought Dempsey would help if I had met him at that damned slum but . . ." He shrugged.

"Who was that guy who let us in?" asked Darling.

"Don't know. Anyway, I know you're in antitrust but there have got to be guys you know in Justice who know their way around this radical thing."

"I'm trying to think," Darling said.

"Jesus, that could take forever, Lucius. I need it now, not five years from now when you have eliminated every possible alternative to come up with what is probably the best source. And, of course, you'd have eight hundred reasons why that person was inadequate for the task but you'd have fifteen hundred reasons why everyone else was more inadequate. I can't wait, Luke. I'm going under and I need help."

Darling finished his coffee and signaled for the check.

"You know I'd like to help you."

"That, I know, is a 'no.'"

"Well, all right, Ram. No."

"That's not like you, Luke. Why the change?"

"In one week, I am leaving this city and going home to make money and raise my kids in a comfy atmosphere, redolent with all the trappings I used to laugh at. Two cars, season tickets to Ohio State, maybe even the Cleveland Browns, the Troy Country Club, plenty of land, and streets that I can stroll down with Kathy in the evening. We used to like long walks... before we moved to this godforsaken sewer of a city."

MacDonald gripped Darling's wrist and the two men locked eyes. Darling could not remember ever staring so directly at Ram MacDonald. It was almost like a revelation of the man's intensity.

"You're right, Luke. I agree with you one hundred percent. I'm sorry I asked. This is a battlefield. I have no right dragging you in."

When the check arrived, MacDonald grabbed it and waved off Darling's attempts to pay.

"If this is a battlefield, you must be shell-shocked, Ram. I never saw you pick up a check before."

"I did. At Dangles on North Street. I paid for the Milky Way."

"I mean within the last twenty years," Darling said.

"I was feeling guilty. No point in both of us going under. If one of us survives, maybe you can get me a job. I can retire in a couple of years. Still a colonel, of course, but with pension and another job, I could make out."

Darling was quiet. He knew it might be the best investment of his life to demand that he be allowed to pay the check. He saw the guileless smile on MacDonald's face and felt the small punch of comradeship.

"Hey, cheer up, Lucius sweetheart, the darling of civics class. I'm a big boy. I'll survive."

"I just can't help you, Ram."

"I know that," said MacDonald sweetly. "That's why I'm feeling bad for asking you. You're in antitrust anyhow."

From the Mayflower Hotel, they walked along Constitution Avenue, toward the Justice Department, and Darling tried to cheer up his boyhood friend.

"Anyway, Ram, you still have your Marine reserve officers' group to play around with. You still with them?"

MacDonald nodded glumly. "Still their unpaid advisor. That is, until that flyboy bastard finds out about it and makes me stop."

"You know, I think that's when we started to drift away from each other," Darling said. "You were always flying somewhere to swap lies with those other fake heroes."

"Just keeping my hand in, Luke. How am I going to run for president if I don't keep my power base? You know, you never told me what you were doing down at that warehouse."

"Same as you. Supposed to meet Dempsey."

"Yeah. But why?"

Darling explained that currently he was working on something allied to what MacDonald had been thrown into. But not the same thing.

"How's it different, Luke?"

"It's different."

"Everything's different from everything else," said MacDonald. "How is it the same?" Without waiting for an answer, he walked over to the large display window of a chain bookstore. "Look at this shit, Luke," he said, pointing to a book that was opened in a display. "That shows you how to blow up a house. And they got the key thing too...the bearing walls. Look. Who publishes this crap?"

"Freedom of speech," Darling said. "It's the law."

"I also thought the law was that you can't incite to riot. Isn't there a law against treason too?"

"That one question is a week, Ram. It varies," Darling said.

"I've got time."

"I don't," Darling said. "But I'll tell you, I wouldn't rely on that movie your friend Dempsey provides."

"Too kooky for you?" MacDonald asked.

"Too kooky for anybody."

He couldn't very well try to shake MacDonald in the elevator leading to the second floor of Justice, but he did make a very nice attempt at Miss McGirr's desk.

"I'm jammed this afternoon, Ram. Incredibly jammed," said Darling, picking up a schedule on Miss McGirr's desk.

"Let me see," said MacDonald, grabbing for the schedule.

"Get out of here," Darling said.

"Just looking."

"McGirr, I want to speak directly to the director of the FBI and I want you to listen in to make notes."

"Why don't you tape it, Luke?" MacDonald said. "Everybody else tapes everything in this city."

"C'mon, Ram," said Darling, trying to generate real annoyance, but it was something he could never do with MacDonald.

With all the single-mindedness of a Boston Celtic setting a pick, McGirr dialed and announced she had the director's office on the line. This allowed

Darling to rush into his office to take the call, free of MacDonald. He had to wait momentarily until Miss McGirr really did have the director's office and then he spoke to a secretary, telling her that he had been trying to reach Agent Calvin Dempsey for three days in connection with an assignment from the attorney general himself and that he was sure the director would facilitate the liaison between Justice and the bureau by having Dempsey contact Darling soon. Thank you. No, there was no need to speak to the director himself since Darling was sure the director was as busy as Darling was. Darling simply wanted to speak to Dempsey.

Waiting on his desk was a progress report prepared by Miss McGirr. The five young lawyers had worked through the weekend and had cleaned up a lot of the preliminary work and were well along into their first-draft reports.

Gilpert had isolated 122 cases that had political overtones, although not all of them were federal charges. Of those 122 eighty-nine were common criminal charges handled by either state or county courts, including armed robbery, mugging, rape, and burglary. Eighty-two of these cases had resulted in convictions, well over ninety percent.

But in the thirty-three federal cases that fit into their working definition of a political trial, there were only fifteen convictions—and of the nine that had attracted national attention, all were acquittals, including, of course, the four cases handled by Albend which were under direct study by the task force.

Willoughby was deep into his analysis of Albend's courtroom work and indicated he might have something interesting on the man. O'Connell had almost completed the profiles on U.S. attorneys and the judges who had handled the four major political cases under study. And DeBaux had most of the basic information on federal court trends and jury selection.

There was a note appended to the report. It read: "Rothblatt wants to talk with you before putting his radical-trial mockup on paper. Gilpert has almost completed his step-by-step breakdown of the four cases. He is a bear for work, and in my opinion did an excellent job.—McGirr."

Darling made a mental note of Gilpert's competence that he knew would stay with him until the day he died. It was part of an almost subconscious filing system he had developed when he was a merchant seaman and an old salt had told him, "Son, you're not going to stay at sea long. Just by the way you listen, I know that. And I'm filing your name away because if ever I need someone's advice on something, in ten years you're going to be the one. Yes, sir. In ten years. And you're going to owe me too."

"What am I going to owe you?" Darling had asked.

"You're going to owe me for telling you to start your own filing system of people who do things well. There aren't ten men on this ship who know what they're doing and why they're doing it. And that holds for everything. When you find someone who works well and smart, remember him."

Darling had thought of the man as a bit sentimental and in the last few years couldn't remember his name exactly, but he always thought kindly of him. There weren't too many kind people in the Merchant Marine; instead, there were a lot of guys who thought that with a name like his, Darling would be engine room bait. It took his fists to show them how wrong they were.

But the mental filing system had proved useful in Darling's career, and now Gilpert's name went into that file as a man Darling would probably be able to get cheap. Until Gilpert learned to tether his vocal cords, he was never going into the big money.

Darling dialed McGirr on the interoffice phone and asked if Rothblatt were ready now with his report. If they could go over it verbally now, Rothblatt just might be able to go back to his office and prepare his written report early. That would free him to assist any of the other attorneys who might be bogged down.

"I've told Mr. MacDonald that you would try to fit him in this afternoon but that I saw no room on your schedule," McGirr said.

Darling sighed. MacDonald was still outside.

"Send him in. And Rothblatt. Thanks," said Darling.

MacDonald was in the office before Darling could hang up the phone.

"Why are you waiting, Ram?"

"To say goodbye. You rushed into your office without saying goodbye."

"Goodbye," Darling said.

"It all sounds so final. I just might cry," MacDonald said.

"Look," said Darling. "Maybe I can give you a little help. I've got a man coming into this office who has done some work in an area allied to what you've been stuck with. Now, you can listen in, but you can't quote anything you hear. Understood?"

"Sure. Although I think I've bought the package anyhow."

"I think you have too, Ram. I don't see you surviving this mission."

"*Semper fi.* I'm a Marine."

Max Rothblatt knocked and entered without waiting. He was a pale man with large eyeglasses and intense dark eyes. His fingernails were bitten to stubble and his expensive dark suit hung on his shoulders like hand-me-downs. His usual assignment was with Darling in antitrust, and he had also found a place in Darling's mental file—excellent, but undoubtedly too expensive when he went into private practice, if he did. He was the sort of lawyer who would indulge himself only with interesting work. Which was why Justice had him in the first place.

"Rothblatt, this is Ramsey MacDonald, a personal friend of mine who is going to, unofficially, totally unofficially—like he is going to forget he has ever heard this—unofficially listen to your report."

MacDonald smiled, shook hands, and perched on the edge of the conference table in the office. Rothblatt squinted, apparently not comprehending who MacDonald was.

"He's all right," said Darling. "Go ahead."

Rothblatt cast another suspicious glance at MacDonald, then began. As usual, he had culled his presentation down to bare essentials. His ability to simplify was his great strength.

"Bananas," he said. "Rotten bananas."

MacDonald looked at Darling, surprised, and stifled a laugh. Darling did not acknowledge it.

"The issue doesn't matter," said Rothblatt. "It is any apparent injustice that your radical core group looks for . . . call it racism, police brutality, breaking Indian treaties, rotten bananas."

At this point, MacDonald interrupted. "Rotten bananas and racism are slightly different problems," he said.

"Not technically. If I said 'racism,' we might be here until spring arguing about the justice or injustice of the matter. But if I say 'rotten bananas,' then we can deal with it technically and Luke won't feel obliged to defend America and I won't feel obliged to criticize it. So rotten bananas. It's all the same thing."

"It's not the same to me," MacDonald said.

"It is to your hard-core radical. It's just an issue around which they can mobilize people."

"With all due respect," MacDonald said, "I've spoken to radicals and they care about racism. At least I think they were radicals."

"They probably were and they probably did," Rothblatt said. "But you're missing the point. The issue, any issue, is just the tool they use...just a tool for mobilizing people to push for their broader aims. If it were really racism that bothered them, they'd be out protesting about Idi Amin, who chased all the Asians out of Uganda. Or they'd be protesting the Black Muslims who are racist. Or Japan, which mistreats its Koreans. Or Indonesia, which slaughtered its Chinese minority. Or New England, which has a history of mistreating the Irish and still has some places that even a Kennedy can't enter. You see, the issue's not important. It's just what the radical can use to build his base."

"What about anti-Semitism?" asked Mac-Donald.

"Classic example," Rothblatt said. "When the radicals thought they could use Jews, they did. And successfully. Like the Rosenbergs, who stole atomic secrets for Russia. During the Hitler-Stalin pact, you even had Jews saying no one should go to war with Nazi Germany even though Germany already had its ovens working. And then Germany invaded Russia and everything changed. Quick, declare war on Germany. Twenty years ago, Jews used to be the 'in' minority for left-wing support. And today, old Nazi hate sheets are being reprinted by the left-wing underground press.''

"Hey, Ram, thanks," said Darling. "You had to get him going. Do you see now why we should stay with rotten bananas to work with this problem sanely?"

"Take the Rosenwald Foundation which gave millions to black colleges," continued Rothblatt, speaking to MacDonald, whose face remained calm with just the slightest hint of a smile. "Millions. And not only was that discounted, but the radicals are saying the Jews used it to control black minds."

Rothblatt was trembling, his pale face turning the color of pickled beets.

"Enough!" yelled Darling. "Enough. Let's stick with rotten bananas." Rothblatt took a deep breath and seemed to calm himself as Darling told Mac-Donald, "Now you've seen an issue that cuts."

"Rotten bananas and the Jewish problem," MacDonald said, laughing. "I'm sorry," he said to Rothblatt.

"Who the fuck are you anyway?" Rothblatt said.

"I'm a colonel in the United States Marines."

"Oh. I thought you might be somebody," said Rothblatt, and his obvious lack of guile and the sincerity of his own form of prejudice hit MacDonald like a pail of cold water in the face. His smile went.

"Just a minute," MacDonald said.

"Rotten bananas," said Darling, laughing. "Rotten bananas."

The phone lit on McGirr's channel. It had to be important. Darling picked it up.

"Two simultaneous calls," said Miss McGirr. "Agent Dempsey on line one and your wife on two."

"What does Kathy want?"

"She said something bad happened and she wants to know what to do with your Barcalounger."

"What's the bad thing?" Darling asked.

"I think she just wants to hear your voice."

CHAPTER ***** 10

"YES, KATHY." DARLING HAD TOLD MCGIRR to tell Agent Dempsey he would speak to him in exactly one minute. He avoided MacDonald's and Rothblatt's glances as if, not seeing them, he could assure himself privacy.

"Luke, Billy isn't sleeping at night. He has nightmares."

"They're back again, huh?"

"Yeah. And Luke . . . ?"

"Yes."

"I'm not sleeping well either."

"Neither am I," said Darling. "I'm coming home tonight."

"Are you through with the job?"

"No. But tonight I'll see you. Pick me up at Vandalia. I'm sure I can get the TWA flight."

"Usual time?"

"Yes. Seven forty-five," Darling said.

"And Luke, I don't know if I can let you go again once you come home."

"And I don't know if I'll be able to leave. I love you, Kathy," he said without self-consciousness.

"I love you, Luke."

Darling switched to Agent Dempsey and waited for the FBI man's secretary to put him on.

Dempsey's voice was cigarette raspy with the cold consonants of the northern plains states.

"What can I do for you, Counselor?"

"There are two things. One, I saw a movie of yours and I'd like some information on how it was made, where I can get clips of it, and how those clips were obtained. And two, I have to talk to you about Wounded Elk and your work there."

"I have two answers, Counselor. One, I'm not sure what film you're talking about and two, I would be most happy to meet with you. Say November first at the bureau."

"We've got to make it sooner. Say tomorrow here," Darling said.

"I'm sorry, but I'm on special assignment until November first."

"I'll only need a half hour."

"I wish I could give it to you but I am not, at this time, able to meet with you," Dempsey said.

"That's unfortunate because there are some very unfortunate implications about your conduct at Wounded Elk and I thought, in all fairness, you should answer allegations made against you and the bureau before I bring them to the attention of the attorney general."

"What allegations?"

"I can't go into it on the phone," Darling said.

"I am more than prepared and I will memo this to your office with copies to my director and to the attorney general to discuss any matters with you . . . any matters . . . to the best of my ability. On November first."

"That's two weeks away. You're creating a logjam here at Justice."

"I regret any inconvenience," Dempsey said.

"Well, could I come over to see you for just ten minutes? Ten minutes is what you're spending talking to me."

"That's correct. I interrupted a very busy schedule because of my desire to cooperate. I don't have this ten minutes either."

"I want the film clips," Darling said coldly.

"What film?"

"In the building at four-fourteen Barclay Street."

"I don't understand," Dempsey said.

"Your secretary sent me there and I saw a film. That film has certain segments bearing on a report I am doing for the AG himself."

"Oh," said Dempsey, as if suddenly illuminated with understanding.

"You can get me the film then?"

"No, no. I still don't know what film you're talk-ing about. There's some kind of garbling here. You have someone on your staff named Gilpert, Ronald?"

"Yes. He requested a meeting with you last week."

"I see. The message didn't reach me because I'm on special assignment, but I see now it refers to an investigation. Yet you say you're making a report for the attorney general."

"As you know, investigation is part of making a report," Darling snapped.

"Well, I'm sorry about all this mixup," Dempsey said. "I'll be free at nine A.M. on the first and I'll be glad to talk with you, Counselor. But as I say, I know nothing of any film."

"Damnit, man...your secretary..." Darling's angry outburst was interrupted by MacDonald's hand covering the mouthpiece of the phone.

"Dempsey?" he said. "About the film?"

Darling nodded.

"Give me that phone," MacDonald said. "Hey, Dempsey. I know you know about that film Darling saw today because your damned office sent me there too. Yeah, this is Colonel MacDonald. Right. Bullshit...bullshit...bullshit...when...what do you mean November first?...uh-huh, uh-huh, uh-huh. Bullshit...right." Then he listened and a mo-ment later smiled as he hung up the phone.

"I'll get you that film, Luke. *And* Dempsey. He'll

bring it over to you himself. Friday okay?"

"This thing is beginning to have loose ends. What did Dempsey say?"

MacDonald gave a quick glance over his shoulder toward Rothblatt. "It's some kind of propaganda film. Overseas. It doesn't belong to the bureau."

"Overseas?" said Darling. "It was in English."

"I know, I know," said MacDonald impatiently, again trying to signal Darling with a glance toward Rothblatt. "I'll get you the film by Friday." His tone suggested an end to the conversation.

Darling sighed but shook his head in resignation and looked over toward Rothblatt. "I think we were talking about rotten bananas," he said.

Rothblatt nodded and rose and backed away so he could face both Darling and MacDonald. He explained that he had chosen rotten bananas as an example of any negative aspect of American society.

"A radical group picks such an issue and uses it as a tool to attack all of society. So they commit some crime and go to trial and the radicals say they had to do whatever it was they did to draw attention to rotten bananas. Gilpert's summary will verify this, but there's always a fight by the defense to get rotten bananas in and an attempt by the prosecution to keep the issue out. The radicals always try to make the trial not murder or kidnap or riot or arson but rotten bananas. That's what they say it's all about. And the press helps them by pushing their viewpoint."

"The press is on their side?" asked Darling.

"Not always," Rothblatt said. "But the press has got to cover the news and the radicals *are* the news. And the trial is part of their program. It draws attention. It gives them a platform . . . save these poor people from that mean old government and its rotten bananas. They roll out the cuckoo movie stars and start raising money and pretty soon, they've got most Americans believing that the worst thing in the world is that the bananas are rotten."

"Okay, I'm new at this stuff," MacDonald said. "Suppose the government does a crash program for *fresh* bananas?"

"Rotten pineapples," said Rothblatt. "The only thing the imperialist U.S. government understands is burning offices and kidnapping. It's the only thing the capitalists will listen to. 'We got you fresh bananas. Now let's get to the root cause of all our troubles, rotten pineapples.'"

"And if the U.S. cleans up rotten pineapples?" MacDonald asked.

"There's a whole goddamn fruit stand," Rothblatt said. "The specific issue's not important; upending the United States is."

"If you were a military commander, would you let one of these radicals speak to your men at an educational session?"

"Officially," Rothblatt said, "I believe in freedom of speech. Unofficially, letting one of those people on your base to talk to your troops is dumber than putting sand down your rifle barrel. Free speech isn't their thing. Speech is a tool. Injustice is a tool. And the goal is to sink you." He paused. "And me. And Luke. And everybody."

"Okay," Darling said. "So that's the prototype and the point is that the trial itself is not some unforeseen accident to the radical, but a planned-for step in their program. Correct?"

"You have a way with words, Luke. Correct."

"Okay. I'll buy all that," Darling said. "Don't bother with a rough draft. Just go ahead with your final version. Can you have it by Wednesday?"

"Yes."

"Okay," said Darling. "Keep in touch if there are any problems."

As Rothblatt was leaving, Darling said, "And you, Ram, did you get anything helpful?"

"I think so. Some of it," MacDonald said.

"It strikes me odd, Ram, for a guy of your savvy— and you have it, short hair and all—it's odd that you're so unaware of this."

"I'm a Marine," MacDonald said.

"Seriously."

"I am serious. I knew this was something military men should stay away from and I always did."

Rothblatt was out of the office now and Darling

said, "Okay. What did Dempsey say?"

"He said it's a film the FBI seized in a raid on some Cuban group. Who made it and how they made it, they don't know. That's Dempsey's special assignment—to find out. In a way, I guess, maybe he's working on the same kind of job you are."

"Why didn't he just tell me that?"

"Luke, you seem to have gotten into the place by accident and Dempsey was afraid you'd raise hell because the bureau was fooling around with something that might be international. Plus, he doesn't know you. Me, he remembers from the White House and he knows I'm top secret cleared. I'll have the film for you on Friday. But if you use it, you've got to protect Dempsey as the source."

Darling nodded.

"Is it going to help you in your report?" MacDonald asked.

Darling shrugged. "I don't know. It would have if they were FBI films. Now, I just don't know. But I want it anyway. And I've got to talk to Dempsey about something he did at Wounded Elk."

"Well, you'll have them both Friday. Unless, of course, you change your mind, go home tonight, forget this assignment, and never come back."

"Not much chance of that," said Darling. "My future depends on it."

MacDonald shook his head. "You dutiful types always annoy me."

When MacDonald had been out of the office for a good fifteen minutes, Darling signaled Miss McGirr.

"Did you get that Dempsey conversation?" he asked.

"Yes. I thought it might be important."

"Okay. Read me your notes."

It was as Ramsey MacDonald had explained, Dempsey wheedling with the explanations and Ram pushing him. Except for one thing. Just before MacDonald had said "right," Dempsey had asked if they were speaking on an open telephone line.

Darling thanked McGirr and hung up the telephone knowing one thing: he would not trust Special Agent Dempsey if his life depended on it.

At Dulles Airport, Darling—his briefcase packed with segmented reports from his five young lawyers—eyed a pay telephone and resisted an urge to call. One of the most common misconceptions was that pay phones were not bugged because too many different people used them. But he knew from his years in Justice that certain pay phones were prime for bugging for just that reason. Pay phones outside courthouses. Pay phones near bookstores were, for some reason, also good. Pay phones in taverns and inside courthouses were, surprisingly, not often worth bugging because people watched their conversations there.

But pay phones at airports, especially Dulles, had undoubtedly filled more tape than Elton John or the Grateful Dead. With his uneasy feeling about Agent Calvin Dempsey, Darling passed up the phone and waited for his flight to Vandalia Airport and home.

He bought a candy bar and changed a dollar bill. He bought a newspaper and changed another bill. Bought *Time* and enough gum so that when he gave the clerk two dollars, he got back ninety-five cents. A Coke in the cocktail lounge got him the rest and when he boarded the flight, he had four dollars in change in his pocket.

He tried to concentrate on his vodka martini, his reward for a hard day's work, but his mind kept drifting back to the film and to Dempsey. He opened his briefcase and, from the hit-and-miss notes he had made, began to expand his description of the film. A word would bring back the image and the thoughts he had had on it, and he would write down the expanded version.

What struck him as strange was the bleeps where there obviously had been profanity. If this were a propaganda film prepared by some foreign government, it would seem that taking out the profanity weakened the impact of the film. And if it was meant to be shown overseas, most countries had more liberal attitudes than the United States toward rough language.

But why would a foreign government make such

a film? And how had they gotten those films, films that were shot closeup, by concealed cameras? Was America so riddled with spies, all of them cameramen, all of them staked out in closets and bedrooms coast to coast?

Darling did not trust Dempsey, his explanation, or least of all his promise to deliver the film by Friday. Yet, if he went to the attorney general and complained, he might really be treading on something top secret. And after all the interdepartmental squabbling was finished, Darling's two weeks would be stretching on to three or four or more. And goddamnit, he wasn't going to do that; he wasn't going to give Walthrop one more minute than he had promised. He would deal with Dempsey a different way, he thought as he idly ran his fingers through the loose change in his jacket pocket.

As the passenger jet circled over Vandalia, Darling thought of Clark State University just a few miles north. He tried to remember when the Guardsmen had shot the rioting students, and he was fairly certain it was at the time of the Cambodian invasion. With an okay from the Cambodian government itself, American and South Vietnamese troops had raided North Vietnamese supply bases inside Cambodia.

It was a simple military move that probably should have been done years before—that is, assuming America should have been in Vietnam at all. It had all the social significance of folding a hand in poker. Yet the students, alive with passion, charged guns with rocks. Students who had been to a left-wing pep rally just the night before.

The Cambodian invasion had been "rotten bananas," in Rothblatt's phrase, Darling thought. And yet weren't the Civil War and the freeing of the slaves rotten bananas too? And the Bill of Rights? And the Magna Carta and even Social Security? There were good things that needed doing, injustices that *did* need correcting.

But kids charging National Guard guns with rocks over a military move in a war they did not like?

Kathy was waiting by the railing, wearing a little bandana around her head and a trench coat. As soon as Darling kissed her he knew she had been crying. They held each other and soothed their longing and he kissed her hard. He saw that their station wagon still had District of Columbia license plates.

"God, I missed you, Luke."

"It's good to be home, Kathy."

"There's some trouble with the project," she said suspiciously.

"No," said Darling, dropping his briefcase in the back seat of the car, next to a rake with the price tag still on it.

"I know there's trouble. It's going to take longer, isn't it?" she said.

"No. Where do you get these thoughts?" he asked.

"I know when things aren't going right," she said.

"I'm just tired," he said.

"All right." She kissed him on the cheek, which was her way of saying she did not believe him but would not argue.

They ate dinner with their best china on their laps. The dining table had to be moved to the dining room, and Luke did not have the energy and Kathy did not have the strength. He knew, and she did not mention, that part of the dream they shared was unpacking together in this house on Hobart Street. This house was the vacations they had missed, the new car they had delayed, the restaurants they had avoided because of the high prices. And sometimes, when frugality had pinched, she had described how they would unpack together. They had been leaving Washington for the last five years of his career with Justice. And now her hopes were delayed yet again, after so many earlier delays.

Eight-year-old Billy thought Troy was great. He asked if his father had played down by the Miami River and Luke said yes, and if Luke had lived in a house this grand and Luke said no, because his father was a lathe operator for Hobard, and did he play football for the high school?

"Daddy was a star. He could have gone to Ohio

State. He was asked by Woody Hayes himself."

"Woody Hayes himself?"

"Yeah. I was a pretty rough fullback."

"All-state," Kathy said.

"You could have been a professional football player?" Billy asked admiringly.

"They weren't as important in those days, son."

"Ah, you should have done it. You could have played for the Redskins, and instead you became a lawyer."

"Your father became a lawyer instead of some old brokendown football player. You know most of them make less than your father and almost all of them will."

"Will what?" asked Billy.

"Make less in the future than your father will. Now, I'm not one to judge things by money but I just thought you should have a perspective on this, Billy," said Kathy.

Darling laughed.

"Well, I'm *not* one to do that," she said. "And you shut up, Luke."

"I'm not saying anything."

"The hell you're not."

"Daddy, why didn't you play for Ohio State?"

"I went to sea."

"Oh, yeah. Couldn't you go to sea after you played football?"

"No."

"Why not?"

"It's just the way life is," Darling said.

"Could you have played after you went to sea?"

"Not after. No. I didn't want to."

"Why?"

"Now, Billy, that's enough," Kathy said.

"I didn't want to afterwards because I just couldn't believe a football game was important anymore. That's why."

"Oh," said William Cole Darling.

After Billy joined his younger brother Tommy in bed, Kathy showed Luke his den. He felt sad when he saw that it was the only room in the house which was fully furnished, polished, and draped. There was a small couch in the den. Kathy drew the drapes and they made love there. She was saving the bed for when he came home for good.

"That'll be soon, precious," said Luke.

They had a cup of coffee and Luke said he wanted to take a little stroll before he went to bed. On the corner of First and Main streets, Luke stepped into a telephone booth and dialed a long distance number. In three rings it answered.

"Do you recognize this voice?" said Darling.

"Yeah." The voice was deep, almost leaden, like a wheeze from a tomb.

"Eleven A.M. tomorrow?" Darling said.

"You know the place," the voice wheezed.

"Yes," said Darling.

The phone clicked dead in his ear.

Darling continued his stroll around the town he was born in. It was a clean town where those who didn't come from money but wanted to make it had to leave, establish a reputation, and then come back. Without his stay in Washington and his record in Justice, Luke would always have been Silas Darling's son who might have, at best, become a junior partner of McAdow and Brown just before retirement. But even more likely was that he never could have entered that firm.

Ram was different. The MacDonalds always had money. Old money. Land money. Darling had only himself and Kathy, who had always moved with the wealthier set. Yes, it was social climbing. Their marriage contract included an unspoken rider which required Luke to return her to the tight stratified social system of Troy, several strata above where they both came from. There had been worse deals made in marriage and they loved each other, so to hell with it. He was keeping his end of the contract.

It felt good to walk on a city street at night, a strange sensation to anyone who had lived recently in Washington, D.C. He found himself going down Main Street, past a diner he used to frequent, past the local newspaper office with the two funny trees in front of it. He didn't remember the trees and they didn't seem like any he recognized. He went past the large houses of what used to be the best section of town.

"Luke! . . . Luke, darling. How are you?" It was a woman's voice.

"Oh, hi, Bea," said Luke, thinking that if he had to choose someone he would not want Kathy knowing he spoke to, it would have been Bea Whittaker. The woman was leaning out of the driver's window of an old Chevrolet. The face was a little fleshier now, but still smoothly beautiful. Her lips were meaty, petulant, still outlined in the garish red lipstick she had favored when both of them were young. Her white blouse was stretched tightly across her bosom, across those breasts that young Luke had dreamt about many nights.

"How you doin'?" she said. "I heard you moved back."

"Yeah. Yeah, I'm back."

"Jesus, you look good. Not a day older."

"Well . . ." he drawled.

"Still bashful? Big federal guy like you?"

"Sort of," he said. "Nice seeing you again."

"Hey, Luke. C'mere," Bea Whittaker said.

"What do you want?"

"C'mere."

Reluctantly, Darling went to the car window. If he had walked away, he knew she would have followed. Now he could establish permanently that the past was the past and held no promise for the future.

"What do you want?"

"C'mere. Don't be afraid."

Darling leaned down into the window. He saw Bea's hands reach to the hemline of her skirt and pull up, showing two white thighs and a small darkness of hair tucked between them.

Darling yanked back his head and walked away from the car.

"Hey, you still don't want some of that, Lucius?" she called after him. "Think you're too good for it now? Huh? Hey, lawyer. It wasn't your kid I had to flush away. What are you running away for?"

In her car, she followed him down Elm Street, still calling out, and he knew he had to do something. He stopped and whirled toward the car. Bea opened her mouth in shock and reached across the seat to put her hand on the passenger's door handle.

"Wait," said Luke.

"Not if you get that crazy look in your eyes," she said. "What do you want?"

"I just wanted to tell you you were a great piece of ass. Goodbye."

"Ha ha," laughed Bea, her ego salved in one of the many wounds it carried. "I'd tell you the same, but I can't quite remember which one you was, Lucius."

Darling laughed with her and she wished him luck and drove away. He watched her car depart.

Coming home was not all dens and lovemaking.

Tuesday, October 25: The Ninth Day

In the morning, he made sure to tell Kathy about how Bea Whittaker had followed him in the car, even mentioned her yanking up her skirt.

"What a mouth on that whore. God, I hope she doesn't talk around," said Kathy.

"Sure she talks. She screwed the whole male population of this city."

"Awful," said Kathy.

"Yeah," said Luke, who had now established that Kathy would not hear of his meeting from anyone else first. He did not tell her how he had gotten rid of Bea Whittaker.

At Vandalia, Darling took the flight to Washington which continued on to New York. He would be in Delsace's Bar in Queens, fifteen minutes from LaGuardia Airport, at 11:00 A.M.

He was to meet Anthony Mottodocio, just retired from the New York City Police Department, a man who may, by himself, have occupied the top slot in Lucius Darling's mental personnel file.

CHAPTER ***** 11

The Near Future

HER COLUMN WAS CALLED "SUNDAY BOOK-person," which was also her name. Not that it had always been.

When Lonzo Gates first met her in the late 1960s, her name had been Sara Bookman. She had long, shiny black folksinger's hair, a wide mouth, and dark house-counting eyes. She fascinated him because she refused to go to bed with him. Early one Monday morning, after a weekend drug party at a friend's house in California at which Sara Bookman still remained chaste, they were married on the beach by Tyrone Johnson, who was then calling himself the Eternal Priest of the Eternal Church of the Eternal God of Everybody.

That afternoon, the newlyweds borrowed another friend's house for their "honeymoon," and Gates found out why their relations had been pure for so long: his new bride had no sexual interest, at least in men.

"Look," she had tried to explain, "I screwed my way through the sixties. I balled politicians and black basketball teams and rock singers and I got the clap from some goddamn Hollywood stuntman who screwed me in a hot air balloon over the Mojave Desert, and it's all too much of a hassle. I've been used and abused and treated like a spittoon by you cock-wielders. I don't like other people's juices in me; I don't like sweating; I don't like men much anymore. And especially, I don't like you."

"Then what the fuck did you marry me for?"

"So you would help me with my career," said Sara Bookman, smiling her wide-mouthed smile which Gates, for the first time, noticed was more of a smirk than anything else. A few months later, she changed her name to Sara Bookwoman because she "refused to wear the label of the oppressor." She stopped wearing makeup at the same time.

A couple of years later, after her feminist "support group" had voted thirty-four to zero that it was impossible for a woman ever to be successful in such a corrupt, racist, sexist, ageist society, she decided to change her name again, this time to Bookperson.

By this time she was writing a column of anonymous book reviews for *Sappho's Children*, a fringe publication whose readers seemed equally interested in novels about women who castrated men and in nonfiction books on the health benefits to be derived from not shaving one's legs. The publication appeared free in lesbian bars on sporadic Sundays and so Sara Bookwoman, nee Bookman, made the final decision that she would not be *Sara* Bookperson, but *Sunday* Bookperson.

Gates and she still shared an apartment, rents being what they were, but he resolutely refused to help her career in any way. In fact, he took pleasure in bad-mouthing her work whenever he ran into a magazine or newspaper publisher that he thought might be considering picking up her column. Despite his efforts, though, her column had seemed to thrive and eventually she was being published in fifty newspapers and magazines across the country each month. Even some mainstream magazines subscribed to her lesbian twaddle, although those reviews were printed anonymously.

It was not true that she and Gates never had sex together, as she often told her friends. Occasionally—and Gates noticed it was usually after reading a book in which rape seemed to play a big part—she would forego her own bed and slip in alongside Gates and invite him to hurt her. For a few years, he generally complied. But slowly it sank in that the more he hurt her, the more she liked it, and since he was determined not to give her pleasure in any way, and since Southern Comfort then was becoming much more interesting than sex, he stopped sleeping with her at all. He had no doubt that she was getting her itch scratched somewhere else by a lot of women and an occasional man, but he just didn't give a damn anymore.

During Christmas week, 1979, while she was away at a seminar on "A New Decade for the New Woman," she had him served with divorce papers. They arrived on New Year's Eve and he went in and peed on her bed, packed his suitcase, and left. He got a copy of the final decree in the mail.

But in the years since then, Gates had stayed in touch with her, and they were probably closer than seemed logical for two people with nothing in common. He had wondered about this for a while, about his reaching out to talk to her, until he understood it for what it was: that Sunday Bookperson, with the ongoing exception of Richard Nixon, was the only person in the world that Lonzo Gates could feel morally superior to.

She was wearing satin pajamas when she answered the door and let him into the apartment they used to share. The black hair was still long and thick but now had strands of gray; her dark eyes seemed sunken, and her wide-lipped mouth was now bordered by scowl lines. As he looked at her, the word that came to mind was "sour."

She did not even offer the usual courtesy of a welcoming smile.

"Come on in," she said. "I hope this isn't going to take too long. I'm doing a bunch of reviews and my roommate will be back soon."

"Oh, I won't be long," he said. "I wouldn't want to offend George. That is her name, isn't it?"

"Very funny," she said. She turned her back on him and went back to sit at the makeshift desk she had constructed out of a flush door and two filing cabinets. It was strewn with books, all looking fresh and new. Most of the dustjackets lacked pictures or photographs on the covers and bore only printed titles.

Gates picked up one of the books. It was entitled, "Sisters Through Life; Sisters Through Death . . . A Free Woman's Diary," and he said, "Still doing the lesbian lockstep?"

"I prefer to think of it as a feminist fandango," she said. "Go ahead. Write a book. I'll trash it. That'll help sell a lot of copies to your neanderthal friends."

"Read it first?" he said.

"No need to," she said. "You are an incorrect person with incorrect thinking. Your book will be incorrect and will have to be savaged."

Gates smiled wryly at one of the few times he had remembered his ex-wife ever telling the truth. Her book-reviewing procedure was very simple. Books by heterosexual males were routinely torn apart. Homosexual males could get by if they were politically "correct." Lesbian writers or women who gushed a lot about sisterhood got rave notices. Women writers—who seemed to like being feminine or—largest sin of all—were reported to be happily married were accorded the back of the hand by Sunday Bookperson.

She never read a book all the way through; at lunch one day, she had told Gates that she had too many reviews to do to have time to actually read anything.

"How can you review a book you don't read?" he asked. She had smiled a real smile and explained her "guiding principles," and Gates found himself admiring her. She could spot deviation from the feminist party line in a word, a sentence, even a comma. She swore that she could tell by the punctuation of a book if the writer was truly supportive of the feminist movement or if he were just a posturing faker, trying to cover up deep-seated macho beliefs.

"How?"

"It's easy. Take dashes," she said. "Macho writers . . . well, they try to cover it up sometimes, but if they use dashes, it exposes them. Because a dash is like an erect little penis . . . pushing forward into the rest of the book . . . forcing you to follow their little dicks wherever they go. Once you realize that, you're on to them and you don't have to read their dismal books to recognize them."

"You really believe this shit, don't you?" he said.

"I know it to be a fact."

"What about me? I use a lot of colons. Does that mean I'm an anal retentive?"

"Actually, it means you don't know much about

punctuation. You were always sort of a primitive about the niceties of the language."

Now, at her worktable, she had a book in front of her and was drawing large x's with a red marker across a page. "More crap," she grumbled and without looking up asked again, "What do you want, Lonzo?"

"Are you still seeing that guy in the U.S. attorney's office?"

"That's why you're irrelevant and time has passed you by. Nobody says things like 'seeing somebody' anymore."

"You still fucking that guy in the U.S. attorney's office?" Gates rephrased.

"Our relationship is based on greater things than sex," she said, still wielding her marker over the book pages like a sword.

"Oh. He's a fag too?"

"How coarse you are. But in the hopes of cutting this short, yes, I still converse with John occasionally. I still have dinner with him once in a while. I still find him intelligent and stimulating and all the things you're not. Why?"

"Because I need you to do me a favor," Gates said.

She dropped the marker and began to laugh. The paroxysm went on so long that Gates for a moment thought that the woman had suddenly snapped and gone crazy before his eyes. Then the laughter stopped as abruptly as if it had never occurred.

"Why should I?"

"Because if you do, I'll take one of your favorite fag books and plug it in my column at *Mossback*," he said. "Maybe give you a chance to crawl between the sheets with some young little chickie you've got the hots for."

"You'll do that?"

"I will," he said.

"You'll let me write the review?" she said.

"Yes," he answered instantly, knowing that he would never do such a thing but just as sure that there was nothing wrong with lying to a lesbian.

"Okay," she said. "What do you want from John?"

"He's an assistant U.S. attorney, right?"

"Yes."

"I want him to find out what he can about Lucius Darling."

"That sounds like a children's book," she said.

"It's a man's name. He is, or was, an assistant U.S. attorney. I want to know what Fagola John can find out about him."

"Such as?"

"Anything. Personal stuff, professional, where is he now . . . anything."

"How long do I have?" she said.

"I'm on a tight deadline," he said.

"Will this get John into trouble?"

"No. I'm just trying to find out where to reach this Darling."

"Did you look in the lawyer's registry?" she asked.

"He's not in it. That might just mean that he's not in private practice. Look. There's no trouble for John. I just need a lead."

"And I get to write any review I want?"

"Yes," Gates lied again.

"Get out of here, Lonzo. I have to call John."

CHAPTER ★★★★★ 12

The Mid-1970s

Tuesday, October 25: The Ninth Day

ON HIS WAY TO DELSACE'S, LUCIUS DARLING thought about the man he was about to meet. If Darling's mental file of competents had been put on paper, the entry next to the name of Anthony Mottodocio might look like this:

Keeps his wits—Doesn't panic. Never talks confidences in someone else's presence. Doesn't bother with unnecessary paperwork. Has the right tools before they're needed.

Gets things done—Won't overload you with information but will tell you when somebody important was seen talking to somebody else important. Automatically weeds out the stuff that isn't admissible, like subject's sex life. Can find anyone or anything and especially who paid whom what and what for.

Knows people—Can judge character. Knew, before *The Godfather*, that racketeers weren't all dumb thugs, and after *The Godfather* knew they weren't all Robin Hoods either.

Thinks in advance—Wont' require a twenty-man stakeout when an observant drugstore clerk will do. If he's going to make phone calls, makes sure he carries change. Also isn't gun crazy and doesn't believe in conspiracies either.

Mottodocio was drinking orange juice and club soda and nibbling peanuts when Darling entered Delsace's, a dark clean bar with black formica tables, a clean mirror, and rows of expensive liquor with cheap plastic pouring spouts. The place smelled of CN Disinfectant. Mottodocio's huge belly hung draped in a starched white shirt between two very fat legs. He seemed to be out of breath from sitting.

"Luke. Sit down," he wheezed.

"Good to see you again," said Darling. "Still drinking that slop?"

"Yeah," said Mottodocio. "Diabetes has a way of not going away."

"I have a problem," Darling said.

"So have I. I haven't been allowed a drink in five years."

"Mine's worse. I want to be out of Washington in six days. I'm going into private practice."

"Yeah?"

"But I saw something in Washington yesterday

that may delay me. I need a club to hold over some-body's head just in case he tries to screw me up."

"Yeah?"

Darling told him about the project, how an agent's name popped up in the Wounded Elk trial, how this agent who might have key information had all sorts of ways of becoming lost.

Finally, he said, "It might take me a month of memos and interdepartmental warfare to corner this guy. If I were staying in Washington another year or two, it wouldn't matter. Eventually, I'd get what I wanted."

"Sure," Mottodocio said.

And Darling told him about the film he had seen and the building at 414 Barclay Street. He told him how sections of the film might well have been used in the four cases in Darling's project—cases the gov-ernment might not have had to lose.

He told of Dempsey's promise to present himself and the film on Friday and told Mottodocio he didn't believe Dempsey's explanation that the film had been seized from some Cuban group.

"First, I don't believe those film clips could have been shot by Cubans. Second, that building on Bar-clay Street was set up like a theater. That film was meant to be shown to somebody. And I don't know who and I don't know why and I don't know what and I don't even know if any of this concerns me at all."

"You want me to get that film?"

"If you can. But I was thinking that that building has to be registered, owned by someone, and I'm sure there is some kind of asshole cover operation going on. When we know who really owns the building, we can find out who really owns the film. I'm sure someone has done something wrong or improper and I can use it to get me what I want. Which is cooperation from Dempsey. Pronto."

"The club," said Mottodocio.

"Right. The club. If I went through my own staff, everybody'd know in an hour and I don't want that. I just want a nice piece of dirt about that building or this guy Dempsey. That's my club."

"I think you're right about the building," Mottodocio said softly. "I think that would be fastest. But tell me some more about this film."

Darling took out his legal pad and read his notes aloud. Mottodocio ate peanuts and grunted, "Uh-huh . . . uh-huh . . . uh-huh."

"And then bleeps again," Darling said.

"How long was this thing?"

"I saw about eighteen minutes of it before MacDonald interrupted me."

"And bleeps for all the swear words, right?"

Darling nodded.

"That's a television show you seen," Mottodocio said.

"What?"

"Sure. The only people what uses bleeps nowadays. When was the last time you seen a movie? They got everything now. Swearing's nothing. And it's for this country." Then Mottodocio had a few more questions about Dempsey and Ramsey MacDonald and how well did Darling know this guy MacDonald.

"We went to high school together."

"So how well do you know him?"

"I know him well."

"You trust him?" Mottodocio asked.

"Yes."

"I don't. How are we going to work finances?"

"Two hundred and fifty dollars a day plus expenses, a hundred over what you spend," Darling said.

"I'd rather have one-fifty and two hundred over."

Darling said, "I don't want to be kept in Washington, wrestling through an expense voucher."

"I got my police pension," the fat man said, "and I could get troubled by too much accountable money."

"Then make it just two days."

"For two days I should get a bonus."

"You got it," Darling said.

"How you going to work it?"

"I don't know but you've got it, okay? Anything else?" asked Darling, checking his watch. The whole meeting had taken eleven minutes.

"One thing," Mottodocio said.

"What?"

"What you're not telling me, Luke."

Darling shrugged. "I don't know what you're talking about."

"You don't know you came in with a tail on you?"

"No," said Darling, careful not to take a sudden glance toward the street.

"Then you also don't know how long you've had one?"

Darling nodded. "What should I do?" he said.

"Go back to your office and finish your report."

"What does the tail look like?"

"About five-feet-four, a hundred-thirty pounds, red hair, black persian lamb coat, and a yellow print dress."

"A transvestite?"

"Nobody's gonna tail nobody with no queer. You never heard of a lady tail?"

"No," said Darling.

"Well, in truth, I never did either, but she's on you and she's not bad. She had you coming in, dropped you onto somebody else, and picked you up again. I bet the dropoff takes you back to Washington. Five-foot-nine, two hundred pounds, light brown hair, pockmarked face. Purple tie and white shirt."

"Male?"

"Yeah," laughed Mottodocio. "Go home. I got work. For two fucking days, I don't have wasteage."

"Thanks."

"And next time, don't make a whole big trip out of your way. If you have to meet me, tell me it's personal and we could like make it in your office. This is like waving flags."

"I was afraid that whatever's happening would drag you in."

"I understand, but I'm in now. Go to the john."

Darling left his briefcase beneath the bar and walked to the back, where he entered the men's room. While there, he washed his hands and examined his face and, when he heard the water running, had to urinate. Returning to the bar, he saw Mottodocio hang up a telephone and hand it back to the bartender, who put it under the bar.

"Go," said Mottodocio. "If I have to reach you privately again, the name is Felner. See you in a couple of days in any case."

"Okay," said Darling and did not break stride as he picked up his briefcase and left the bar. He saw a pockmarked man with a purple tie eating a hotdog at a corner pushcart. The pickup tail.

A New York patrol car pulled up to the hotdog cart and two patrolmen got out, asked the man for identification, and made him lean against the side of the building while they frisked him. Back down the street, Darling saw a redhaired woman also leaning against the wall with a policewoman patting her down for weapons.

All that and Anthony Mottodocio had not left his stool in Delsace's bar. Apparently, he had sent the assistant attorney general of the United States to the bathroom so he wouldn't hear the names of Mottodocio's police contacts.

Back at Justice, all hell had broken loose. Attorney General Walthrop had been trying to reach Darling all morning. Miss McGirr had attached a *Washington Post* news story to the three memos of the AG's phone calls.

There was also a note on a telephone conversation with "a Mister Felner who says the tails themselves may prove a super lever." That was followed by McGirr's written question: "Luke, we into undercover or something?"

And there was a note McGirr had taken verbatim from Kathy. Bea Whittaker had been spreading nasty gossip about Darling. Kathy had heard it from Gwynn Brown, who had heard it from Nancy Sleighter, who knew everything. "Miss you madly. Love, Kathy."

Darling read the *Washington Post* story while walking to his desk. It was one of those informed-sources things that said Justice was investigating why it was losing so many political trials. The informed source said that Darling, formerly of antitrust, was in charge and rushing to a judgment. There was also a quote from the informed source:

"This is a crash, helter-skelter operation that is going to miss the primary fact that Harold Albend is probably the finest trial lawyer in America today and he has been pitted against only political hacks. We already know why we lose and no one is ever going to read it in our official report," said the informed source. He noted that it would be "years before fresh, innovative legal talent might transform the lopsided legal battle but by then the new high-quality crop of young lawyers might just be worn-out political hacks themselves."

Darling dialed McGirr. "Get me Gilpert."

"I've got him on the line already."

"Send him into my office."

"He's at home sick."

"With what?" Darling asked.

"Probably *Washington Post*-itis. He says migraine."

"Put him on . . . hello, Ronny."

"Oh, hi. I'll be all right in a couple of days."

"I have a home assignment for you," Darling said.

"Yes, sir."

"Give me an explanation for the attorney general, who undoubtedly wants to know why he didn't have a chance to announce our task force's work before he got slammed on it in the *Post*."

"I don't know. Maybe you could say you didn't know anything about the leak. It was a leak, wasn't it? I get the *Post* delivered to my door, you know."

"Yes, it was a leak."

"I get the feeling you think I had something to do with it, and I resent being judged guilty without even a charge or a chance to defend myself."

"Ronny, in this town you not only have been judged guilty but you've already been sentenced."

"What sentence?"

"Who'd trust you again?" Darling said. He heard Gilpert gulp.

"The reporter promised. He gave me his word. He just wanted background. He knew about our project."

"I believe you. Come on in and get back to work."

"You trust me?"

"I trust you didn't know better but now you do. I don't know how many people will be willing to trust you in the future."

"So I *have* been sentenced."

"Yeah, but you might get time off for good behavior. We'll see how smoothly the report goes from here on in."

"You know, the reporter misquoted me. I can announce that. He did, Luke. I swear. He didn't get one word right."

"You stay away from reporters."

"He lives in my building. He told *me* about the project. He said he just wanted to chat about it. I didn't even know he was getting a story. I can sue him."

"You stay away from reporters, Ronny. I'm not going to say it again."

"Yes, sir. I'll be right in."

Darling's explanation to Attorney General Walthrop was brief. There was a leak, apparently in his own staff, and he apologized.

"I know it's a leak, damn it. Who?"

"I've got it narrowed down."

"I want his name."

"I'm working on it."

"I want his name and I want him out of Justice today."

"I'll get on it."

"See that you do. I've got a small—hopefully, a small—press conference this afternoon. I'm going to confirm the study you're doing. But after that story this morning, you can't leave in any week. Figure December."

"But the report'll be done Monday."

"I don't accept 'rushes to judgment.' You've got to give me that report in December," Walthrop said.

"I don't know if I can do that. My marriage took a hell of a strain with just these extra two weeks. I can't push it to December."

"Commute to Ohio," Walthrop said.

"No."

"I didn't leak that story, Luke."

"I am going to do my report, hand in my resignation, and you can delay it with someone else in charge."

"Hmmm. Possibly. *If* the report's good enough. But I'm going to have people run up and down every comma on every page looking for a rush job. If there's shoddiness that can be interpreted as haste, you can consider these extra two weeks no favor to me. I think you understand my position."

"Yes, I do."

"Did you find the conspiracy yet?" asked Walthrop.

"Not yet, but I'm looking."

"All right, Luke. I'll handle the clowns from the Fourth Estate. Always could. Good luck, son."

"Thank you."

Kathy was in tears on the telephone. She repeated what she had told Miss McGirr, only she sobbed from the hello. She didn't know what to do about the gossip. Maybe it was true that you can't go home again.

"Honey, I have a bit of a shock for you, but you've got to listen. It has to do with Bea Whittaker."

"What? What?"

"A. Things have changed in attitudes but B, even if they hadn't, the salient feature of this whole thing is that people really don't care that much. It's just some good dirty gossip. Everyone has something to hide and everyone has to live with it."

"But I haven't done anything wrong," Kathy said.

"I have, dear."

"I didn't mean it that way."

"I know you didn't," Darling said.

"Oh, Jeez. What am I worried about? It's nothing. Everyone knows that Gwynn Brown went down on the colored football player back in senior class. Went down on him. And she's Mrs. Brown. My God, it's nothing when you think of it. I'm Mrs. Lucius Darling."

"And you're always going to be, dear. Goodbye."

Darling knew the country still had racist attitudes marrow deep and that he probably suffered from some himself. But he still could not quite comprehend why the color of a man's penis had some qualifying moral effect on the act of fellatio. He never would understand this absurdity.

It was at this point that Ronald Gilpert slammed through the door unannounced and insisted upon rendering his full apologies and, if necessary, his personal resignation.

Darling threw him physically from the office, then told Miss McGirr that when the reporters called, he would be available for interviews next Tuesday.

"But you're going home Monday."

"Yes, I am, McGirr. And don't you forget it."

CHAPTER ★★★★★ 13

"IT'S SEVENTEEN AFTER TEN. AT TWENTY-seven after, call me back on a tight phone."

The caller had not given his name but he didn't need to. Darling knew no one but Tony Mottodocio whose voice sounded like air leaking from a tire.

Darling hung up the telephone in his barren hotel room and looked at the self-winding calendar Timex with the heavy leather band that Kathy had given him a few years before because it made him look "young and groovy."

"Anybody who uses words like 'groovy' is too old to have a young husband," he had said that night.

"How about sexy?" Kathy had asked.

"I don't need a wristwatch for that. Not unless I was posing for dirty movies."

"Black socks," Kathy said.

"And a mustache."

"And an equipment change," Kathy said.

"Oh, you evil castrating bitch you," Darling had said.

"Don't worry, Luke. We'll show the picture on a wide screen," and she had laughed and he had laughed and they had made warm and wet love on their living room floor.

Why was it that every time he was alone for more than a couple of hours he began to think about his and Kathy's love life?

The watch read 10:14 and he reset it to 10:17 because if Mottodocio said it was 10:17, the Greenwich observatory had better check its clocks.

At 10:27 Darling was in a phone booth inside a drugstore four blocks from his hotel. He had bought a carton of cigarettes, taken the change from the ten-dollar bill in quarters, and had dialed Mottodocio's number direct.

"Is your phone tight?" asked Mottodocio, his voice wheezing as if he had just run across a street to answer the telephone.

"Yes."

"What's the number?"

Darling read the number off the round white tab in the center of the dial on the old-fashioned black wall phone.

"All right, wait there. I'll call back in five minutes."

To amuse himself, Darling checked the second

hand on his watch. Three hundred and two seconds later, the telephone made a sound as if it were taking a deep breath before ringing and Darling lifted the receiver before it had a chance to ring.

"All right," Mottodocio said. "I don't know how good my other phone is anymore. Where are you?"

"Drugstore near my hotel."

"Anybody else in the store?"

"Just the owner."

"All right. You got my message at the office?"

"Yeah. What'd it mean?" Darling asked.

"The two tails that were on you. They belong to Americans in Readiness. Ever hear of it?"

"No," Darling said.

"It's some kind of civil defense thing made up of volunteers, but they get paid expenses."

"By whom?"

"The funding's private," Mottodocio said. "For once, you Washington thieves aren't picking up the tab."

"Well, what are they? They sound like air raid wardens."

"I'm trying to pin it all down. The funding goes through a foundation and then gets lost. I should have it, though, in a while. Anyway, these people are supposed to be able to locate important people in an emergency." Mottodocio paused and took a deep sip of air. Darling could hear the asthmatic wheeze like a whistle over the phone. He waited.

"In case an enemy attacks, they're supposed to be able to get messages to big shots. They practice by finding somebody and tailing him for a while."

"That's bullshit," Darling said.

"I know it, Counselor. But that's what they think they're doing. Those two on you got your name and were told to follow you."

"All right. Get me what they're doing, connect it to that building where the film was shown, get the building connected to Dempsey, and you will have done your job in beatific splendor," Darling said. "With that lever, I can get Dempsey's underwear if I want. I can clear out all obstacles. Beautiful. Beautiful."

"Don't you want to know why they were following you?"

"I can tell *you*. Dempsey is involved in some security nonsense thing. And like all security nuts, they tap and tail everything that comes their way. I don't know what security thing Dempsey has but he will give me what I need for my investigation, just so I don't blow the whistle on him."

"It don't bother you, Luke, that somebody put a tail on you?"

"No." Darling looked at his watch and saw the date in the window slowly beginning to change. "I don't have time to worry about that. All I want to do is finish and go home."

"Counselor, are you leveling with me about

what we're doing?" There was suddenly a sharp edge on the retired policeman's voice.

"You know damn well I am. If you watched television tonight, you saw it ... the attorney general talking about my project."

"Then what's Jericho?"

"Jericho?" Darling echoed. "Joshua fit the battle ... blew down the walls. The Bible."

"That's all it means to you?"

"That's all. What's bothering you, Tony?"

"I always thought you was one of the good guys."

"I am," Darling said.

"How can you tell?"

"Because I just want to do my job and get the hell out of this cesspool of a city."

"Then I think you would know ... being not only a good guy but a smart guy ... that to dangle me on a limb somewhere is not the wisest of all things to do," Mottodocio said.

"I know that."

There was a long pause before Mottodocio said, "All right. Just so's you know it. Watch yourself going home. You'll probably be tailed."

"Hey, wait. What is this ... ?" But the phone clicked dead in Darling's ear. He sat in the phone booth. Had someone gotten to Mottodocio? No. Mottodocio was not like that ... at least not up until now. More likely something had happened to Mottodocio that he didn't want to trust Darling with.

All right, what? Jericho. What was that? A place called Jericho. Mottodocio had found something called Jericho and thought Darling was holding back that information from him.

Jericho.

As Darling looked up and met the storekeeper's eyes through the windows of the phone booth, the man moved closer to the cash register. The counter on which the register rested was armor-plated to prevent the storekeeper from being shot in the legs through the counter's panels. Under the counter would be stashed a gun. In a back room, at least on check cashing nights, there might very well be another man with another gun. Those were some of the costs of doing business in big cities nowadays. It was passed on to the consumer in an extra penny for aspirins.

And the cost of coming near some kind of security nerve, some kind of secret operation, was picking up a tail and maybe having your phone tapped. The cost of that too was passed on to the public—like right now when an assistant attorney general of the United States decided he was going to look the other way and ignore something that might just be illegal because he didn't want to do anything except go back home to Ohio.

Darling pushed open the piano-hinged door of the old booth, slid from the wooden seat, and, looking neither left nor right, walked quickly from the store and out onto the sidewalk.

He stopped in front of the store, reached into the narrow tube of a paper bag, and ripped open the end of the carton of True Blue cigarettes. He removed a pack and took a great deal of time in opening it: carefully removing the cellophane from one end, peeling open the foil at one corner, tearing off the foil and neatly rolling it into a ball with the cellophane before dropping them on the sidewalk. With the middle finger of his right hand, he squeezed up on the bottom of the pack, forcing the first three cigarettes to rise. He raised his hand to his mouth and clenched one of the popped-up cigarettes between his teeth, then pulled the rest of the pack away.

And his eyes kept scanning. His side of the street, opposite side, left, right, and then all over again.

He lit the cigarette with his disposable lighter. As he dropped the pack and lighter into his side pocket, he saw a figure in a doorway, diagonally across the street.

His tail.

Mottodocio was right.

Darling hesitated, dragging deeply on the cigarette. He thought about what he would like to do. What he would like to do would be to walk across the street, grab the person in the doorway by the throat, and twist out of him just who he was and why he was following Lucius Darling. And with his luck, the tail would start screaming and a platoon of police would just be passing by and Darling could see the story in the *Washington Post*:

> Lucius A. Darling, the assistant attorney general in charge of finding out why the government is losing political trials, faces a trial of his own in the future. He was arrested late last night for assault.
>
> Darling, whose study has been criticized within his own department as a "breakneck rush to justice," apparently tried to speed up justice again last night when he leaped upon and began to pummel a man standing in a doorway in downtown Washington.
>
> "I thought he was following me," Darling said. His victim, The Rev. Cadwallader Fortney Barnes, minister of All Saints Episcopal Church, said, "Nonsense. I was just taking my evening constitutional and thinking about Sunday's sermon."
>
> Darling was ordered held, pending psychiatric examination.

Just what Luke Darling needed—more newspaper publicity. He wouldn't be able to get into Bob Brown's office disguised as a Western Union man if something like that happened.

Darling walked to the corner in the direction

away from the tail, turned left, then broke into a run. He didn't turn to see if the tail was following him; he just ran.

At the next corner, he saw a cab coming down the street. He jumped out from between parked cars and waved at the cab. The driver swerved to the left, like a hockey player skating around a check in his own zone, but then hit the brakes and stopped, apparently after seeing that Darling was white.

Darling clambered quickly into the back seat. The driver turned. He was a black man.

"Where to in such a hurry, mister?" he said. His voice came out electronically crisp in the car, and Darling realized he was talking through a loud-speaker to the back seat. A heavy wired-glass plate separated the two men.

More of America's wonderful freedom, thought Darling. He wanted to tell the driver, "Troy, Ohio, and there's an extra five bucks in it for you if you get there in twenty seconds," but instead he said, "A nice quiet bar. Someplace away from here."

"I saw a brown Chevy cruising around here. He following you?" the cabbie asked.

"Probably," Darling said wearily. "Let's just lose him."

The cab driver decided on a place called the Shamrock Bar. Darling thought that an old-fashioned Irish saloon might be just the place to do some serious drinking.

But the Shamrock let him down. It had become a go-go bar with the go-go part of it suffering stretch marks right down into her green sequined G-string. That was at the far end of the long black formica bar top, a special stage with blue and white lights. At the other end of the bar was a color television set, perched on a thin plywood platform. Five men and a B-girl sat at the bar, listlessly consuming hard drinks.

Darling sat down, getting two vacant stools between him and the others, ordered a Beefeater martini, and sighed. Even the dull beer peace of the traditional Irish bar had been violated by change: the woman with bangled breast and sequined crotch grinding on a plastic stage while Johnny Carson interviewed a former astronaut at the other end of the bar and people in between drinking scotch. They should have been drinking beer, slowly, while Mel Stottlemyre pitched the Yankees into insignificance in a late-inning night game and the bartender took bets for tomorrow's races at Bethesda.

Even the Irish bar was gone, along with the friendly neighborhood storekeeper, the chummy cab driver...and assistant U.S. attorneys who would be offended by wiretaps and tails.

"Another martini," said Darling while thinking, *I am a long way from home and the hour is late. A long way from home.*

The dancer worked to a jukebox behind her and,

being largely ignored by the customers, took refuge in the sight of her own moving feet, the traditional hoofer's defense against an uninterested audience. She was long of leg and her thickened middle hinted of a full-term pregnancy somewhere along the line. It had happened to Kathy. After the child, no amount of exercise or dieting had brought back that long thin, tight waist. Gone into the mists of memory.

"Make it a double," Darling told the bartender. He had gotten a small square napkin with his other drink and now wondered if he would get two napkins with his double. He didn't. He clicked open a ballpoint pen from his inside jacket pocket and doodled a big "2" on the napkin to commemorate the receipt of his drink. He doodled "JW" to commemorate the attorney general of the United States, who was keeping him in Washington. And an "HA" for Harold Albend, who was beating the pants off the United States government—to be specific, Justice.

Darling wrote out Justice in full, very careful to underline the J so that he wouldn't be writing the concept of justice but the label of a government department. For if Darling were dealing with concepts of justice, who then would speak for the old Indian woman whose church had been fouled by human waste? Or for that matter, for Mottodocio, who might be approaching senility?

Are you a good guy, Lucius Darling! he asked himself. Mottodocio had asked it. And Darling answered now, privately in his mind.

I refuse to answer that question on the grounds that it might incriminate me. More importantly, however, I am not a bad guy. There are no bad guys in this world. No good guys. Just guys who want to go home where they belong, to Troy, Ohio, and live wealthily ever after because they deserve it.

Jericho, Darling wrote, followed by *Walthrop, Movies, Dempsey, MacDonald, Mottodocio,* and *Miss McGirr.* A big "virgin" next to Miss McGirr. And it occurred to Darling that for some strange reason he had always thought of the Virgin Mary as Irish.

Virgin Jericho. The Virgin of Jericho. Good Guys vs. the Jericho Virgins. No virgins need apply.

The dancer was looking at him. Somehow their eyes had locked and she was smiling. Darling smiled back. Sweat glistened on her globular breasts. Would that his tongue could explore those breasts. Tongue to breast, groin to groin, he could pretend she was Kathy, even unto orgasm.

And by pretending, maintain his marital fidelity, even telling Kathy she was far superior. *Lucius Darling, my good and old friend, you are besotted drunk. Hail Jericho, full of Grace.*

"Everyone pays and no one collects," said Darling softly to no one and turned away from the dancer toward the television because he was a faithful husband, because he and Kathy had something good, and

even in his drunkenness he was not about to jeop-
ardize it for a go-go dancer who was not nearly as
good in bed as Kathy. No one collects. Why? Why
this?

"Another double?" asked the bartender.

"No," said Darling. "A double."

"I said a double," said the bartender.

"Yes, you did," said Darling. "I heard you."

"Right," said the bartender with a sigh and Darling looked at the television screen. A gracious
screen with a fine movie. The title in white over
shots of green forests was: "A Matter of Growth."

Miles of green forest raced across the screen, the
shot taken from a plane.

"This?" asked the announcer. "Or this?" And
the shot changed to mile after mile of burned-out
forests, blackened stumps, the grisly ghosts of what
once were trees, the ground itself scorched and
charred into blackness.

"Or this?" the announcer's voice said, and the
film cut to new houses being built in a typical American suburb; then to high-speed presses spewing out
thousands of copies of a daily newspaper. And the
voice-over saying that "Behind America...behind
America's growth is wood."

Snatches of sentences now, random words, heard
with half an ear, pictures watched with half an eye.
The lumber companies of America, not cutting down
trees just to make a profit by selling them, but re-

planting and reforesting America. Research to make it stronger, bigger, more beautiful trees, all paid for by private enterprise.

More pictures.

More words.

Then the legend at the end of the film: "Prepared by the American Lumber Users' Institute."

Darling watched as the screen darkened then spilled into a commercial for liquid drain cleaner.

Of course, private lumber companies should run the lumber business. Why should the government, with its arbitrary and sometimes silly standards, interfere? That was the message of the film. It was an unpaid commercial, prepared by the lumber barons to justify their rape of the land. Darling thought the film had been familiar and realized why. It was the style . . . the style of the film he had seen earlier in the empty warehouse building on Barclay Street.

Darling tried to collect the focus of his mind. He had stumbled onto something here in the bar, something that told him what that crazy film with the clips he needed was about, but he couldn't quite turn the corner on his fog.

"No. No more," he said to the bartender who was holding his glass. The lumber companies were convincing you that they were good for America. The film asking "Why?" at Barclay Street was trying to convince you of something else. What? What was it doing? It was doing something. It was pushing you to a conclusion. What? Why this? Why the film?

What was its conclusion?

Trouble was bad for America.

That was no conclusion.

Wednesday, October 26: The Tenth Day

In the morning, his head filled with pain and his mouth with the putrescence of the night before, his carton of cigarettes scattered over the hotel room and his phone ringing, Darling thought of exactly what the films meant. Lumber companies were good for America. Radicals were bad for America, and especially bad for those they claimed to help.

So why is the phone still ringing?

"Uhhh," groaned Darling and picked up the receiver. "Yes?"

"Luke, this is Miss McGirr. Are you all right?"

"Yes, yes. All right."

"It's nine-thirty and you're usually in early."

"Yes. Early. Coming in," said Darling and when he finally got into the bathroom to wash out his mouth, the first glass of water made him drunk again from the night before. He looked back out into the hotel room. The bed was empty and there was no green-sequined G-string or anything to tell him he had been with a woman the night before. *Good*, thought Darling. *It could have been worse. Good. Could have been worse. Much worse.*

At the office when he smoked his first cigarette of the day, he found a cocktail napkin stuffed into the pack of True Blues. It had a message on it.

Jericho.

He threw it into the wastebasket.

CHAPTER ***** 14

WHEN DARLING HEARD THAT RAMSEY MAC-Donald was in the outer office, he groaned. Ramsey MacDonald was not to be mixed with hangovers. He was born laughing. Loudly.

Miss McGirr waited by Darling's desk for an answer. She held a sheaf of papers. She had brought black coffee. She had walked quietly. She had lain papers to be signed, gently down before Darling. She knew suffering, and she cared.

"Chase Colonel MacDonald," said Darling. "And on the DeBaux report . . ."

"I heard that," came MacDonald's voice.

Darling looked up to see MacDonald entering his office. "What'd I do to make you sore at me?" the Marine asked.

"Ram, not today," said Darling. "I'm just up to here."

"Don't let me stop you. I only need a minute. Christ, you look awful. What happened to you?"

"McGirr," said Darling. "Please tell DeBaux I'll see him in exactly fifteen minutes..."

"Too long," said MacDonald. "Tell him ten, Miss McGirr. I'll be done in ten and I'll go peacefully."

Miss McGirr looked at him, then questioningly at Darling.

"It's all right, McGirr," Darling said. "But if he isn't out of here in fifteen minutes, call the police."

Miss McGirr nodded, grimly serious. As she passed MacDonald in the doorway, he stood aside for her with exaggerated courtesy, which forced her to smile despite herself.

The door closed behind her and MacDonald walked toward Darling's desk.

"Well?" Darling said.

"'Well?' Why 'well?' between friends?"

"I told you, Ram, I'm busy."

"I would have sworn you were hung over, the way you look. You been tying one on?"

"Something like that."

"You're not going to find out why the government can't beat the radicals in court that way." He plopped into the chair in front of the desk. "But what the hell, you're not interested in the truth anyway ...just in rushing ahead to justice. A rush to justice. A—"

"Please, Ram, no needles today. And two of your fifteen minutes are gone."

"Ten's all I need," said MacDonald. "First, I wanted to tell you that that Rothblatt is some smart guy. That idea of rotten bananas. I've gone back to my reading about the radicals and that's just what it is, you know. Rotten bananas. Any issue, just so they can use it."

"Careful, Ram, you're talking to a lawyer. Don't confuse court cases with movements. There's been a lot of real movements in the past that qualified in somebody's eyes as just rotten bananas. Women's rights, emancipation, child labor laws...they were all somebody's rotten bananas at one time. We're just looking to see what effect it has on trials. But don't make a mistake. Just because a radical calls a banana rotten doesn't mean it *isn't* rotten."

"Good old Luke," MacDonald said. "Just when I find the truth, you've got to start watering it down and fudging it with your whereases and howevers and never let it be forgottens. Screw you, lawyer. It's all rotten bananas to me."

Darling put his hands over his eyes, pressing palms against closed eyelids. The splash of bright lights inside the eyeball was restful.

"Christ, you do look terrible."

"Ram, is that all you wanted? To tell me my staff is brilliant and I'm hung over? 'Cause if it is, you can go now." He looked at his Timex. "Nine minutes left." He covered his eyes again.

MacDonald ignored the ultimatum. "I think

you've been away from home too long," he said. "You look like you need to get laid."

"Thanks. I needed that like a spinal fracture."

"Now that the press has worked you over, why don't you tell them to stuff their job and you just go home?"

"Because I don't do things like that," said Darling. "It's not the Marine way."

"All right. But don't say I didn't warn you. I'm going to a meeting tonight and you're coming with me."

"A meeting?"

"Yeah. An open meeting at the Washington Graphic Arts Center. A protest group."

"Ram, I'm tired."

"Yeah, I know, but you've got to find out what you're reporting about. Otherwise, your report's not going to be any good."

"I'm tired, Ram."

"Right, but you can't ever ignore the value of research into rotten bananas."

"I am tired."

"Right. And the rotten banana that they're going to be protesting tonight is you."

Darling's hands dropped from his eyes and he looked at MacDonald sharply. "Me?"

"Right," said MacDonald, a smile creasing his handsome face, obviously pleased with himself for piquing Darling's interest. "I have it right here." He fished a piece of pink paper from inside his suit jacket and began to read aloud: "'A people's protest against a plot to imprison political opposition.' They spelled political with two L's, Luke. 'Hear the truth about the Justice Department scheme to railroad into jail anyone who opposes the fascist establishment.' Et cetera, et cetera." MacDonald looked up. "That's you, kid. The fascist establishment."

Darling glanced at his watch. "Time's up. McGirr'll have the cops here in three minutes."

"Fine. I'm just leaving. I'll pick you up at your hotel at nine o'clock," said MacDonald, rising and walking lightly to the door.

Darling said "Ram," but when MacDonald turned around, Darling changed his mind. He just wasn't up to arguing with MacDonald. "Nine o'clock," he said.

"Right," said MacDonald and then was gone before Darling had a chance to tell him what hotel he was staying at. Good, he thought. If MacDonald couldn't find him, maybe he'd get some sleep. Already he had second thoughts about the wisdom of going to a radical meeting, even one concerning himself. For all the talk about getting "firsthand, grassroots, ground-level knowledge" of an issue, Darling thought the other approach made more sense. You could not be objective when you were emotionally involved. The door had been closed behind Mac-Donald for only thirty seconds and Darling was already regretting having agreed to go to the meeting. And Ram *would* find the hotel. He found everything.

He pushed aside the pile of blue interoffice memos. With a key from a heavy metal ring, he opened the lower drawer of his desk and took out his file on the radical investigation. It was thicker than it had been yesterday; McGirr must have made some additions to it.

The first page inside the dark green folder was his original memo to Attorney General Walthrop and he looked down the list he had prepared of possible causes for the government's poor performance.

Research and definition of political trials. Next to it, McGirr had penciled in the name "Gilpert" and after it had made two check marks. That meant both his preliminary and final reports were in.

Unique aspects of political trials. Max Rothblatt. One check mark. Max was still working on the final draft of his rotten bananas analysis. Since discussing the report with Rothblatt, Darling had become convinced that there was not really anything unique in the new wave of political trials—at least not enough to explain the government's losing record.

There had been rotten banana issues and rotten banana trials before. Defense attorneys, he recalled, had slipped rotten banana issues into the Sacco and Vanzetti trial. The nation's hatred and fear of anarchists. Anti-Italian prejudice. Dislike of people with beards. The jury had listened to every rotten banana issue that came up, but Sacco and Vanzetti were legally guilty and the jury convicted them and they fried. A radical trial today was no different from a radical trial fifty years ago. Except today, the government always seemed to lose.

He took his black felt-tip pen and drew a line through *unique aspects of political trials* and then through *research and definition of political trials*. Neither of those reports would tell him why the government lost.

Performance of judges and federal attorneys. O'Connell. One check mark. The preliminary report was in. Darling flipped through the back of the file and found a stapled pile of twelve pages. O'Connell had summarized his conclusions on the top sheet and Darling read them quickly. As he expected, the radical trials had been handled by good judges and bad judges, judges who knew the law and judges who couldn't recognize the law if it were water and they were swimming in it. Judges who were rich and judges who were poor. But no judges whose stock holdings or paid-up life insurance or bank balances had shown any marked jump before, during, or right after a radical trial. Judges, in other words, who hadn't been bought. Good, bad, smart, dumb, but unbought. The same for the federal prosecutors. Maybe a little more dumbness than one ought to expect, but no indication that any of them had tried, systematically, to lose.

Darling drew a line through *performance of judges and federal attorneys*.

Jury selection. DeBaux. No check marks. He should be waiting outside with his preliminary report.

Performance of defense attorneys. Willoughby. No check marks.

And, of course, *Conspiracy*. Walthrop's reason. Darling smiled as he closed the folder and dialed McGirr to send in DeBaux. "And tell O'Connell his preliminary report on judges and prosecutors is okay and he should get cracking on the final draft."

"He already is."

"But where's Willoughby's report on the defense attorney? On our friend, Harold Albend?"

"Willoughby's sick today, Luke. But I talked to him on the phone and he's working at home. He'll have it all wrapped up for you tomorrow."

"Okay. Send Fred in."

DeBaux entered carrying a container of coffee and Darling asked him to share it.

"Take it all, it's for you. Miss McGirr said you'd want it."

"Good for her. Sit down, Fred. When you go into private practice, remember one thing: fancy offices you can do without; a fifty-thousand-volume library you can do without; what you can't do without is a secretary who knows what she's doing."

"Can't do without clients either."

"Get a good secretary and you'll have so much of a reputation, clients'll be knocking down your doors," Darling said.

DeBaux was fussing with a large, reddish envelope tied with rust-colored string. Slowly he began to remove papers from it.

"So, jury selection," Darling said. "What's the bottom line?"

"The bottom line is zero. Nothing." DeBaux was a gaunt, big-nosed shambling young man who wore tweed suits. His family was moneyed. Darling had not been able to classify him and Miss McGirr had offered none of her usual impeccable opinions except to say that he was competent. Darling would have to hear him out.

"What's zero?" Darling asked.

"Item. Albend uses public opinion polls before the jury is selected."

"Why?" asked Darling, sensing that DeBaux wanted to explain it systematically.

"A trial is the United States versus so-and-so, but it's really just the people of a district who sit on the jury who decide for the government or for the defendant. Albend uses polls to find out the local prejudices in the trial neighborhood, then tries to tie them into his defense tactics."

"For instance?"

"For instance, suppose he finds people in one area are crazy nuts about federal tax policies. Paranoid about it. Well, armed with that, he can tailor at least part of his defense to make it look like the government has been trying to screw the defendants on taxes. He can tailor his defense issues. He did that with the screwball minister who led the riots against the army recruiting booths. He said the government was trying to get a tax case against him. The judge let it in and the jury acquitted."

"Got you," Darling said.

DeBaux went on as if he had not heard. "In other words, he finds a jury he can jerk off." He looked up at Darling, who nodded.

"Albend also usually has a psychologist at the defense table with him when he's selecting a jury. This fellow's supposed to help him reject people who have a thirst for vengeance . . . you know, automatic votes for conviction."

"He's thorough," said Darling, admiringly.

"He can afford to be. He's never short of defense funds. But you know what's most interesting of all?" DeBaux asked.

"What's that?"

"It's bullshit."

"What is?"

"All this crap about new jury selection methods, it's all bullshit, press talk. They fancy it up with psychologists and public opinion polls, but it's the same thing lawyers always do." He cleared his throat and turned over one of the sheets of paper and read aloud:

" 'If the client is a landlord, a banker, a manufacturer, get a juror who looks neat and trim and smug. He'll be sure to guard your interests as he would his own. Every knowing lawyer seeks a jury of the same sort as his client.' "

"But—"

"Just a minute, Luke, there's more." He continued reading. " 'Keep Irishmen on the jury in trials of "the state" versus anybody. Irishmen always imagine themselves in the dock. Get rid of Presbyterians. They're as cold as the grave. They know right from wrong but seldom find anything right. Baptists are even more hopeless. They distrust everybody who doesn't live next door to them. Lutherans and Scandinavians are almost always sure to convict. Keep Jews and agnostics. Skip prohibitionists. Never take a wealthy man in a criminal case.' "

Darling tapped his felt-tipped pen on the green desk blotter. DeBaux looked slightly embarrassed. "And so on," he said quickly. "Anyway, there's your modern jury selection techniques. From Clarence Darrow in 1936. And he did pretty well without psychologists and public opinion polls."

"In other words, you're telling me Albend just does what every other skilled lawyer has done?"

"Right. No more, no less. It just looks fancier

when he does it because the press is always sucking around to make him look good."

"You don't find any reason in there for us to be blowing these cases?"

DeBaux shook his head. "None at all. If jury selection was a factor, we'd lose every time we faced a good attorney who knew how to pick a jury. But we face a lot of them and we generally win. It's just these political trials that give us trouble."

"Any possibility of jury tampering?"

"None. I checked everything. FBI files, talked to judges, talked to jurors even. No way."

"How long will it take you to write the report?"

"I'll have the final draft to you tomorrow."

"Good enough," said Darling. "I'll take your preliminary."

DeBaux handed over a sheaf of papers into Darling's hand, then shuffled toward the door.

"Good work, Fred," Darling said and the young lawyer's face brightened as he left.

Darling skimmed quickly through the report. It seemed solid. DeBaux had not gone into the question of the federal attorneys' process of selecting jurors because as lawyers, both he and Darling knew that federal prosecutors were stuck with whatever jury they happened to get.

In a multidefendant trial, each defense attorney had a number of peremptory challenges which allowed them to throw out any juror they didn't like, without even giving a reason. The government, on the other hand, had only a few such challenges and couldn't get fancy. The prosecutors were fortunate to be able to keep bomb-thrower types off the jury.

A layman might think it was unfair, that the cards were stacked against the government, against the prosecution, and he would be right, Darling thought. Sometimes laymen forgot that the cards were supposed to be stacked against the prosecution. It was never supposed to be easy to send someone to jail.

Darling put DeBaux's report at the bottom of his green folder and with his pen, went back to the list at the start. Through the words *jury selection*, he drew a black line.

Only one category left: *Performance of defense attorneys*. That was the Albend report due from Willoughby tomorrow.

No. Make that two categories left. There, in red ink, was Walthrop's own category. *Conspiracy*.

Screw conspiracies. Lucius Darling dealt in facts.

Four of the five categories had not given a lead yet on why the government lost these cases, but Darling was only slightly disappointed. He had not really expected any gigantic breakthrough, any single reason that someone could point to and say, "Here. Here it is. This is what we've been doing wrong."

The truth was always more complex than that, always a welter of actions and interactions. And he was sure that the truth of the unsuccessful prosecutions would turn out to be a little bit of this and a little bit of that, and he would amalgamate them all into some logical, sensible pattern and make a string of hard-nosed recommendations to Walthrop that wouldn't be flashy but would be effective.

Not flashy but effective. It sounded like something appropriate for Luke Darling's tombstone.

Swell, he told himself. Except for one thing.

Jericho.

What the hell was that all about?

CHAPTER ★★★★★ 15

RAMSEY MACDONALD CAME FOR DARLING at precisely 9:00 P.M., thumping on his hotel room door loud and long until Darling got out of the shower, tossed a towel about himself, and opened the door.

"Hi, Luke, what a dump."

"Only a couple more days. Then I'm going home."

"Now I know why you can't wait."

"I'll get dressed right away. What time's this Get-Darling rally supposed to start?"

"An hour ago but take your time. The first thing the radicals are going to do away with is clocks. Another tool of capitalist repression. They never start before ten o'clock. Waiting for their crowd to show up."

MacDonald was right. When he and Darling arrived at the Graphic Arts Center meeting room at 9:30, there were only about forty persons there but in the next fifteen minutes another seventy showed up. All the folding chairs were filled and a dozen people standing at 10:00 P.M. when the meeting was called to order, if what ensued could be called coming to order. What it meant, as far as Darling could discern, was that the level of noise was reduced somewhat. Among the last arrivals had been two television crews who had set up at the far left side of the room.

Darling and MacDonald sat in the back row. Darling had expected longhairs, hippies, types whose appearance alone was enough to cause a warrant to be issued for their arrest. But here they were only a sprinkle. The majority of the audience were adults, in their late twenties and thirties. Many wore suits, and the ones who wore jeans and denim jackets wore the kind that said unmistakably that they had been purchased in those quaint little shops around quaint little corners where quaint old junk was sold at ripoff prices.

Darling felt relieved that he did not recognize anybody.

Even the chairman of the meeting was too long in the tooth to be considered young, although he tried hard. Darling guessed his age at the early thirties. He wore almost black sunglasses, dirty khaki pants, army brogans, and a fringed leather buckskin jacket. His red, curly beard did not quite seem to match his long, straight blonde hair which Darling thought was another tipoff to his age because as the age increased, the hair stayed straight but the beard got darker and curlier.

"I'm Timothy Blalock, president of Students Against Repression and chairperson of your meeting tonight. We are here to protest the latest in a long series of government steps to silence any criticism of its racist, genocidal criminal policies."

From front left a voice called, "Right on."

"Right on," someone else responded.

MacDonald leaned over to Darling. "Hey, you drew yourself a biggie."

"Who is he?" asked Darling.

"Berkeley violence, Kent State violence, antiwar violence, he's been in all of them."

"I've never heard of him," Darling whispered.

"Not many have."

Blalock had reached to a small table behind him and picked up a copy of the *Washington Post*. A story just below the fold of page one was circled in red marker.

"Here's the evidence," Blalock said, "the government itself admitting that it's trying to find ways to convict anybody who doesn't agree with its policies. It seems they're not satisfied with what they're doing now. Not satisfied? They're never satisfied. They raped the people at Attica. They raped the people at Wounded Elk. They raped the people in Berkeley. In Watts. In Chicago, they used their local goons to try to kill us on the streets. But are they satisfied? Was it enough for them?"

"No," came the voice from the front of the room. Darling spotted its owner now. It was a young woman in the third row. She had been the first to yell "right on." Now her "no" was picked up by a dozen more voices.

"No."

"No."

"Never enough."

"No."

"No."

"Fucking right," yelled Blalock. "Nothing's ever enough for the pigs. Nothing ever. And now they're trying to find a way to pervert the jury system, one of the last vestiges of democracy, to their own evil ends. What they want is a state where a government accusation is proof of guilt. And now they've turned loose one of their right-wing hacks..." He paused and glanced at the newspaper in his right hand. "...a right-wing hack, Lucius Darling. Can you believe that name?"

There were titters of amusement through the audience. MacDonald applauded.

"A right-wing, racist redneck hack named Lucius Darling to put more people in jail. People whose only crime is to have the courage to stand up and tell the government: No! Here we stand, motherfuckers, and you go no farther."

"Hey," MacDonald whispered into Darling's ear. "They're making you famous."

"Shhh, Ram," Darling said.

"Well, again . . . again, we tell the motherfuckers: NO! What do we tell them?" Blalock demanded.

The crowd roared back, one voice. "NO!"

Darling was shocked at the violent level of the language. Not from an excessive sense of prudery, but from the casual nature of the profanity and the casual willingness of the audience to join in it. Darling had learned at sea that profanity generally covered an inability to express one's thoughts clearly. It was the fucking ship and the fucking old man and the fucking mail call and the fucking this and the fucking that. Eliminating the use of the accurate, specific statement also eliminated the need for accurate, specific thought.

But then so did slogans, and obviously profanity was the radical's all-purpose, all-weather slogan.

The crowd continued to roar "NO!"

The thin blonde woman in the third row jumped to her feet, raised her fist over her head, and shouted "No" again.

"He's brought a cheering section," Darling said to MacDonald softly.

"S.O.P.," said MacDonald.

The woman next to Darling stood trembling, tugging at the pocket of her brown tweed walking suit. Her eyeglasses had teardrop-shaped tortoise shell frames and her hair was pinned atop her head. He thought she looked like a librarian.

She bellowed, "We tell the motherfuckers no."

It took three or four minutes for the screaming to die down and then Darling heard voices in the aisle to his left. The men standing around the television cameras were mumbling to each other. One of them walked forward toward Blalock and spoke softly to him.

"Comrades," Blalock announced. "Wouldn't you know it? The media can't cover this meeting if we use, as they put it, profanity."

"Fuck the media," shouted the girl in the third row. Before anybody could pick up the chant, Blalock wheeled toward the young woman. Even with the dark glasses, the look of fury on his face was plain. The woman slipped back into her seat even more quickly than she had jumped up.

"I agree with your policy," Blalock told the audience. "But I don't think we should give the pig-owned press a chance to shut us off from reaching the people out there. People who believe with us that this country still can be saved. All they need here is an excuse to cut us off, and I'm not going to give them one. And besides. We wouldn't want to offend the president or the Congress, would we? And we all know that none of them use pro-fan-i-ty."

He lingered over the word, drawing it out, as if in mock horror. The audience tittered again.

Then the camera's red shooting lights came on and Blalock started over again, holding up the newspaper, repeating almost word for word his blast that it was a plot to suppress opposition and jail dissenters. He repeated his denunciation of Darling as a right-wing redneck hack and said again: "We tell them no." This time all expletives were carefully deleted.

"This is incredible," Darling whispered to MacDonald.

"I know. I liked it better when he called you a motherfucker."

"Shut up, Ram. These people believe this bullshit. I'm some redneck. From Ohio yet. And these people believe it."

"Not just them. Remember, I've been studying this thing. By tomorrow or the next day, a poll would see indicators that tens of thousands of people . . . in just a couple of days . . . would believe that there's a fascist cop conspiring to persecute people who speak up for their rights."

"You seemed to have learned a lot pretty fast," Darling said.

"I was always a quick study," MacDonald responded.

Darling saw Blalock look off into the audience, giving the cameraman a good low-angle shot. The speaker had confined himself to half-a-minute, a discipline Darling knew was calculated to get his statement uncut on national television. A person who rambled for three or four minutes or longer guaranteed himself an editing at the studio with newsmen picking what they wanted to run. But a person who kept himself to a few brief ideas could get exactly what he wanted.

Blalock nodded to the cameraman, signaling that he was done, and rested his hands on the little podium. An errant breeze caught his army field jacket. Someone coughed in the last row. The red lights on the television cameras went off.

"I am fucking ashamed, fucking ashamed to be an American. I am fucking ashamed of what we did in Southeast Asia. I am fucking ashamed of what we did in Greece. I am fucking ashamed of what we did in the Middle East. I am fucking ashamed of what we do with our food. But all that is nothing compared to the fucking shame I feel at the fucking scummy putrescence called the Justice Department."

Darling nudged MacDonald. "Imagine how he'd feel if he worked there a week," he whispered.

"You don't get offended easily, do you?" MacDonald asked.

"I'm offended," Darling said. "But what am I supposed to do about it?"

Blalock was also asking a question. "What are we going to do about Justice, about the agents of fascism, about the beast Darling?"

"Burn his children," screamed a woman who,

until then, Darling would have trusted as a babysitter.

"Picket," came a voice from the second row.

"A sit-in at the attorney general's office."

"Write the president," came a voice near Darling. That suggestion was greeted with laughter.

"Fuck the president," somebody shouted in correction.

"Right on," shrieked the young woman in the third row, obviously having suffered long enough watching her language. "Fuck the pig motherfucking cocksucker president."

The logic of the statement was so pure and clear that it was approved by acclamation.

"Fuck the motherfucker."

"Fuck the cocksucker."

Voices around the room seemed to vie with each other to be the most vehement in their denunciation. The woman next to Darling seemed to have carefully weighed the policy and culled from it that part she found most worthy.

"Fuck everybody," she said softly. "Fuck everybody." Over and over. "Fuck everybody."

Darling turned away and smiled. There was at least one other person in Washington as sexually frustrated as he was, and he felt sorry for her because his frustration would end in five more days when he stepped off that plane in Troy, Ohio.

A young man had come from the back of the hall

to whisper something in Blalock's ear. The bearded man tossed the *Washington Post* back onto the table behind him and raised his hands for silence.

"Brothers, sisters, comrades, we have a surprise tonight and a special honor. One man has stood against this tide of terrorism and repression by the pig government. One man has had the courage to fight on, despite the odds, against the overwhelming power of Washington. That one man is with us tonight, comrades. Back from his victory at Wounded Elk. Harold Albend."

The room erupted with cheers. People jumped to their feet and turned toward the door. The woman next to Darling leaned over and told him, "Come on, get up. That's Harold Albend."

Darling just shook his head but she had already turned back and joined in the roar. Albend, immaculate as ever, walked down the center aisle toward the podium. The cheers grew louder. Some reached out just to touch his sleeve. A few thrust their hands into his.

He had conquered the crowd as surely as John F. Kennedy had taken West Berlin, thought Darling, who glanced at MacDonald, sitting placidly. The Marine's face showed no disgust, no anger, no amusement. It was the face of a surgeon looking at a tumor.

At the front of the room, Albend let the applause drain itself. He raised his hands for silence. A few people sat down, then everyone sat. The woman next to Darling remembered to glare at him, and Darling shrugged.

"We have met the enemy and he is ours," Albend said, his voice soft, without strength, but the words were enough to set off another explosion of cheering.

Blalock moved away from Albend and leaned against the wall near the front of the room.

Darling watched Albend carefully. The radical lawyer obviously had prepared no remarks beyond his opening sentence because he started to ramble, without verve or flair, and Darling thought that it certainly was not by rhetoric that Albend had won his cases.

Unless Albend were toning himself down because the television cameras were there. But the cameramen were still packing. Quietly, droningly, Albend recited the events of the trial at Wounded Elk and told how the government had entered into a conspiracy of silence—whatever that was—to try to convict the innocent but that somehow the government had failed.

Darling paid more attention when Albend said he did not share the alarm of the audience over the "rush to justice" in the attorney general's office.

"What it means is that the fat cats are getting panicky," Albend said. "It means that we must guard ourselves. We must be careful. They have tried every dirty trick in the past, and now they are ready to try more dirty tricks. Even dirtier. We not only must expect that. We can know for certain it is coming.

"But it is not a show of strength. They are acting from their weakness, because they know their end is almost here. This government of corrupt men, presiding over a corrupt governmental machine that spews forth corruption as its only product—their end is coming. And only when that day comes . . . that this government of filth and evil and cruelty is no more . . . only then on that day may free men freely walk this land again."

The flight of eloquence was so in contrast with the flatness of the rest of his talk that Darling was convinced it was an ending to a speech he must have used many times.

The crowd jumped to its feet to cheer. Darling saw two television reporters applauding. Albend soaked up the cheers and Blalock came forward and spoke to him, then raised his hands for quiet.

"The counselor of the poor and oppressed has agreed to stay and answer any questions any of you might have and to share with us his knowledge of this giant crime which is America today."

Everyone sat again. MacDonald rose and raised a hand. Darling looked on, stunned.

"Yes, sir," said Albend, talking over the heads of the crowd, which turned to look at MacDonald.

"Mr. Albend, I'm not quite sure I understand the nature of the protest against the Justice Department.

Isn't it the function of the Justice Department to prosecute?"

"No, sir," Albend answered. "It is the function of the Justice Department to find justice."

"But if the department thinks someone is guilty, then, constitutionally, it has a duty to prosecute, is that right?"

Albend cleared his throat. "You might say that."

"Well, sir, this is the part I don't understand. Isn't this study of why the government is losing cases just a question of the government trying to make itself more efficient in carrying out its duties?"

"No," the young woman in the third row shouted. Other "no's" followed.

When silence returned, Albend smiled and said, "The people have answered you. But let me add that your point might be well made if we were talking about a legitimate constitutional government and not the cesspool of corruption, avarice, and repression that exists in this country today."

"Right on," came a shout near Darling.

"Fuck the motherfucking government," shouted the woman in the third row.

"Fuck everybody," called the woman sitting next to Darling. "Fuck everybody."

Brazenly, MacDonald waited on his feet until the noise had stopped. He smiled too and said, "I just want you to know, Mr. Albend, that I think it's wonderful that despite this government being so repressive, you are still able to freely defend people in actions against the government. I mean—"

"I know what you mean," said Albend, showing a small flicker of temper. "But let me tell you that there is nothing contradictory about that. The government just hasn't figured out how to silence me yet. They've tapped my phone and intercepted my mail and they have stooges following my every step. But so far they have failed. And they will continue to fail."

A broad smile swept across MacDonald's face as he sat down.

The TV crews headed for the door. Albend immediately pleaded a prior engagement and begged off answering further questions. Blalock took over the meeting again and profusely thanked Albend.

MacDonald tapped Darling on the shoulder and suggested they leave. Walking outside, Darling asked, "Why didn't you want to stay till the end?"

MacDonald shrugged. "It's always the same. They'll shout a little more. Then Blalock'll tell them to go home and await further instructions."

"You *have* done a lot of studying. Maybe you can tell me what was the point of the meeting if there's no action?" Darling asked.

A blue and white Chevy van rode away from the front of the building and MacDonald pointed after it. "There's the point. News coverage. Just keep the pot boiling. Hey, dummy, you forget? It was your guy who told me about the technique. Rotten bananas."

Darling shrugged. They stopped at the bottom of the steps to light cigarettes. The door opened at the top of the stairs and Albend sauntered out, putting on his topcoat as he walked. It did not cover his trademark cravat. Near the bottom of the steps, he saw and recognized MacDonald. He looked hard at Darling as if trying to place his face.

"Good evening, gentlemen," he said, pausing in front of MacDonald. "Of course, I remember you from inside, but have we met before?"

"I think not. I'm Colonel MacDonald."

"Oh," said Albend, obviously taken aback. Military men did not attend this sort of meeting. He glanced toward the top of the steps to see if anyone was up there who might be able to help him if he needed help. *He's afraid*, thought Darling. *The apostle of violence and revolution is afraid of violence. He...*

His train of thought was interrupted by MacDonald, who said, "And this is my dearest friend, Lucius Darling."

"Oh, oh...I see," said Albend. "Well, I'd best be on my way." He turned.

"Do you mind if I ask you a question, Mr. Albend?" said Darling.

"I will not discuss my cases with you," said Albend.

"I wouldn't bother," said Darling. "I just wondered. What did America ever do to you that you hate it so much?"

Without waiting for an answer, Darling walked away from Albend. MacDonald followed him, and after a few steps said, "Luke, maybe you ought to pack it in and go back to Troy tonight. You're getting emotionally involved."

"Ram, it makes me sick. Tonight, this was like watching a cartoon." But that was not exactly correct and he sat thinking quietly in the car as MacDonald drove him back to his hotel and just four blocks from the hotel, Darling said, "Ram, what did tonight remind you of?"

The Marine shrugged. "Visiting day at the asylum? Open house at the zoo? I'll bite. What?"

"That film we saw," said Darling. "Dempsey's film. The radicals and the screamers and the rioters. Tonight reminded me of that."

Pulling up to a red light, MacDonald shook his head. "Wrong, Luke. These tonight are garbage. Except for Albend and Blalock, just hangers-on. Camp followers. Tomorrow, if their leadership was gone, they'd find new leaders and a new movement and it wouldn't matter which one. Become vegetarians. Zero-population growers. Whatever. There's only a handful of leaders to the whole thing. The rest are just simps."

"You believe that?" asked Darling.

"Believe what?"

"That if their leadership was gone, they'd go away?"

"Yeah. I believe it, Luke."

"'Tis a consummation devoutly to be wished," said Darling softly.

"You believe *that*?" MacDonald asked.

"I don't know. They make me sick."

"Me too," said MacDonald. He seemed to be waiting for Darling to say something more, but the lawyer was silent. A moment later, MacDonald pulled up past a parked cab to the front door of Darling's hotel.

"Want a drink?" he asked.

"Not tonight, Ram. I've got to get some sleep. You've learned a lot in a few days."

"You too, Luke. Sweet dreams."

CHAPTER ★★★★★ 16

DARLING WAVED AT MACDONALD'S DEPART-
ing car before turning to walk into the sparsely dec-
orated hotel lobby. A man with a peaked cab driver's
cap sat in one of the worn plush chairs facing the
door, reading a copy of the *New York Daily News*.

He studied Darling's face, then stood up and
walked to him.

"Mr. Darling?"

"Yes?"

"You're supposed to come with me." The man
moved past Darling for the door.

"Wait a minute," Darling said. "Why am I supposed to come with you? Who says?"

The man turned. "Look, all I know is I got fifty
bucks in advance and I been sitting there waiting for
you."

"Who gave you the money?"

"Fat guy. Fattest man you ever saw."

"Let's go," said Darling. He followed the driver

from the hotel and walked with him to the cab parked just short of the hotel entrance.

"Get in front," the cabbie said brusquely.

Even though annoyed at being pushed and pulled around in Washington, Darling did as he was told. The driver started his cab's motor but did not move. He was looking toward the corner.

Darling followed his gaze to see what he was staring at, then realized the driver was watching the traffic light. But it was green already.

Just as the light turned amber, the driver peeled off from the curb with a rip of tires, flooring the gas pedal, and made a skidding right-hand turn at the corner, passing through the red light. He drove fifty feet, then jammed on the brakes.

"Get out," he snapped.

Darling looked to his side. Another cab was parked there and its rear door on the left side quickly opened.

Darling got out of one cab and into the other. Mottodocio, whose bulk seemed to fill three-quarters of the back seat, reached across him and slammed the door shut. Darling heard the other cab pull away down the street.

"Sit low," said Mottodocio.

Darling slumped in the seat. The street was quiet and uncrowded and fifteen seconds later a car passed them, going in the same direction as Darling's first cab.

"There goes your tail," Mottodocio said. "Okay, buddy, let's get out of here."

The driver made a giant U-turn from the curb to drive off in the other direction. As he pulled away, Darling leaned forward to look around Mottodocio at the car that had been following him. It was a brown Chevrolet.

He chuckled.

"What's funny?" Mottodocio asked.

"That poor bastard. This is the second time in two nights he's lost me. If he's in training, he's going to wash out."

"He hasn't lost you yet. Left at the corner."

Two blocks later, Mottodocio said, "Stop right here. By the red Plymouth."

"Come on," he said to Darling when the driver stopped. "We can take my car and drive down to the Capitol park. It's a good place to talk." To the driver, he said, "Thanks, buddy."

"Anytime, mister."

Mottodocio got out of the car quickly for a man of his bulk and Darling slid out the curbside door after him. The retired cop waited until the cab had driven away before reaching into his pocket for a set of keys. Then he led Darling across the street and into a gold Ford whose seats and dashboard had the new, but not for long, look of rental cars.

Mottodocio drove away and turned right at the corner.

"This isn't the way to the Capitol," Darling said.

"That's right," Mottodocio said.

They drove away from the center of Washington. Darling tried to make conversation but Mottodocio was silent. A few minutes later, they were on Route 50, the six-lane divided expressway, heading northeast toward Baltimore.

Five minutes along Route 50, Mottodocio pulled into a deserted rest station off the right side of the road. A faint light illuminated the doors to two restrooms built into a concrete blockhouse. Behind the building, black trees loomed against a black sky.

"So?" said Darling, as Mottodocio put the car in neutral and pulled up the handbrake. "Have you got my lever against Dempsey?"

"Yeah. I got your lever right here," said Mottodocio and his fat hands moved so smoothly, so precisely and naturally, that Darling only saw the pistol when it was pointing at him.

"Counselor, I thought you had smarts but you fucked the wrong guy."

"I hate guns. Get that away from my face," said Darling. "I mean it. On either side, I don't like guns."

"You didn't want no lever against the FBI and Dempsey. You're part of it," said Mottodocio.

The gun stayed in Darling's face and the lawyer said, "If you're going to shoot me, shoot me. Just get that gun away from my face. One way or the other."

Darling watched the hammer go back under a

fat thumb, then heard it click safely back into position. He suddenly became aware of the smell of dirty toilets and the faraway light of the Washington Monument. Mottodocio slid the pistol back under his belt.

"All right," he said.

"All right," said Darling. "What do you want to know?"

"What'd you get me into?"

"You're the investigator."

"Don't be a wiseass, Counselor."

"I mean it. I had a problem. I needed some film clips. I needed to talk to an FBI guy who was dodging me. I knew it was some undercover thing and I wasn't about to get any help without a lever. You were the lever. That's all it was."

"That's it?"

"In my whole life, I've never gone near this spy hoopydoo undercover nonsense. It's not me, Tony, and you know it. I was antitrust because I wanted to be. I wanted to get into the guts of business. I want to make money and retire rich. I've got everything I want back in Troy. I don't need tails and I don't need meeting second cars and I don't need phoning from tight phones."

"Then why'd you come to Queens secret?"

"Because I knew I had stumbled into this kind of shit, you dumb bastard, and you were supposed to help me get out. I've got an attorney general on my ass. I didn't volunteer for this shit."

"Well, Luke, you're in it."

"No. Not anymore. I'm sick of this garbage. We're just going to back off. I'll do my report without Dempsey. I'll list him as uncooperative and let it go at that. You go home to Queens, I'll go home to Troy, and we'll let these people chase themselves in circles. Maybe they'll find some Communists, who knows?"

"Sounds easy," Mottodocio said. "But I don't think so."

Far off, a light went out in a high building. A large jet changed pitch of engines overhead, heading for Dulles. The Baltimore Expressway was silent. Darling sighed. He lit a cigarette and offered one to Mottodocio, who shook his head.

"Can't drink *or* smoke, Counselor."

"Well, I need a drink. I have had a hangover since morning and I am tired. No. Tired was what I was this afternoon. I've gone beyond tired. Let's find a bar somewhere."

"You got a drinking problem?"

"No, but I intend to."

The two men drove to Annapolis with Mottodocio talking. Darling knew of a late-night spot there.

It had all started when Mottodocio had checked out the building on Barclay Street.

"Not with the tails in Queens?" asked Darling.

Mottodocio shook his head. "No. That was covered. The cops let them find out they were believed to be muscling in on protected gambling territory. People will always believe dirt, especially about cops. So what they found out was this Americans in Readiness thing. I can't tell you how, but I've got a list of the members."

But Mottodocio himself had been picked up by a tail when he started looking into the building on Barclay Street.

"Who owns it?" Darling asked.

"Nobody owns it."

"This is America. Everything is owned by somebody."

"Right. This used to be owned by somebody. And then the government closed down on a lot of mortgages and started buying up property for some kind of urban renewal crap and this building was one of them that they bought. The Housing Department told me they didn't have a record of owning it, but the old owner showed me his receipt from the federal government. So the building's owned by you guys, the feds, but you guys don't know about it."

"I've been in Washington twelve years," Darling said. "Sounds like your normal, garden-variety fuckup. Any connection to Dempsey?"

"None."

But Mottodocio's stomach had begun telling him things. It told him he was in traffic.

In the cocktail lounge in Annapolis, he kept talking.

Darling, gulping down the vodka martini, felt the energy drain from him, that force of will that had kept him going all day. The strange thought kept coming to him that if he got killed, he wouldn't be able to go home to his family. But why should he be thinking of getting killed?

Mottodocio sat looking at the tray in front of him, with one glass of orange juice, another glass of club soda, and a third glass to mix them in.

He built his drink and sipped it with the delicacy common to men who were fat as a matter of choice.

"First off, I'm gonna tell you something I never told a fucking prosecutor in my life, 'cause what I'm telling you is the least admissible evidence in the world. But I swear by it. We're into something so big and so slick we're over our heads. My stomach tells me."

"Listen," Darling said. "Get out of this thing. No hard feelings from me. No complaints. I don't want complications. I just want to go home."

"In for a dime, in for a dollar," Mottodocio said.

"Do you think there's physical danger to you?"

The ex-cop shrugged. "When you don't know what you're dealing with, anything's possible," he said.

"Then I don't want you working on this anymore. That's final."

"Go stuff it," Mottodocio said. "I told you I'm in. Besides, I haven't had so much fun since the Knapp Commission came sniffing around trying to prove I was a corrupt cop."

"Were you?"

"Would it matter to you?"

"Not a stick," Darling said.

"Then I'll tell you what I told them. 'I respect-fully decline to answer on the grounds that . . . ' You know." He shoved his thick wrist out through the finely tailored blue jacket and looked at his watch. "Will you stop bullshitting? Time's running away."

He took another big drink of his orange juice mixture, then placed it carefully on its own wet yel-low ring atop the tan plastic tray.

"I told you that those two tails in New York belonged to this Americans in Readiness thing. I've done more checking. They're volunteers but they get paid a little bit for each assignment. Expenses, any-way. The funding looks private."

"Funding? A couple of people, a couple of bucks," said Darling.

"Maybe. You ever hear of Bryant Marine Base?" asked Mottodocio.

Darling thought a moment, then nodded. "Train-ing center in World War II. Down in Virginia. Closed down about five years ago."

"Supposed to be closed down," Mottodocio cor-rected. "One of the tails we picked up on you in New

York said he was expecting to go there for advanced training."

"What kind of training?"

"He didn't know."

"Who was he, this tail?"

"Nobody. Stock broker. Ex-Marine. Veterans associations. Lives in Manhattan. Gun nut. Silver Star in Korea."

"Tony, you're not telling me anything. I wanted to know what Dempsey is doing in that building with that film and you're not giving me anything."

"Counselor, I'm giving you *everything*. Just so you can look at all the pieces and if you just look at pieces and don't see anything but pieces, then you're too stupid to be a federal prosecutor." Mottodocio seemed angry.

"Sorry, Tony. Go on. What about Bryant Marine Base?"

"There's been people using it, but I don't know who or what for." He looked at his watch again. "Anyway, that's where I'm going. To find out what's happening there."

"And you think this has something to do with that film?"

"I know it does. It's all wrapped up together somehow. I know it. The tails. Americans in Readiness. A building that nobody owns. A film that nobody ought to have. A Marine base that nobody ought to be on. It's all tied up together."

Darling swallowed. He had waited too long to ask the only question he had really wanted to ask.

"And what about Jericho?" he said.

"It's a day."

"What does that mean?" asked Darling.

"The tail we picked up in New York. The guy. He had a note on him. It said . . ." Mottodocio drew a leather-covered notebook from his inside jacket pocket and flipped through pages. "It said 'Bryant. Jericho Day.'"

"What does it mean?"

"I don't know."

"What did he say it meant?"

"He talked about a training exercise but he didn't make any sense."

"Do you believe him?"

"Yeah. I think it was just a name he picked up someplace along the line. I don't think he knew anything more than just the name."

"And you think it's important?" Darling watched Mottodocio's face carefully.

"Counselor, I *know* it's important."

"Your stomach?"

Mottodocio nodded. "My stomach."

Darling was disappointed. He did not know what he had expected from Mottodocio but he had expected something more, something tangible. He had wanted a lever against Dempsey but he still did not have one. Mottodocio accused Darling of seeing only pieces, but damnit, he could hardly even see the pieces. So what that the Barclay Street building was owned by the federal government? So what that some tail was going to go to Bryant Marine Base? And so what that the old base was being used for something? Old bases were always being used for something. So what that there was a civil defense group with a little private financing?

The thought stuck in his mind again. A *couple of people, a couple of bucks.*

"What about the private funding for the tails?" he said.

"Yeah. You thought a couple of tails, right? Well, I got a list. A thick list. It's more than a couple of tails and a couple of bucks."

A *list*, Darling thought. *Something tangible.*

"Let me see it," he said.

"I don't carry around things I wouldn't want to lose. I mailed it to you."

"When?"

"Today. And I didn't know if your mail was safe so I sent it to your secretary, the Irish one, what's her name?"

"McGirr?"

"Right. It's addressed to her. Marked personal and the return address is Felner. You should get it tomorrow." He looked at his watch again. "Make that today. Unless your mail's like New York's and then you probably won't get it until next year."

A list. It wasn't much but maybe something, Darling thought. His face must have registered his disappointment because Mottodocio saw it and recognized it.

"Luke, let me tell you something. I know you've got all this education and polish but I've been around and I know something too. Life is really kind of a simple thing. When you start digging around in it, no matter how complicated it is on the surface, no matter how many loose ends seem to be sticking out of something, you usually find out that there's one reason for the way things are happening, one knot that ties all the loose ends together."

"Where is it?" asked Darling.

"When it's hard to find, Luke, it means that somebody's trying to make it hard to find. We're fooling with something big." He finished the last swirl of orange drink in his glass. "Big," he repeated. "That tail on you?" he added. "You know who it is?"

"No," said Darling. "I think he's got mud on his plates."

Mottodocio brushed his pants leg. "Yeah, mud. That's two bucks you owe me for dry cleaning. When I find out whose car it is, I'll let you know."

He stood up suddenly at the table. "You'll have that list in the mail. What you do with it is your business. I'm going to find out what's going on at Bryant Marine Base." He smiled, an unaccustomed event in his large round face. "By the way, that list cost me five hundred dollars."

"Two hundred," said Darling.

"No. Five hundred for real. I laid out my own money."

"I'll get it for you," Darling said.

"Okay. Don't forget. And watch your ass, Luke. You're good to work with."

"Good?"

"That means you ain't a nillytwat like most."

"Thanks," said Darling. He watched Mottodocio leave. He had another vodka martini, then called for a cab. He slept in the taxi all the way back to Washington. It was Thursday. He would be back home in Troy in four more days.

Fuck Jericho Day.

CHAPTER ★★★★★ 17

Thursday, October 27: The Eleventh Day

MISS MCGIRR BROUGHT IN THE WRITTEN RE-
port on Harold Albend at the same time she brought
Darling his morning coffee. He was staring at the
soundless TV flickering in the corner.

"Willoughby is the shy type," she said. "He had
this on my desk this morning. If you have any questions, he'll come over to talk to you."

"Shy? A shy lawyer?"

"The modern generation, I guess. You terrify him
for some reason. But read the report first."

"Okay. By the way, when does the mail come
in?"

"When they finish fooling with it in the mail-
room, about ten o'clock."

"Okay. There's going to be an envelope addressed to you and marked personal and the return

address is going to say Felner."

"Right," McGirr said.

"When it comes, it's for me. Don't open it. Just bring it in."

Miss McGirr's look was halfway between surprise and hurt. "Luke, when I asked you on that memo if we were into something undercover, you never answered me."

"That's right, McGirr. I never answered you."

Willoughby's report was detailed and thorough and not shy at all about drawing a conclusion in the matter of Harold Albend.

Albend was a shit lawyer. That conclusion jumped from the double-spaced, neatly typed blue pages.

Willoughby preceded his report with two quotations:

"If Harold Albend were defending Eichmann, I might find a couple of good words to say about genocide."—Professor Aaron Rothberg, Harvard Law School professor emeritus.

"Mr. Albend, your ignorance of the law is so monumental that it is matched only by your rudeness to this court and its traditions of justice."—Associate Justice Bartley Haimes, United States Supreme Court.

Willoughby's report started:

"With most men in the public limelight, a broad spectrum of opinions is not only possible but normal.

Certainly, a highly publicized attorney is no exception.

"The typical public view is that such a defense attorney is an avenging angel, but this is purely a public relations image and much too subjective for analysis.

"However, a lawyer's skill *can* be measured. The opinions of his peers, the opinions of the bench, the attorney's background, his behavior in court—all these things are objective and can be measured and thus the attorney himself can be measured.

"In each and every one of these categories, Harold Albend is defective."

Willoughby went on to trace Albend's career:

He was graduated from John Marshall Law School in Jersey City, now defunct, a school noted neither for the difficulty of its curriculum nor the brilliance of its professors. Despite this, Albend graduated near the bottom of his class. He took the New York state bar exam three times before passing it.

He then applied for positions at, apparently, every large Wall Street law firm but was rejected by each. To support himself, he began his own criminal practice. In short, he was an ambulance chaser unsuccessfully peddling justice in the city's police courts.

During his free time, of which he had

much, he wrote a book examining an unsolved ten-year-old murder case in the Midwest and came to the conclusion that the murder had been committed by the local American Legion unit, which he described as a neo-Nazi organization. The book was too polemical and sold poorly, even though it did win Albend some praise from various far-left literary journals. The crime was solved three years later; the victim's business partner had contracted to have him killed.

The slight literary praise did nothing for Albend's practice, however. And then he got a simple armed robbery case involving a black man in Harlem. Albend lost the case, as was his usual practice. This time, however, the defendant's family put up some additional money and Albend appealed the verdict. To the surprise of everyone, the conviction was overturned because the police had used "contaminated" evidence—in other words, evidence illegally obtained.

This occurred at the period of time when the U.S. Supreme Court seemed to be seizing any case which might be before it and using it as a vehicle to make sweeping changes in criminal law.

The press commended Albend for the

"victory." He became an instant media hero. Somehow forgotten in the encomiums of his brilliance and well-paid perseverance was the fact that the Supreme Court had rejected every one of the issues Albend had raised in the appeal and, in fact, had called some of them "clownish." They had freed the defendant by a study of the trial record, on grounds they themselves raised. In other words, even though he won that case, Albend actually blew it too.

But it did not matter. Well-heeled antiestablishment types began to flock to him. He won a number of the cases despite himself, often through more Supreme Court "lawmaking." Now, in the last eighteen months, he seemingly has come into his own, winning four major antigovernment cases for radical defendants. (The four cases Justice is studying.)

However, a careful review of these cases shows that Albend today remains what he always was—a slipshod, careless, ill-equipped lawyer whose only strong point is his lucky ability to be in the right place at the right time.

Looking for the cause of why Justice loses these radical trials, Albend's performance—on a scale of zero to ten—is a zero.

He has performed stupidly and sloppily.

The question is raised then: if Albend has not won these cases by his skill, how have they been won? The answer to that question is beyond the scope of this report.

Darling slammed a fist angrily down on the blue-sheeted report. He picked up the phone and jerked the dial.

"Yes?"

"McGirr, get me Willoughby."

Within sixty seconds, his phone buzzed.

"Willoughby is on two," and Darling hit the flashing button second from the left.

"Willoughby?"

"Yes, sir."

"I've just read your report on Albend." He paused and the young attorney on the other end of the line said nothing. "Why didn't you draw the conclusion that was necessary?"

"I'm sorry, sir, but my assignment was to give a critique of Albend as a lawyer. Nothing else. I thought it would have been presumptuous—"

"It was presumptuous of you to have an opinion about this study of ours and not to share it with me," said Darling. "Damnit, this isn't a contest. It's a puzzle and we're all trying to solve it together."

"I'm sorry, sir. I thought I was doing the right thing."

Darling remembered that Willoughby was young and black and apparently awed at being in Justice. He brought his voice down into a lower register.

"All right," he said. "No real harm done. And forget my screaming. I apologize. It's just been that kind of a morning. Anyway, you say, let's see, that Albend performs stupidly and sloppily. You dodged the question but it's obvious you've got an opinion: if he hasn't won these cases, how have they been won?"

Willoughby cleared his throat. "Albend," he said, "*was* sloppy and stupid. The government was sloppier and more stupid. The cases weren't won by Albend or anyone else. They were lost. By us. In my supporting documents, there's an analysis of each one of these four cases. I took Gilpert's summary and I pulled from it the step-by-step of all actions that I thought were significant in the not-guilty verdict. I think, sir, you'll see the point if you read it. Maybe I should have spelled it out more clearly."

He stopped and waited.

"Okay, Willoughby. Thanks. By the way, good work."

"Thank you, Mr. Darling."

Darling leaned back in his chair, propped his feet on his desk, and began to read Willoughby's report again. This time he read it all the way through, even the thick appendix which contained detailed, intelligent summaries of the major points of each of the four trials they were studying. He paused in his reading to call Miss McGirr to see if the mail had arrived yet. It had not.

After reading, he tossed the report onto the desk blotter, pulled his feet from the desk, and sat up. Then he took the dark green folder from his bottom desk drawer and opened it.

The memo that was the first sheet in the folder seemed to jump at him as if it were an accusation.

The possible causes of the government's losing:

Research and definition of political trials. Crossed out.

Unique aspects of political trails. Crossed out.

Performance of judges and federal attorneys. Crossed out.

Jury selection. Crossed out.

And now Albend. He took his pen and drew a line through *performance of defense attorneys.*

And all that was left on the page was Attorney General Walthrop's suggestion: *Conspiracy.*

He stared at the sheet of paper as if the word offended him and he would glare it off the page. He looked over at the television set, flickering soundless on the bookshelf. It seemed to be a presidential press conference. He debated himself for a moment on whether or not he should turn up the sound. He decided not to. He no longer cared what was going on in Washington. He was going home.

Quickly, he began to sketch out on a yellow legal

pad the outlines of his report. It would be very simple. There was no one cause why the government was losing these cases. A lot of little errors were the reason, and sharper administration by the government would eliminate those errors and start Justice winning cases again.

Miss McGirr entered silently and put a brown manila envelope on his desk. Darling looked at the return address, saw the name "Felner," and without opening it, stuck the envelope in his top desk drawer. One thing left. When Mottodocio called, Darling would tell him to go back to Queens, sip orange juice, watch his health, and grow old gracefully.

He began to sketch out recommendations for Attorney General Walthrop on how to tighten up performance by Justice in the radical trials.

The intercom buzzed.

"Yes, McGirr."

"Felner. On one."

"Good," said Darling. He hit the lit button and said, "Hello."

"Mr. Darling?" said a voice. It was not Mottodocio.

"Yes."

"Mr. Lucius Darling?"

"Yes. Who is this?"

"I believe we have a mutual friend. Mr. Felner?"

"Yes," said Darling, pressing the phone tighter to his ear to try to hear the caller, whose voice sometimes seemed lost in a maze of background noise. But the voice seemed strangely familiar.

"Would you describe Mr. Felner for me?"

"Now what the hell—"

"Please. You see, I don't know you."

"All right," Darling said. "Five feet nine. Three hundred pounds. Wheezes like a worn-out tornado."

"Yes," the caller said. "And if he asked you for a drink, what would you give him?"

"Orange juice and club soda."

"Okay. Mr. Felner asked me to give you the name of an owner of a brown Chevrolet."

Darling pursed his lips in annoyance. He didn't want to know. Screw whoever was tailing him. All he wanted to do was to go home. Enough.

"The car is owned by Dempsey. A Calvin Dempsey."

"Swell," said Darling unenthusiastically. "Where's Tony? I've got to talk to him."

"Mr. Felner is dead."

CHAPTER ***** 18

The Near Future

"THIS IS SUNDAY."

"No, it's not," Lonzo Gates replied. "It's Thursday."

"Sunday Bookperson, you asshole," his ex-wife's voice snapped over the telephone.

"Oh. Sorry. You caught me unawares."

"Caught you shit-faced on Southern Comfort is more like it. I've talked to John."

"And?"

"He couldn't find out anything. This Lucius whatever his name is . . . there's no personnel file on him at the Justice Department."

"That's impossible," Gates said.

"I can only tell you what he told me. There's no personnel file."

"He's got to be one lousy U.S. attorney if that's the best he can dig up for me," Gates said.

"He did what I asked him to do, and I won't ask him to do anymore," the woman said.

"Fine. And don't ask me to do anything for you either," Gates said.

"Which means?"

"If you want to review fag books, do it in your own column, not in mine. You don't need to give her a good review to get into some little twat's underpants. Give her a Swiss army knife. That always used to work."

"You promised, Lonzo," she said accusingly.

"I lied."

"You are a manipulative prick."

"And don't you ever forget it," he said.

He had just hung up and barely had a chance to luxuriate in his victory when the telephone rang again and he decided that if she pleaded, correctly, and got that faggot U.S. attorney back on Lucius Darling's trail for him, he would give in and give her the review space she wanted.

"This is Lonzo Gates," he said into the telephone.

But the caller was not Sunday Bookperson.

"This is Joshua," came an oil-slicked voice and Lonzo stifled a groan. It was his editor.

"Joshua," he exclaimed with a heartiness he did not feel even a part of. "How are you?"

"Well, we're sort of wondering how you're doing with your new piece. What is it . . . Jericho Day?"

"Right," Gates said. "I'm plugging away at it,

but they're trying to cover it up. They're closing doors right and left."

"Can you tell me anything about it yet?"

"No, Josh . . . Joshua. I can't. But pretty soon."

"We're saving space in the next issue," the editor said. "That means you've got a deadline next Tuesday."

"I'll try to make it," Gates said, his heart starting to pound faster in his chest. How the hell could he make a deadline only five days away? He didn't have a word yet that he could write.

The editor was slow in answering and then said, in too casual a voice, "I'd really try to make that deadline if I were you. You know, I've got investors and editorial boards to consider and, well, I don't mind telling you, Lonzo, there are some of them who think your stuff may be just a little . . . dated. A good punchy piece now might change their minds."

And what if they don't change their minds? What if I don't get this piece in on time? Does that mean that after twenty years I'm going to be tossed out on my ass into the snow like some freaking bag lady? After all I've done for you?

That was what he thought and wanted to say. Instead, he said, "I understand."

He had another couple of drinks and then jotted down some notes and picked up the telephone and dialed Western Union.

"This is a telegram to the attorney general of the

United States. Yeah, personal, by name. Yeah. Here's the text: 'Under the Freedom of Information Act, *Mossback* Magazine demands full access to the records of one Lucius Darling, assistant U.S. attorney, and to his study fifteen years ago on radical court cases. Failure to comply with this request will be viewed by the journalism community as a government coverup.' Right. Sign it Lonzo Gates."

CHAPTER ***** 19

the mid–1970s

Thursday, October 27: The Eleventh Day

MOTTODOCIO WAS DEAD AND THE CALLER would not say how or when but only that Darling should know it and that the body was at a morgue in Virginia.

"What town?"

"Bryant."

"How did he die?"

"Hey, Counselor. I ain't stupid."

And the phone was dead. Some silent quiz show with hysterically happy housewives going through their joy in pantomime played on his television. His ashtray was full of True Blue butts and it was raining outside on Constitution Avenue. Under his drumming fingertips was the outline of the report to Walthrop that would take Darling home, even more desirable now because it would be away from all this.

The report was also, in all probability, a lie, a grievous lie, and he knew it because Mottodocio was dead.

"Goddamnit," snarled Darling, who was not at
this time ready to confront any major moral crisis.
He had always thought of himself as basically an
honest person with the wisdom to avoid those sit-
uations that presented only the alternatives of dis-
honesty or disaster, and in that way he had intended
to grow old with respect, decency, and reasonable
wealth.

And now, Anthony Mottodocio, in getting himself dead, had presented Darling with the kind of
choice he had so successfully avoided all his life. If
Mottodocio had died violently, then there was evidence, more than Mottodocio's hunch, that Darling
had stumbled into something big, more than likely
connected to why the government was losing political trials. Because it was this investigation that had
triggered a whole apparatus against Darling and Mottodocio.

And if there was something bigger than government ineptitude involved in these cases, the report
on his desk, waiting to be written, was surely a lie.

If Mottodocio had died violently.

"Goddamnit," said Lucius Darling, who wanted
very much at that moment to be the sort of person
who could just send in the report. How much more
convenient life would be.

There was, of course, also the possibility that

Mottodocio, grossly overweight and suffering from diabetes, had been brought down by a heart attack or a stroke.

Hey, Counselor. I ain't stupid.

Why did that son of a bitch have to say that? Because Mottodocio had undoubtedly died violently and that person was a lot smarter than Mottodocio himself. He didn't want to stay connected a second longer or even one bit of information deeper with Darling. A wise choice.

When Darling told Miss McGirr he was leaving, she asked where he would be.

"You don't want to know."

"I'm not afraid, Luke," said Miss McGirr.

"I am."

The Bryant County Morgue was a mixture of stainless steel and white paint. In the refrigerator room, Darling met Dominic Sansalone, an obsequious, small, black-suited man with a pinstripe mustache and clutched hands ready to share your grief.

"You knew Mottodocio?" asked Darling.

"He's going to my funeral home in Queens. But he's not ready," said Dominic Sansalone.

"He's as ready as he's ever going to be," said Darling.

The bright fluorescent room smelled of chemicals. The floor was tile. The room was chilly.

Brushed steel doors, slightly larger than file drawers, precisely marked the large steel box at the left. There were six drawers.

"Uh, how did Tony die?" asked Darling, being too casual and knowing how stilted he must sound.

"Car accident," said Dominic Sansalone, approaching one of the drawers.

"Oh," said Darling, aware now of how relieved his voice sounded. An auto accident was . . . well, accidental. If Mottodocio had died in an accident, a man who had been increasingly nervous and suspicious, a man who just might have gone off the emotional deep end, then that was reasonable. That was highly reasonable. Unreasonable would be to think he was killed because he was threatening someone or something. That was unreasonable.

But then, why did the man who informed Darling of the death want to get off the phone that quickly?

Perhaps he was a friend of Mottodocio's. Maybe Mottodocio had slowly been going insane and with him having so many loyal friends with great power, that man had not been about to defame the dead.

Hey, Counselor. I ain't stupid.

Hell no, thought Darling. Not stupid at all. After a long life of cool nerves, Mottodocio had succumbed not to any conspiracy but to frayed nerves. The constant surveillance had pushed him emotionally off the edge.

"Cause of death, however, is none of my business," Dominic Sansalone was saying. "But there will be a coroner's report and you could wait for that. It's coming in tomorrow, I'm told."

"Except that I'm a funny guy," Darling said. "Sometimes I don't believe what I read. I like to see it and touch it."

Sansalone nodded as if he understood and agreed.

"There's what is and then there's what you think what is, right?" he said.

"Right," said Darling. "You're right and I want to make sure I'm right."

The big Mottodocio belly came out of the cooler like a snow-capped mountain under a white sheet.

"It'll have to be a closed coffin. It was a messy accident," said Sansalone. "Even I can't make the remains presentable."

Darling felt the moisture in his clenched hands. He had never gotten used to bodies. A man was supposed to look on a body without fear or disgust, but Darling could only pretend to do that.

With crisp, polished fingertips, Sansalone motioned for Darling to remove the sheet. Darling had hoped this would not happen. As though declining an honor, Darling said Sansalone could pull back the sheet if he wished.

The first thing Darling saw was the head. Half of it. The right half. The left was a purple swelling of brains and skull chips with the left eye turned back up, looking into the skull. Blood was smeared from the open head down the left side across the expanse of white shirt. The bronze belt buckle was flecked with three brown spots. The pants remained creased neatly; the shoes shined.

"He had a gun too. It's upstairs," said Sansalone. "It wasn't fired."

A bitter reek came from the open brains, like whiskey left overnight in a tumbler. Darling kept his chest very still lest the contents of his stomach, already perched just under his throat, came up into his mouth.

"You feel all right?" Sansalone asked.

"Yeah, yeah," said Darling.

"The car went through a guard rail and fell maybe twenty, twenty-five feet."

"Uh-huh," said Darling.

"Car wasn't too banged up...but accidents are funny, right?"

"Mmmmm."

"You sure you feel all right?"

"Sure," said Darling, finding that was too much of a word. He ran retching to a waste basket he had spotted in the corner and heaved up breakfast and other remnants of twenty-four hours of food intake. He wiped his mouth and face with his handkerchief and it got so soiled, he threw that into the waste-basket too. He apologized to Sansalone, who told him it was nothing...that it happened all the time.

"Whew," said Darling. It was over. He had shown his lack of manhood. Well, over was over. There was work.

Why, asked Darling, did the rest of Mottodocio's body seem so untouched? Sansalone shrugged. Had Sansalone ever seen dead bodies like that before? Yes, Sansalone had. In auto accidents? Well, sometimes. Accidents were funny things.

Darling lowered his face to Mottodocio's head. He sniffed. With his forefinger he gathered moisture from Mottodocio's half-a-mouth. He sniffed his finger.

"Booze," said Darling.

"Drunken driving, say the police."

"You know Mottodocio?" Darling asked.

"Everybody in Queens knew Tony. He was a good man. He had respect. You WASPs think the only people we respect are gangsters. That makes you feel better that you think we think like that. But, Mr. WASP, we respect good men. Anthony Mottodocio was a good man."

"Yes, he was," said Darling. "I never knew him to drink."

Sansalone shrugged. "It's your government. I'm just a little funeral home owner come here to collect a friend. The cops here say drunken driving."

"You never knew him to drink, did you?" asked Darling.

Sansalone shook his head.

"You've seen other bodies like this?"

"Twice," said Sansalone.

"And they didn't come from auto accidents, did they?"

Sansalone shook his head again.

"Somebody got very close and then banged in the head with a blunt instrument. No powder burns. No broken arms or legs. Not even a messed shoe from a hammer caving in a head," Darling suggested. "A hammer, maybe?"

"Drunken driving, say the police," Sansalone repeated.

"Goddamnit," said Lucius Darling. His stomach felt weak again.

Darling parked the office car in a lot a block from the Justice Department building. As he walked back to the office, another thought came to him and he walked into the street to hail a cab.

Answer time.

Mottodocio wasn't just dead. He had been murdered. He was a diabetic and didn't drink. Liquor in his mouth was just liquor that somebody had put in his mouth.

And Dempsey. Always Dempsey. Dempsey's car had been tailing Darling. And maybe Dempsey had picked up Mottodocio's identity. Dempsey? A killer? An FBI man?

Darling needed answers about a lot of things.

About the film. About the screwups in the radical trials. About Americans in Readiness. About the tail using Dempsey's car. About Mottodocio...yes, about Mottodocio's murder. And Dempsey would answer those questions or Darling would rip his god-damn throat out.

So help me God.

Ten minutes later, Darling's cab pulled up to the old factory building at 414 Barclay Street. He left his briefcase on the back seat. "I'm going into that building over there," he said to the driver, pointing. "If I'm not out in fifteen minutes, I want you to call this name and this number and tell him I'm in trouble." He scribbled Ramsey MacDonald's name and home phone number on a paper and pushed it through the slot.

"And what's your name?"

"Darling," he replied, and at the cab driver's look, added, "Lucius Darling. Remember. Fifteen minutes."

"You better pay now," the cab driver said.

Darling yanked some bills from his pocket and pushed a ten through the slot between the seats. "Here. This'll hold you. Remember. Fifteen minutes."

He took a deep breath as he stepped slowly up the brick steps to the building. He had not noticed before how faded, lime-white the brick was. He hit the button for the doorbell, but he heard no sound from inside.

He pressed it again. There was still no sound. The silence shouted at him. He had remembered the brutalizing alarm that had sounded the first time he had come to this building.

Darling touched the doorknob and the door fell back open slowly. Cautiously, he stepped inside. The hall was empty.

"Anybody here?" he called out. His answer was an echo of his own voice. The hall was dully illuminated by sunlight coming through a small window. On the wall next to him, he found a switch and flipped it but no lights came on. He walked along the hall to the elevator. Where was that pockmarked bastard who had answered the door the last time? The temper was beginning to rise in his throat.

The elevator's doors were closed and when he pressed the "up" button, it did not light. Nor was there an answering whir of machinery.

He swore under his breath and went to the stairs and up them slowly, pausing at each landing to listen. But the building was silent, empty. And the movie room too was silent and empty. The chairs were gone. The room was dark because it had no windows, but enough light creaked in through the door for him to see that the slots in the wall through which the film had been projected were still there.

He had not been dreaming. It had happened. He had seen a film here.

He went through every office in the building as rapidly as he could, but there was nothing. No phones, no lights, nothing, not even a scrap of paper which might indicate that someone had ever been here, doing something, whatever it was, and that that something had led to the murder of a retired New York City police officer in a brutish little town in Virginia.

He glanced at his watch and realized he had already consumed ten minutes. He did not want the cab driver to go off without him, so he ran down the steps and out the door of the abandoned building, just as the cab driver started away from the curb.

"Hey!" Darling shouted.

The cabbie heard him and stopped and Darling jumped into the back seat.

"Take me to the Justice Department. And I'll take my note back."

"Everything all right, Sherlock?" said the driver.

"Don't get smart with me. I'm not up to it. Just give me the fucking note and take me to Justice."

Back at his office, Darling asked Miss McGirr to come in.

"Of all the lawyers we've got working on this, who do you think is the best?"

"Gilpert."

"The most logical thinker?"

"Gilpert."

"The one least likely to tailor his facts to fit his opinions?"

"Gilpert, Luke."

"Okay. Send Gilpert in."

Gilpert entered Darling's office warily, as if unsure of his reception. The day's *Washington Post* had carried another story about the "rising protest against the government's 'rush to justice' probe."

"Stop looking like that," Darling said. "I've got a job for you."

"Yes?"

"This is confidential," he said, and Gilpert winced. "I mean, even from our own staff. I don't want one of our guys thinking that I'm checking up on his work."

"Oh, I see."

Darling handed forward a part of the appendix of Willoughby's report on Albend.

"Take this," he said. "Now this is a step-by-step summary of major actions in each of the four cases we're looking into. It was prepared by Willoughby from your master summaries. I've drawn some conclusions from it, but I need another opinion. You're the best lawyer on this assignment and I want to know what you think."

Gilpert sat up straighter in the chair. "What do you want me to do, Luke?"

"Take the rest of the day off. Take this summary

home. Read it and read it and read it. Think. Don't talk to Willoughby. Don't ask anyone else's opinion. All the facts are there. Think. Then be here at eleven-thirty tomorrow to discuss it."

"Do you want anything in writing?"

"No," Darling said.

"What should I be looking for?"

"The reason we lost these four cases."

"But that's what this whole project is about," said Gilpert.

"That's right. And it's been done very well too. I think I've got the answer now, but I want an overview to go along with mine." He smiled inwardly at his use of the word "overview." He *had* been in Washington too long.

"What is your view?" asked Gilpert.

"I think it would be less inhibiting to you if you didn't know that," said Darling. He stood up. "Ronny, do this one carefully. It's important."

"I will," Gilpert said, rising also.

When the office was empty again, Darling took the brown envelope from his desk drawer. It was marked to Miss Mary Ellen McGirr and the return name was Felner, but there was no return address.

He ripped open the top of the envelope and pulled out a pile of about twenty pages, eight-and-a-half by eleven, white. There was no note with them.

The papers were a listing of names and addresses of people by states. It started with Alabama and listed three names, skipped Alaska, went on to two names in Arizona. The names were numbered consecutively. Darling turned to the last page. The last number was 187.

He turned to the center of the list. North Carolina. North Dakota. Next was Ohio. There was only one name listed.

"Bea Whittaker, Troy."

He looked at it for a long time, then dialed McGirr.

"McGirr, get me a reservation right away for Troy."

"Good for you," she said. "Take a break. Should I call Kathy and have her pick you up?"

Darling thought, then said quickly, "No, let's make it a surprise. That way if I get sidetracked, well, you know . . ."

The earliest plane was at 6:00 P.M. Darling was at the airport early and from a telephone booth called FBI headquarters.

No, Mr. Dempsey was not in. He was out of town on assignment. No, the nature of that assignment could not be revealed, but yes, of course a message could be gotten to Mr. Dempsey.

"All right, get a pencil." Darling waited. "This is Lucius Darling. I am an assistant attorney general of the United States. Mr. Dempsey will be in my office tomorrow morning at eleven. If he is not, criminal charges will be filed against him by me. Do you have that? I said *criminal charges*. Make it very clear that I am not talking about some interdepartmental disciplinary bullshit. I am talking about fucking criminal charges. That's right, sweetheart. The name is Darling. Lucius Darling. If you want a reference, call Mr. Walthrop. He is the attorney general of the United States. Your boss, in case no one over there at the bureau has ever told you."

He slammed the phone down, with a dull malevolent pleasure at having worked out some of his anger on someone, even an innocent.

Dempsey would be there tomorrow. He had better be.

CHAPTER ★★★★★ 20

IT WAS DARK WHEN LUCIUS DARLING GOT to Vandalia Airport outside Troy. He rented a car, drumming his fingers impatiently, wishing that the clerk would hurry up so he could be out of the airport before seeing anyone who knew him.

"Can we step it up a little, Miss?" he asked the plasticized brunette at the typewriter.

"Coming right up, Mr. Daring," she said.

Daring. After ten minutes of computers and credit card checks and a typewriter that she talked to while typing, this one still thought that he was Mr. Daring.

Why are you worried about cars and computers and dumb clerks? he asked himself. *Because I don't want to think about what's going on.*

And what is going on? he asked himself as he finally got his keys and headed quickly for the side door that led to the parking lot.

What is going on is I don't know. But a man I

*gave a job to is dead and I've been tailed and I'm
on to something big and . . .*

And what?

*And I don't think Attorney General Walthrop is
such a fool anymore.*

He drove from the airport lot and took the familiar road toward Troy. His lights carved a thin
yellow cone from the unlit highway darkness. Bony
corn stalks, left over from early fall, loomed stolidly
on both sides of the road, seeming to watch him, he
thought, like row after row of starved soldiers.

Easy, Luke, you're getting spooked. Corn is corn.

But he checked the rearview mirror anyway. The
road behind him was dead black and empty.

Darling stopped at a phone booth outside a
closed-for-the-night gas station. It was nice to be
back in America. There was a telephone directory
hanging under the telephone shelf and the pages had
not been ripped out or pissed or puked upon. There
still was an America where people believed that telephones were for making telephone calls, not for protesting against a corrupt capitalist racist fascist
society.

He looked up the number and dialed. The phone
rang twice, three times, four times, and he was growing impatient when it stopped ringing and a woman's
voice answered. He knew the voice well; it was gruff
and it told about too many balls and beers, too many
rolls in the hay, too many cigarettes after. It told all

that just by saying, "Hello. Who is it?"

"Bea. How are you?"

"I'm fine," said Bea Whittaker. "The rent's just been raised, a decent girl can't make a living in this town, the price of Ramses jelly is going out of sight, the pill gives me kidney problems, and you ask how I am. Who are you anyway?"

"This is Luke."

"Luke, huh? What's the matter, Luke? Kathy got the curse? Tell her to blow you."

"Bea, it's important. I've got to talk to you."

"Important, huh? It must be important for a big national figure like you to want to talk to me. I've been reading about you, Luke. You're on page one. And here I've been waiting to find you on the comic pages."

Although early in the evening, she was already half drunk, Darling realized.

"Please, Bea," he said.

"You know where I live," she said and hung up.

He skirted the center of Troy, stopped at a tavern and bought a fifth—"no, bartender, make it a full quart"—of Cutty Sark, and hated himself while it was being put into a brown paper bag.

Bea Whittaker lived on the far side of town, in a two-room apartment behind a grocery store which took most of the first floor of an old two-story frame building. The owners of the store lived upstairs. Bea had her own entrance, down along the side of the building and up three wooden steps. Darling found the pathway and knocked softly.

"It's open," came her husky voice.

Darling pushed open the door and stepped into a kitchen, originally white but now dirtyish gray and made grayer by the puffs of dust that stuck to the globules of grease high overhead, the kind of dust and grease that would probably defeat all but the most meticulous sort of housekeeper.

Just inside the door to the right, half the wall was taken over by bookshelves filled with mostly paperbacks. Darling could not see any of the titles, but red, white, and blue appeared to be the predominant colors on the covers.

From under the bookshelves, four thin streaks went across the kitchen floor to the far left wall where Bea Whittaker stood, pushing a couch into position. She patted down the couch cover and did not turn around.

"I knew it was you, Luke. By the walk. You have a kind of Nazi thump to your walk. Do you know that somebody's face is only ten percent of how people recognize him?"

"Funny time to be moving furniture. How are you doing, Bea?"

"Everybody I can," she said. "I'm just moving this 'cause I'm expecting the editor of *House Beautiful* any minute. So I don't have much time to spend with you. What do you want?"

"Are you inviting me in?" he inquired softly. Bea gave a finishing pat to the faded brown and green flowered spread on the couch, stood up, and turned to Luke.

She wore a thin pink sweater that was stretched tightly over her large bosom, with a short black skirt that reached down only to mid-thigh and high spiked heels that accentuated the lines of her long, pretty legs. Her bleached blonde hair had been cut short and pushed back casually, but it was tightly curled and hung ringletted around her face.

They were the same age and he knew life had not dealt her a lot of winners, but she was still good-looking, exciting-looking, in a gaudy kind of way, the way she had been when he had knocked her up, God, how many years ago?

"The big lawyer comes bearing gifts. Just close the door."

Darling pushed the door shut and walked to the sink. He took the bottle of Cutty Sark from the bag which he crumpled and dropped into a straw basket, without a liner, which held the supper garbage, then asked where she kept the glasses.

She pushed by him and said, "Go sit down. I'll do that."

He avoided the couch and sat at the kitchen table near the door. He looked over the table, through the window, out into the backyard, just barely brightened by the illumination from a street lamp a block away.

She brought two glasses over to the table.

"Sorry, I'm out of soda," she said. "I used water." She stirred both glasses with her right index finger and put one of them in front of Luke. She sat at the center of the table, at his left hand.

"Luke," she said, "no bullshit. You really look good."

"Thanks, Bea. I'm looking forward to getting home."

"I did read about you in the papers, you know. Are you really trying to figure out how those Communists keep getting off?"

He nodded and sipped the drink. It was too strong for his taste; the liquid in Bea's glass was even darker and she drank half of it at one gulp.

"Good," she said. "Get the bastards."

He felt her knee brush against his under the table and fought his instinctive impulse to recoil, left his leg there for a moment, then moved it out of the way by extending the leg straight out in front of him.

"Bea," he said, "what is Americans in Readiness?"

"Who wants to know?" she said, looking over the rim of her scotch glass, poised at her lips.

He smiled. "Lucius A. Darling, assistant attorney general of the United States of America." Her eyes did not soften and he put his left hand over her right hand. "A friend," he added and smiled again.

She left her hand under his on the table. "How long's it been, Luke, since we were friends? Fifteen, eighteen years ago?"

"Twenty," he said.

She changed positions by putting her hand on top of his.

"That's right. You were the conquering hero. Goddamnit, Luke, you looked good in that football uniform. Good enough to eat." She giggled. "I think I told you that then too," she said. "You wouldn't let me, though."

She drank some more, gazing at the window, out toward the darkened yard, as if in a private dream that he could not enter.

"Bea. Americans in Readiness?"

If she heard him, she did not show it. Instead, she said softly, "You know, Luke, it was your baby." Her eyes searched his face. "Yours," she said. "Ours."

He did not know what expression to try for. He attempted to look moderately concerned, reasonably sympathetic.

"Our baby," she said, sipping more of her drink. "And I killed it for us. I killed our baby, Luke." She looked back toward the window and tears sparkled in the corners of her eyes. "I killed that poor fucking baby, Luke."

"Bea. You had an abortion. It wasn't a killing. Don't blame yourself."

"Fuck you, Mr. Lawyer. It was a killing. It was our baby, Luke, and I stopped it from living and that's a killing."

It was his turn to look toward the window.

"You were never sure, were you, Luke? You didn't know, did you? But I knew, Luke." She finished her drink and yanked her hand away from his and stood up and walked back to the sink. This time she filled her glass full of straight scotch.

"You know how I knew, Luke?" she asked. "I knew because I was faithful to you, Luke. You were just so fucking beautiful and you fucked me and made me pregnant and it was beautiful and I knew it was always going to be beautiful and Luke, from that day on, all summer long, I didn't sleep with nobody else. We were going to make it." She walked back to the table and sat down again, this time erectly, staring out into her yard.

"And then it got close and you panicked and went off to sea...Luke, you prick, you just sneaked out of town without saying goodbye, and there I was with this big belly growing and the father ran away."

"I went away, Bea. You knew I was going."

"Did you have to sneak away without even saying goodbye? I hated you then, Luke, and that's when I got Doc Vandener to knock it out. You know what he wanted to get rid of the baby, Luke? You know what his price was?"

He looked at her face; tears coursed down her cheeks.

"You don't want to know, Luke, about that awful old man. You don't want to know."

Luke squinted his eyes at the thought.

"Hurts you, Luke? It didn't hurt me. It made me strong. You were off at sea. And then you went to college. But I was getting a real education." She looked back toward the window, her gaze drifting into infinite focus as if there were something out there that she should see, and she raised her glass to her lips again and drank deeply and Luke covered her hand again with his and said, "Bea, I'm sorry."

She slammed the glass down on the table. "I don't want to hear about it," she snapped. "You want to know about Americans in Readiness? What's it worth to you?"

"Bea, I—"

"Make love to me, Luke. I want you in me."

"Bea, I can't," said Darling, knowing it was a lie, knowing now that he had expected it, maybe even looked forward to it.

"Yes, you can. You'd be surprised. I'm good at it, Luke."

Bea slid her chair back from the table and moved forward onto her knees. She reached her hand out and fumbled with the zipper on his trousers. As she brought her face toward him, he wanted to push her away but he didn't; he let her, and after a while she said with a smile, "Come on, Doc. On the couch."

He stood, feeling foolish, erect through his open fly, and he looked toward the door, toward the light switch, but Bea said, "With the lights on."

She pulled her sweater over her head in a fluid, practiced movement, revealing that she wore no bra. Her breasts still had the firmness of youth. She stepped out of her short skirt and now was wearing nylons and high-heeled shoes and nothing else. As she lay back on the sofa, she said, "Come on, Luke. I'm clean. You don't have to worry." He moved to her and she made his softness hard again and then guided it into her and finally, just before his moment, she reached up over her head and flicked another light switch, plunging the room into darkness.

"Go ahead, Luke. Live your fantasy. Imagine somebody else."

And he did. He imagined the someone else was Bea Whittaker twenty years ago when she was the most beautiful girl in town and everybody lusted after her, but he had her, and the world was all clean and different then. And then with a rush and an explosion he was gone deep into her. Through it all, he did not say a word.

He rested on her, breathing heavily, and her voice brittled through the dark. "Not bad, Luke. Best so far this week."

He put his face close to her ear. "Americans in Readiness."

"Fuck you, Luke."

"Please, Bea."

"Fuck you, Luke."

"You're supposed to be able to reach people in an emergency. Why? Who are you assigned to?"

"Fuck you, Luke."

"When did you join? Who signed you up?"

"Fuck you, Luke."

"Do you know Bryant Marine Base?"

"Fuck you, Luke."

"Jericho Day?"

"Fuck you, Luke."

He pulled away from her and stood towering over her in the door. He zipped up his fly and she laughed. "You can go, Luke. They always go, right after."

"Goodbye, Bea," he said.

At the door, her voice stopped him. "Luke?"

He turned. "Yes?"

"I always knew I'd get a chance to screw you good and proper." Her voice trailed off into a low, rumbling laugh and when Darling closed the door behind him, he could still hear it in the yard. As he walked past the kitchen window he could still see her form on the couch in the dark, and from the blob that was her form, the high-pitched laugh still came.

CHAPTER ★★★★★ 21

DARLING DID NOT CALL KATHY. HIS PLANE touched down in Washington shortly after 1:00 A.M. The anger he had carefully restrained in Ohio had come back, but now it was different, mixed with guilt, as he thought of Mottodocio's murder and how Lucius Darling, the wonderful Lucius Darling, had avenged the killing by flying to Troy, Ohio, and getting laid.

So when he got to the airport, his mind was made up. He rented another car and drove past Washington on Route 211 and through the night out into the Virginia countryside.

Mottodocio had accused him of seeing only pieces. But that's all there was to this. Just pieces.

There was Americans in Readiness. And Bea Whittaker. Scratch that. Bea Whittaker was a foul-mouthed whore and Americans in Readiness could not be doing anything important if she had a piece of it. Mottodocio's death? Not them, not her. Sentimental old whores weren't killers.

The tail on him? Dempsey again. Somehow, Dempsey was the key to this. The FBI agent had blown the Wounded Elk trial by his stupidity. And when Luke started looking into things, Dempsey had panicked and had him tailed. First by the Americans in Readiness types probably, and when they had screwed up, probably by FBI men. Maybe by Dempsey himself.

But so what?

What did that have to do with Mottodocio's murder? What about Bryant Marine Base? Was Dempsey somehow connected with that base? Was something going on there, something that Mottodocio found out and wound up getting killed over? Was it possible he had stumbled onto a secret government operation?

And the film. What did that have to do with the FBI? Whose film was it? He heard that familiar echoing, metallic voice of the narrator in his ear again intoning "Why?"

Yes, indeed. Why?

Why did all this have anything to do with him and his simple little report on political trials?

Why?

Jericho Day.

Why? Why? Why?

"Sorry, Tony," he said aloud in the speeding car.

"I can only see pieces because there is nothing else but pieces."

Bryant Marine Base was ninety-seven minutes out into the Virginia countryside, outside a small town which had boomed when the base was there and whose thriving residents had amused themselves by constantly complaining about Marine influence in their town and the tough hillbilly leathernecks and what a terrible influence they were for children and how they were desecrating their nice, historic town. They complained so loud and so long that they finally convinced the local congressmen to press for the elimination of the base. It finally happened in the mid-1960s and when the base went, so did the growth and the town.

The town of Bryant was now a string of mostly closed stores, boarded-over restaurants, and hotels converted to rooming houses. A narrow two-lane road led out of the town and, two miles out, Darling found the old base.

The grass was grown high now outside the cyclone fence that set the boundary of the camp. He followed the road past the fence and rode along, parallel to the fence, for about 300 yards, when the fence made a sharp right turn back away from the road and headed back toward some trees far off in the distance. A quarter-of-a-mile down the road, Darling found a wide spot, made a three-swipe U-turn, and headed back slowly. He had not seen any gate in the long strip of steel fencing.

Deep in the back of the base, he could see the outlines of buildings, black against the black trees against the black sky.

Almost at the end of the fence, he saw the gate he had missed before. Once a paved road had led to the break in the fence, but the pavement had broken up. From gravel it had come and to gravel returned. Darling shut off his lights and made the left turn up to the gate.

He got out of the car to look around. The gate itself was made of the same material as the fence: twelve-foot-high steel with a two-foot-high strip of barbed wire jutting outward from the top to discourage visitors.

He grabbed one of the chains and wrenched but there was no give. As he touched the fence with his fingers, he noticed that the galvanized iron still had a smooth chrome slickness, the feel of a fence before it becomes coated with the dulling gray powder of age. Darling walked along the fence for fifty yards in both directions. The fencing was all the same.

A military base, closed down for ten years, and it had a new fence around it.

He pressed his face close to the gate and peered inside. The buildings, 150 yards back from him, seemed to take shape as if to reward the intensity of his stare. To the right were the low-level barracks buildings that served on military posts as housing and office space, hospitals, and post exchanges. Slightly to the left was a higher building that he recognized from its round quonset-style roof profile as an old military field house—a combination gymnasium and indoor drill field.

There were no lights anywhere.

Darling got back into his car and backed slowly out to the road. Leaving his lights off, he began even more slowly to drive away from the base. About fifty yards away was a wide shoulder of road, and Darling pulled off there. He searched the glove compartment but found no flashlight. He got out and locked the doors. The night was crisp, but not cold, and he left his topcoat on the front seat of the auto. He rummaged through the unlit trunk for a flashlight but— damn American rental cars—there was none. All he could find was a magnesium warning flare which he slipped into his side pocket.

He left the keys to the car on top of the vehicle's roof so he would not lose them if he had to try to climb a fence. Then he ran across the black roadway. There were no headlights in either direction and in the clear Virginia night, he could have seen them for miles on this flat patch of land.

Moving up to the corner of the fence where two sections met at a right angle, he squatted close to the ground, screwing his eyes tightly shut, trying to milk out of them one more trace of night vision.

Then, still crouching, he moved along the fence toward the gate.

Thirty yards from the corner, he found a hole in the fence and felt it with his hands. The edges of the twisted steel were sharp, as if they had been cut. Was this how Mottodocio had entered the base? He knelt and slipped through the break in the fence with room to spare. It might have been Mottodocio's entry point because it would admit a man much bigger than Darling. The high grass on both sides of the fence would cover the hole over and make it almost impossible to find, unless somebody went over every foot of fencing carefully.

Inside, Darling tried to rip out the high grass, to create a flat spot so he would be able easily to find his way back out. The grass was tough and wiry on his hands. Uprooting it was hard because its roots would not let go, and breaking it was harder because the grass was flexible. Finally he settled for stomping it down, cracking it underfoot. He felt his hands covered with tiny paper cuts from the grass and thought to himself, *Luke, you've been away from the farm too long.*

Trying to make no noise, Darling came up on the windowless side of the sentry box inside the main gate and crouched there, listening, until he was sure beyond certainty that there was no one inside the small booth.

The door to the shack opened easily, without a

squeak, and Darling peered inside. Moonlight bathed the booth with a pale light but Darling could find nothing—no telephone, no book of weekend passes, no clipboard stacked up with general orders.

He turned away, then stopped again, squatted, and inspected the floor of the booth. It was littered with cigarette butts. When he twisted the tobacco end of one between his left thumb and index finger, the paper crackled but the tobacco rolled smoothly out of the open end. The tobacco was fresh; the cigarette butts were recent.

He headed off down the busted-up macadam road toward the buildings in the back of the camp. He held the flare in his right hand, and with his left patted his shirt pocket to make sure his cigarette lighter was still there. He heard the sound of his own crunching footsteps and moved off into the grass bordering the roadway. The grass here was shorter than it had been near the fence and it muffled his steps without rustling. The moon beamed brightly on him and he could see his own shadow moving ahead of him on the ground. He turned the flare over in his right hand so that the spike end, designed for sticking into the ground, was out in front of him, like a spear, and he felt better.

The roadway passed between buildings and on the right, he could now see four barracks buildings. To the left was the field house. The other buildings that once must have been on the base were gone,

probably sold off to junk dealers or building con-
tractors.

Stop.

Did he hear a sound?

Darling crouched against the wall of the nearest
barracks building and listened. He heard the night
wind blow brushingly through the trees. Crickets
chirped and far off he heard something that sounded
like a frog, yelling "ribbit, ribbit." Perhaps there was
water here. A pond or creek.

He heard no other sounds.

He was afraid the darkness was getting to him.
He stood up and walked around the front of the barracks building. The door was open and the steps leading to it were old broken chunks of cinder block.
Just a look inside told him that the building had been
stripped of all its furniture and fixtures and had not
been used since the base had closed down.

The second barracks building was the same.
Empty.

And the third.

And then, as he came out of the door of the fourth
and last barracks, he heard the sound again.

This time it was unmistakable. No frog, no
cricket, no breeze. It was a sharp crack, like a shot.
Darling slipped back into the doorway and froze in
position. Another sound came, this time a voice. He
could not hear it well but it seemed loud and complaining.

The sound had seemed to come from the only other building left on the base, the giant field house that sat fifty yards away on the other side of the roadway.

He knew he was safe here in the shadows and he feared running in the bright moonlight across the road to the field house. Suppose there were more people on the base. What then?

The moon slid behind a cloud and the field house's wooden walls went from luminously silver to black. Darling took a deep breath and, still holding the unlit flare like a track team's baton, raced through the darkness and the grass, across the roadway.

The moon reappeared. Ahead of him Darling saw the field house begin to grow silver again, but he was almost there. One last spurt covered ten more yards and he dropped into a crouch against the back wall, not minding if he breathed hard, but trying not to breathe noisily.

Darling waited to let his breath return. He was at one of the corners of the building. There would be large doors in the middle on each side, and there would be doors on each end. Unless the Marines had lost their senses totally and stopped building field houses the way it had always been done. The building itself was one-half the size of a football field.

He looked around at the building but still saw no light. Then he heard the voice again. Keeping low, he moved along the ground, near the wall, across the back of the building. He stopped under a window and listened.

Crack!

Another shot. Carefully, he raised his head to a corner of the window and peered inside. He was look-ing into a gymnasium. The top was surrounded by a shallow balcony and the moon poured into win-dows behind that balcony and splashed giant blotches of shadows on what was once a varnished gym floor. But he saw no one. He moved his face closer to the window and peered to the right, down the length of the building. The moonlight seemed to vanish halfway down the length of the building and the far half of the gymnasium seemed pitch black.

This should not be, he realized. If windows let in moonlight down at this end, they should do the same at the other end. Puzzled, Darling straightened up and continued to move along the back of the building.

Another shot.

The voice again.

Ahead of him there was another window. He crouched low and moved there, then slowly raised his head to peer inside. But everything was black; he could see nothing.

Still he heard the voice clearly. It *was* coming from inside and it was yelling.

"The Big Inch," it yelled. "The Big Inch."

But why couldn't he see? What had happened to the moonlight?

He moved to the next window. Halfway up the window, he could see a little glimmer of light and he put his face as close to it as he could and realized that the inside of the windows had been covered with some sort of heavy black sheeting.

But this piece had torn slightly, probably when it was being nailed up, and through the hole alongside the nail, he could see a brightly lit gymnasium floor.

He tried by moving his head to see more but could not. He squatted and thought.

The inside of the field house had been divided in half. Only the back half was being used and someone was in there with lights on.

Over his head, he heard the voice yell again.

"Goddamn it, move up close!"

Was this it? Was this what Mottodocio had found? If so, what was it?

"Sorry, Tony," he mumbled to himself. "Still just pieces."

Darling rose to his feet and walked quietly back to the far end of the building, in the direction from which he had just come. There he paused and peered around the corner to make sure no one was there, before moving out into the bright moonlight. A third of the way along the wall he found a door and Darling stood against it before realizing that he would be

silhouetted against the moonlight like a shadow figure. He slumped back toward the ground. Slowly
now he raised his head. There was no one in sight
and nothing but blackness at the far end of the gym.

He turned the doorknob but it was locked.

Pressing his weight against it, the door gave way
easily before him, swinging open with a creak that
he found earpiercing. He skidded inside, pushed the
door shut behind him, and dove for a corner.

At the other end of the building there was silence.

Then a voice yelled, "You hear anything?"

"No."

"I heard something."

"Yeah, sure. The boogie man coming to get you."

"Yeah? That was no boogie man last night."

Darling squatted in the corner. His hands rested
in rubble and paper and when he saw a large barrel
off to the side, he slipped away to hide behind it.
Almost immediately, his side of the field house was
bathed in brightness as a rip of light cut into it from
the other half of the building.

A man stood there, his hands having apparently
separated two heavy floor-length drapes. He was silhouetted against an upside-down V of bright light,
looking into the dark half of the gym. Glancing
around the side of the barrel, Darling could see what
looked like storefronts behind the man, but the angle
was too sharp to make out more than that.

Storefronts? Stores inside a gymnasium?

The curtains were let go and settled back together and darkness swallowed again his half of the gym, like a camera shutter slowly being turned down to closed.

Darling was on his feet immediately, hunched over, moving slowly toward the curtain, the flare still in his right hand. He was careful where he put his feet, careful not to step on a bottle or can that would signal his presence.

He saw the curtain a few feet ahead of him now, a polished black plastic surface glistening slightly in the moonlight from the gym windows. He reached a hand out tentatively to the curtain, felt its almost wet slickness, and ran his fingers along it to the wall. The curtain was hammered into place behind a two-by-four which had been slammed into the gymnasium's old plywood wall.

He heard a voice.

"The Big Inch, I tell you," someone shouted. "You're the last trainee. Don't be our first failure."

With his left hand, Darling grabbed a tiny pinch of plastic between his left thumb and index finger. He pressed the point of the flare against his waist and slid his hand down it until he was holding it by the nail end, like a pencil.

Carefully, he raised the point to the plastic in his left hand. His heart pounded in his chest, sounding to him like a bass drum, bellowing, "See me. See me. See me." He tried to pull a deep breath down into the pit of his stomach and the drumming eased.

Softly, he pricked a hole in the pinch of plastic with the tip of the flare. He twisted the metal tip around to widen the hole. Then he removed the flare and slowly released the piece of plastic between his fingers and it slid back to its original position.

He heard people moving around. A tiny spaghetti strand of light beamed from the other side of the drape toward his face. He moved forward, pressing his right eye toward the hole, leaning awkwardly, trying not to brush the curtain with his body and set it moving.

Spread out before him, like looking through the bubble viewfinder of a cheap camera, was a confusing stew of objects and scenes.

To the left was a movie screen and ten feet in front of it, facing the screen, were three empty chairs. Even farther left was an old wooden desk, apparently original Marine-issue and too worthless and heavy for even scavengers to want to steal. But the rest of the gym had been set up to look like a street. There were plywood and paper storefronts with clear plastic sheets for windows. The shops had stoops and doorways and fuzzily, through the plastic windows, he could see behind the storefronts the mockups of checkout counters, cash registers, merchandise displays. He could see mannequins arranged to look like people strolling down a lit street. A woman dummy with blonde hair looked into an appliance store window. The store had Russian lettering. And something was strange about it. Of course. Russia didn't have appliance stores. The Soviet Union hardly had appliances, and those they had were sold in small sections of Russian department stores.

This was an American street.

"Now remember. The Big Inch." The words came from a megaphone. Upwards. To the left. On a mock rooftop. A man with a megaphone sat there. His legs dangled. Up the street a man in a leather jacket walked quickly toward the appliance store. As he neared the blonde dummy, another man came out of the store. He was short and slim with flaming red hair and freckles that looked like rusty fingerprints.

The man in the leather jacket touched the dummy on her right shoulder with two fingers of his right hand.

Darling hardly saw the young redheaded man change the slow, steady pace of his stride. But then there was the sound of a shot. The dummy thumped forward against the storefront. The redheaded man walked off down the street, quickly, but with no show of hurrying. The man in the leather jacket walked off in the opposite direction. The blonde dummy dropped to the ground.

"That's better, O'Gara," bellowed the man with the megaphone. The redhead stopped, almost under the feet of the man with the megaphone.

"What if you can't tell which person the spotter touches?" he asked, looking up over his head.

The man on the rooftop put down the megaphone.

"Then you don't make terminal contact."

"You let the target get away?"

"That's what you do."

The redhead shrugged, the shrug of the unconvinced. Or the unhappy.

"But you got to remember to move in close, Lieutenant," the man on the rooftop said. "You've been in Nam. You know what I'm talking about. Close up. The Big Inch."

Darling saw the redheaded Lieutenant O'Gara nod. "I'm a pro," he said.

"You're a Catholic too, right?"

"So what?" said O'Gara.

"Still say your Hail Marys?"

"God, country, family, self," said O'Gara.

"All right. This is the windup to training, O'Gara. We have a prisoner who was to be executed by firing squad. Since dead is dead, I asked if we could use that prisoner as your final test. That is, if you think you're up to it."

Darling saw O'Gara's shoulders lift slightly, but the man's voice was smooth. "The Big Inch, sir," he said. "Bring on your prisoner."

"All right. Use a .45. You have one, don't you?"

O'Gara reached into his checkered flannel shirt and yanked out a squarish-looking black pistol and waved it over his head.

The man with the megaphone nodded and O'Gara returned the gun to his shirt.

"All right. Olsen will be your spotter on this one, O'Gara," said the megaphone man. "You won't see the subject until the subject passes you and then you'll have just a fraction of a second. Sit over there. With your back to the store." He waved toward a seat in the center of the gym floor and O'Gara sat in it with his back to the man with the megaphone.

"Now we'll see how good you are with live ammo and live brains coming out of a live skull. Ready, O'Gara?"

The redheaded man waved.

"Said your Hail Mary, O'Gara?" cracked Olsen, the man in the leather jacket. He came out of the appliance store. At his side was a black-robed figure. It wore a sailboat of a white linen hat and beads dangled from the waist. Darling smothered a gasp. Olsen had a nun in tow. She moved alongside Olsen as easily as if she were on wheels. Her white bonnet hid her face, even though her head was erect. Darling felt she carried herself with an almost unreal dignity. She made no sound, moving with Olsen toward the chair on which O'Gara sat, his back to them.

As he steered the nun past O'Gara's chair, Olsen

reached his left arm around and put two fingers on the nun's shoulder.

"Now!" he shouted.

O'Gara rose from the seat like a sudden boil. Darling did not know whether he heard the shot first or saw the flying white chips or saw O'Gara recoil. But even as the young man moved, Darling saw him pull a handful of black cloth down to him with his left hand and with his right put the gun to the side of the white sailboat of a linen hat and fire three times.

Sawdust shot out of the nun's head and wheels spun where her feet should have been. O'Gara continued away from the chair. He had the gun in the shirt and walked away, as though slightly late for a modestly important lunch engagement. The white linen hat burned at the edges and with a sudden whoof became a small orange pyre, ignited by the muzzle blast.

"God bless you, O'Gara, that was perfect," boomed the man with the megaphone.

O'Gara turned back and as he did, Darling saw the man was grinning.

"Perfect," said the man with the megaphone. "The smart move. You helped bring the head to you and your gun. That's what we mean by cool. Use your brains. You don't always have to run up and put the gun where it belongs. You can bring where it belongs to you. And when you do that, even a blunt instrument works. Inside the Big Inch, every-thing works."

Everything, Darling thought. Even a blunt in-strument to scramble the brains of an overweight, retired New York City cop.

"I thought she was a sister. I thought she was a fucking nun. I did. For real. I thought she was a fucking sister," said O'Gara. "Jesus."

"You're my kind of man, O'Gara. A real man."

O'Gara kicked a bit of dust and lowered his head to help conceal his big, booming grin.

"Shit. It wasn't nothing. But I thought it was a fucking sister."

"You're as ready as we can make you, Lieutenant O'Gara," said the man with the megaphone. "Now let's get the hell out of here."

Darling saw him drop to the floor, from the roof of the store. He came out of a storefront carrying a sheepskin jacket over one arm. He walked up and shook O'Gara's hand, then with O'Gara and Olsen, walked to a door in the far corner of the gymnasium and went outside.

The door closed behind them. The silence of the gym seemed louder to Darling than the pistol shots had been. He heard noises. People walking. Voices. He stayed frozen in position. Then he heard a car's motor starting.

They were leaving.

Darling moved along the black drape, across the

gym floor, toward the other side of the building. At the far wall, he felt the plastic curtain, again attached to the wall by strips of two-by-fours. He punched another hole in the plastic and peered around again, but there was no sign of anybody in the lit section of the building. Outside he heard a car start to drive away, its wheels scraping on the broken gravel of the roadway.

He used the flare's point as a blade and ripped a hole in the black plastic, then tore it with his hands. It gave way stretchingly, grudgingly, but soon he had a rip big enough to step through. He paused. Somehow now he felt the danger intensified and his courage seemed to shrivel up into a hard nut and lay leaden in the pit of his stomach.

He ran to the desk in the front left corner of the gym. Perhaps there would be something in the desk. All the drawers were empty until he opened the one on the bottom left.

A blue looseleaf notebook.

He grabbed it. The cover had a hand-printed label:

JERICHO DAY
TRAINING PROGRAM

He reached to open the book but stopped when he heard a sound. Voices. The door from outside opened.

Darling dropped to the floor behind the desk. He moved forward into the knee hole, still clutching the notebook in his left hand.

The modesty panel on the front of the old wooden desk had warped out of its frame by age and there was a thin, pieshaped slice of space through which he could see into the rest of the room.

Outside, through the open door, he heard the car's motor idling.

Olsen and the man with the megaphone came through the corner door and into view. They each carried two five-gallon gasoline cans.

Swiftly and silently, they began to douse the interior of the building with gasoline, Olsen working his way over the old storefronts in Darling's direction. He finished saturating the storefront facades, then splashed gasoline around the rest of the floor and up onto the walls.

His feet were only five feet from Darling when he sloshed gasoline out of the can toward the desk. Drops spilled through the wedge-shaped opening and hit Darling's face. He felt the chill of the gas's instant evaporation. Olsen had seen nothing, however, and kept spilling gasoline onto the chairs. He moved now, alongside the desk, out of Darling's view. Darling was afraid to move and he stayed frozen in position, holding his breath.

Olsen's voice boomed as if he were shouting into Darling's ear.

"I guess that's it, Harry."

"Yeah. Let's go."

Darling pressed his eye to the crack again. The one called Harry was walking toward the door and Olsen was following behind him, each swinging their empty fuel cans.

They were at the door.

"Harry, you got the book?"

"No. I thought you had it."

"Shit. Wait a minute. I'll get it."

The book. The book. The book he was holding. Darling fought back panic. He saw Olsen approach. Darling pressed tightly into the corner of the desk's knee hole. He reached his left hand out and opened the bottom desk drawer as far as he could without it falling onto the floor. Quickly he took the looseleaf notebook in his left hand and put it into the desk drawer. He left the drawer open, then turned his body slightly so his right hand was in front of him. If Olsen saw him, the point on the end of the flare might serve as some kind of weapon.

He heard Olsen's footsteps thumping near. Olsen stopped. Darling heard a hand move the drawer. He held his breath. He could not see the man.

Then he heard his voice.

"Got it, Harry. Let's go," Olsen called.

More footsteps, this time walking away from Darling. He let out his breath in a hiss that was not as silent as he wanted.

He breathed again deeply, trying to untangle the knot in his stomach. He heard a sound. Paper crackling. No. It was fire. Fire.

He pressed his eye to the slot in the wood. Olsen, holding the notebook under his arm, had just tossed a wooden match into a pile of rubble at Darling's right, near the curtain through which Darling had entered. He saw Olsen look up at the curtain, but obviously the rip did not register on his consciousness because he looked away. The rubble broke into crackling flames. Olsen stepped back, moving away. He lit another match and tossed it toward one of the folding wooden chairs. The dried-out wood burst into immediate flames. Darling looked to the other side of the gym. Harry had just ignited the far wall.

Then Olsen called, "Let's move it," and both men ran toward the doors. As Harry went out, Darling saw his hand go toward the wall and then the overhead lights went out.

But the gymnasium was no longer dark because white light was replaced by red light, from flames burning their way through the dry wood of the old structure.

Flames danced in the gym.

Darling stood up. A fire was already raging to the right, behind him, where he had come through the curtain. Ahead of him, the storefront remnants were crackling in fire. Across the gym, the pistol range area leapt with flames. The only way out was through the central part of the heavy plastic curtain that cut the gym in half.

He froze against the wall for a moment. The men might be inspecting their work through the windows of the door. If he ran across the gym floor, they could see him clearly outlined against the brightness of the flames. And they had guns.

He didn't move.

Then he remembered. The door was covered over with plastic too. They could not see in.

Screw it anyway. He did not care; anything was better than ending life as a cinder. He ran away from the wall, picking his way through brushes of fire, toward the center of the drape.

With no time to look for the opening, he swung his right hand over his head and, axe-like, drove the spike on the flare into the black plastic and wrenched downward. Its momentum carried it for eighteen inches through the heavy plastic before it stopped. Then Darling put both hands into the rip and tore, dropping to his knees, using his weight to pull the plastic apart. He drove through the opening, almost in a vault, and landed heavily on the floor on the other side. The smell of smoke followed him. Behind him he could hear the flames but for the moment could not see them through the curtain. Then a lick of flame hit the black plastic in the far corner. He could see the black material slowly mellow into an orange glow and then flare up. The plastic melted and showered burning wettish droplets into his side of the gym. Where the droplets hit, debris began to burn.

To the left was the back door of the field house. But the men had gone out on that side and if they had not left yet, they were probably still there.

He broke right for the main front doors of the field house. Behind him, the black drape gave way with an explosive *whoosh*. A blast of hot air exploded into the rest of the gym, and suddenly the inside of the building was high noon with flames. He slammed his body against the push bars that opened the gym's double doors and as they flew open a blast of chilly Virginia night air hit him in the face. He exhaled the smelly smoke from his lungs and took one deep breath and someone called out: "Jesus Christ. There's somebody there."

He looked to his right and saw a car turn onto the broken macadam roadway from the end of the gym. He was in its headlights.

"Stop! Or I'll shoot."

Behind him was the flame; ahead of him the bullets.

Darling jumped from the front concrete steps of the building and ran to the left, away from the vehicle. He heard it speeding up to follow him.

He darted left at the end of the building, still staying low, close to the wall. He tripped over an old cast-iron drain pipe and scrambled to his feet. No matter what he did, he still had those fifty yards of open ground to cover before he could get to the safety of the old barracks and the high grass around them.

Better now than later.

He broke into a run. He straightened up and headed across the open space for the barracks. Around his feet he saw the flicker of the headlights. The car had turned the corner behind him.

He darted left, then swung back to the right, open field running. Just like the old days. Team Captain Luke Darling leading his team to victory.

Except now it was just Luke Darling, too old for this crap, running for his life.

There was a shot. Darling spun away, hit the ground, rolled, and came up running off in the other direction. There was a pause. The marksman was leading him. Darling stopped and dove. Another shot. Another miss.

And then he was alongside the barracks building. The car was racing toward him. He ran around the back of the building and into the tall grass.

Almost on all fours, trying to keep the top of his body below the level of the uncut weeds and grass, he scrambled for the protective cover of trees. The car was only twenty yards behind him, but then the tall grass was in front of its headlights and he was no longer bathed in their brightness.

He stood up and broke to the right, toward the line of trees that bordered the road, toward the roadway that led to the front gate.

"Shit," he heard a shout from behind him. "Back up this fucking thing." The car ground noisily into reverse. "The fence. He's heading for the fence."

The car spun off down the roadway toward the gate.

"Seal it off. It's the only way out."

Darling dropped down and glanced to his right to see the car, barely fifteen yards away, racing past him, heading for the front gate.

A hundred yards ahead, the car's brake lights flashed on. The vehicle stopped, backed up, then U-turned so its lights were shining back up the camp toward the burning field house. Behind Darling, the night sky began to light as the flames broke through the filmy dry wood of the gym and jumped into the night sky.

Darling saw the car's headlights flash onto high beam.

"Harry, you take the left. O'Gara, stay near the car. I'll take the right. He's gotta come this way. Just shoot the bastard."

Darling crawled, keeping low, toward the fence, toward the hole that Mottodocio had made. He saw Olsen moving off in that direction. Did he know the fence was cut through there? If he did, Darling was trapped. There wasn't a store, not a house within miles of the camp. And this was Virginia. Nobody was likely to be driving by now. People were asleep at this time of the morning.

Suppose more men were coming here to meet the others. It might not be long before they arrived and at daybreak, Darling could be hunted down like a fox.

Screw it. He ran for the area where he knew the fence was cut. He could not see Olsen anymore.

Then he caught the flicker of the flame off the man's automatic pistol. It was nearby. Too near.

And a voice: "I see you. Stop."

Darling crouched, frozen in place.

"Move and you're dead," came the cold, efficient voice. Then louder. "Harry, I got him."

Darling heard the rustle of Olsen's feet through the tall grass toward him.

He was caught. And if he tried to run he'd be shot. And if he didn't try to run, what? A death like Mottodocio's?

"I'm coming," he heard Harry yell. The man was far away.

"Stand up, you. Hands over your head."

Olsen moved in. The Big Inch. He moved an inch too close to Darling.

Darling stood up. Behind his back, he had wrenched the top off the flare and now he put the sandpapered top on his left hand against the fuse of the flare. He stood facing Olsen across two feet of grass.

"Hands over your head, I said," Olsen repeated.

Darling raised his hands. As he did, he rubbed the raw explosive end of the flare against the sandpaper top in his left hand. He felt the heat, heard the *whoosh*, and as his hands came up he thrust his right hand forward, with the flare, into Olsen's face. He saw Olsen's eyes, frightened, glint red, then Darling rolled to the right and hit the ground.

Crack!

Olsen fired, but the shot went where Darling had been.

"Help," the man screamed. He fired again. And again. But Darling was moving back through the high grass now. The flare lay alongside Olsen's feet. An arm was thrown up across his eyes.

Harry ran forward, O'Gara following.

"What happened?" one man yelled.

"I'm blind. I'm blind."

The flare illuminated the three men, dayglow orange against the nighttime sky. Darling backed away carefully through the grass. The other two men were trying to help Olsen and they had forgotten him for a moment. He broke toward the fence and when he was fifty feet from them, stood up and ran.

He found the hole in the fence on the first try. He was through and running hard across the road.

Darling grabbed the keys from the car roof. The auto started instantly. He floored the gas pedal and drove off. In his rearview mirror, he looked to see if headlights were following. But there were none... only the bright flames of a burning old gymnasium lighting the nighttime Virginia sky.

CHAPTER ★★★★★ 22

Friday, October 28: The Twelfth Day

WHEN LUCIUS DARLING ARRIVED AT HIS office, he realized how unusual it was to enter and not find Miss McGirr already there. But there was still an hour to go before the workday actually started.

Darling had driven back to Washington during the night. He had tried to think, but he concentrated so hard on every pair of headlights from behind that he could not think of anything else.

Back at his hotel room, he had showered and changed from his filthy stained suit and, without waiting, fearing he knew not what, left his room. He went to an all-night coffee shop a block from his office and had sat there with pad and pencil and drunk coffee for three hours.

And finally, he had had a chance to think. One

thought came through, clearer than any other: he was in over his head.

He would have to go to Attorney General Walthrop. He would not endanger anyone else's life. Walthrop ran Justice; he had put Lucius Darling into this assignment. He would be the logical one to tell.

But tell what?

That there was an association called Americans in Readiness that went around following people? That Darling was being tailed by someone using an FBI agent's car? That a retired New York City police lieutenant had been murdered?

He could hear Walthrop now.

"Murdered?"

"Well, the police said drunk driving but he was a diabetic and didn't drink."

"I see." Walthrop would lean back in his chair and arch his fingers and look at Darling carefully.

What else could Darling tell him? That he had seen a propaganda movie about revolutionaries? Made with secret film? And if the government had used that film, they might have won some of the cases that they had lost?

That an old Marine base was being used to train people who talked laughingly about murder? Oh, yes. The New York policeman had been to that base.

"The murdered policeman?" Walthrop might say.

"Yes."

"I see."

"And they shot at me there too and tried to murder me and they burned the evidence."

"The evidence of what?"

"The evidence of Jericho Day."

"Oh. I see, Darling. I see. Really I do. That's all very interesting, Luke. It sure is and I'm certainly going to look into it. You can count on that. And now that your report on these trials is almost done, I think you can get ready to leave Washington, Luke. Back to sunny old Ohio and that rich private practice. Sure. In fact, why don't you just give me what you've got on the report and I'll have somebody else put the finishing touches on it. No need for you to waste your time playing literary man. Somebody else can finish it up."

And that would be that and Lucius A. Darling would be stamped for all time as a nut case.

And maybe he was. Maybe this was nothing but a string of coincidences.

No!

He slammed his coffee cup angrily on his saucer and it spun, then tipped and spilled coffee onto the formica table top.

This was no mirage, no conspiracy dreamed up in the head of some lunatic who believed in conspiracy because it was simpler than having to deal with untidy facts.

There *was* a conspiracy out there. There was Jericho Day.

A conspiracy.

But to do what?

He had ordered more coffee. And more coffee. And then went to his office and decided that he would not talk to Walthrop until after he spoke to FBI Agent Calvin Dempsey.

Dempsey was due at 11:00 A.M. And Gilpert at 11:30.

There was a terrible suspicion growing in the back of Darling's mind but he told himself not even to think of it, not until after he got Gilpert's report.

Darling turned on the television in his office, then rooted around until he found Miss McGirr's hot plate and heated water for instant coffee. He settled at his desk with his cup of coffee, and, with his desk control, turned up the TV sound so he could hear the morning news.

There was a woman announcer, the Washington channel's latest experiment in giving everyone an equal opportunity. The last time it had been blacks. Why didn't anyone realize that equal opportunity also meant equal opportunity to fail? They had managed to hire a black who couldn't read the news script. Darling had wondered what had happened to him when he eventually disappeared off-camera, then found in the postshow credits that the man had been promoted to executive producer. If he was bad enough to be a producer, this woman was bad enough to be president of the television station.

She mumbled her words and got hopelessly lost in any sentence which had a comma in it. She apologized three times for being nervous. The apologies seemed to make her more nervous. But she struggled on.

"Harold Albend, the noted criminal lawyer, said last night that it is impossible for anyone with radical views to get a fair trial in the United States.

"Speaking to an overflow crowd at Mount St. Margaret College, Albend said that 'justice is reserved in this country for the rich and powerful.'"

The camera cut to a film clip of Albend, his cravat neatly in place, his long hair thinned on top but swirling about his ears. He spoke:

"The government stacks all the cards against anyone who doesn't share the establishment's point of view. And that means the poor and the disenfranchised and anyone else who doesn't buy their code of capitalist racism."

And as Darling watched, the pampered little sons and daughters of America's capitalists jumped to their feet to give Albend a standing ovation for his denunciation of their families, their parents, and their country.

The film was cut, past the applause, and Albend was again talking: "Only when the entire system of the courts and the law in this country is overturned, only then can we guarantee fairness to all. But that will happen only when—and notice I say *when*, not *if*—only when the government itself is overthrown. It cannot happen too soon for me. And if it takes a gun to do it, then buy a gun."

"Arrest that prick," said Darling aloud in the empty office. "Inciting to riot; preaching violent overthrow of the government; insurrection; sedition. Goddamnit, arrest that prick!"

But there was no arrest. Just another screaming outburst of applause from the people that the Albends of America had made into cannon fodder with their bombast.

Then the woman announcer was back on.

"Police today patrolled the campus of St. Luke's College in Jersey City, New Jersey, where students are protesting the inclusion of religion courses in their curricula at the Jesuit-operated school and demanding an end to 'reactionary superstition.'"

"Goddamnit," Darling mumbled. "It's a private school. If you don't like it, go to fucking NYU."

The announcer again: "Violence flared yesterday when students charged police who were called to the campus by school officials. Decrying 'fascist racism,' students scuffled with cops. No shots were fired, but twenty-seven students were arrested for assault. Leaders of the Free Speech Movement on campus vowed today to close down the school until 'the racist thugs meet our demands.'"

"Rotten bananas," said Darling aloud. "Rotten bananas."

"What?"

He looked up to see McGirr inside the door.

"Nothing, McGirr. I'm just moaning to myself about the injustice of a life in which the boss has to make his own coffee."

"If the boss is going to sneak into the office at all hours of the day and night, he deserves what he gets. I'll get fresh."

She turned to leave and Darling turned down the sound on the television. Enough was enough.

When McGirr brought the coffee back, Darling said, "Please get Kathy on the phone."

"And you just saw her last night? That's love, Luke."

"And that's meddling, McGirr. I didn't see her last night and I'd appreciate it if you didn't mention my trip to her."

McGirr looked surprised but nodded. A minute later she buzzed Darling on the phone and he pressed the second flashing button.

"Hello, Kathy. Christ, I miss you."

"When are you coming home, Luke?"

"Couple of days, honey. How're the boys?"

"The boys are fine. That job is supposed to be done Monday."

"Was that my promise?"

"Yes."

"I always keep my promises. Particularly to sexy young things."

"Just what I'd expect to hear from a racist redneck. Luke, what they're calling you has been terrible. Television. Newspapers."

"Don't worry about it. Six months from now, no one will remember a word."

"I hope not."

"Did I ever tell you that I love you?"

"Not today."

"I love you," said Darling. "Keep that with you."

"Luke. Is anything wrong?"

"No. I'll call you when I know what plane I'll be on."

"Take care, honey. I love you too."

They hung up simultaneously and Darling felt better. Some of the guilt over last night's meeting with Bea Whittaker seemed to ease from him.

At one minute to eleven, Miss McGirr advised him that Agent Dempsey had arrived.

"Send him in. And hold all calls."

Miss McGirr pushed open the door, then stepped aside to let Dempsey enter the room. He was a smallish man with a thin mustache and a pockmarked face. He wore a brown snapbrimmed hat and a checked top coat and carried a highly polished tan attaché case.

The agent's eyes met Darling's with no show of

emotion. He stepped into the office and approached the desk as the door closed behind Miss McGirr.

Dempsey took off his hat and stood in front of Darling's desk. The same plumb line of scalp, showing through the immaculate, precise part in the center of his hair.

The man from 414 Barclay Street.

"We meet again," Darling said. "Please sit down."

Dempsey put his hat on one chair, left his topcoat on, and sat in the other leather chair facing Darling's desk.

"I believe you called me to discuss the bureau's role in the handling of the Wounded Elk trial," Dempsey said. His voice was bored and professionally laconic. He pressed the spring clips on his attaché case and the cover popped open.

"That was a long time ago, Dempsey," Darling said, holding and meeting the other man's eyes. "Other things have come up since then. One. Why have you been tailing me? Two. I want a copy of that film I saw. That'll do for openers."

Dempsey smiled, slightly, at just one corner of his mouth. "One, Counselor Darling, I have not been tailing you. Two, Counselor, what film?"

"The film you let me see in the building on Barclay Street. The film that, if we had it in evidence in some of these trials, might have won them."

"I know nothing of any such film. Or any building on Barclay Street for that matter," said Dempsey.

"Goddamnit, Dempsey!" yelled Darling. He slammed his fist on the desk. "Are you crazy? Nobody can be that goddamn brazen. I saw that film. You and I talked about it on the telephone."

Dempsey just shook his head.

"You spoke about it to Colonel MacDonald. You promised him to have the film to me today. Would you like me to call Colonel MacDonald?"

Dempsey shrugged. He looked away from Darling and raised the top of his attaché case on his lap so it was propped open.

"You want to play rough, Dempsey? All right." Angrily, Darling reached for the phone, dialed nine to get an outside line, then dialed MacDonald's home number.

The phone rang once. A heavy, metallic voice echoed on the other end. "This is Colonel MacDonald on tape. Neither Karen nor I is available right now to answer the phone. At the signal, please leave your name and number and we will call you back as soon as possible."

Beeeep.

The voice. It sounded so unlike MacDonald's. Tape distortion.

"Ram, this is Luke. I've got Dempsey in my office. Call me right back, will you?"

He slammed the telephone back onto the base. "He never answers the goddamn phone but he'll call back. Then we'll see, Dempsey. In the meantime, there are some other things we can talk about. A retired cop named Mottodocio. Americans in Readiness. Bryant Marine Base in Virginia."

"I'd rather talk about films," said Dempsey slowly. He reached into his briefcase and brought out a thin glassine packet of four-by-five photographs. "For instance these. I have the original film."

He handed them forward. Even before looking at them, Darling knew what they were, but he forced himself to look at the top one. His stomach dropped inside his body. There he was, lying on top of Bea Whittaker. Her naked right breast blobbed sideways in the picture, touching the flowered spread of her couch. Darling looked at the second one. Bea Whittaker making him hard, Darling's face looking right at the camera.

At home with Assistant Attorney General of the United States Lucius Darling.

He felt as if he were going to be sick; it took great effort to put the pictures down on the desk in front of him, without tearing them into pieces.

Dempsey snapped his briefcase shut. "You may keep that set, Mr. Darling. I have the negatives. I think you were talking about playing rough."

Darling's mouth began to move before he could think of something to say. Finally, he blurted, "Dempsey, you're a bastard."

"Yes. But I'm America's bastard," Dempsey said.

He stood and took his hat from the other chair. "And now, sir, if our business is completed, I'll be on my way."

Darling looked at him, astonishment mixing with his anger and his shame. Lucius Darling. Being blackmailed in his own office. By an FBI agent.

"But . . . ," he started. He stopped. "Colonel MacDonald . . ."

"Colonel MacDonald?" said Dempsey. "I don't know any Colonel MacDonald."

The FBI man planted his hat on his head and walked toward the door. He stopped there as Darling's weak voice reached him.

"Dempsey?"

The FBI agent turned.

"What's Jericho Day?"

Dempsey met his eyes coldly, his face a blank surgical mask of disdain. "I wish you the best in your retirement, Mr. Darling," he said. He stared at Darling momentarily and, before Darling could say anything else, turned and left the office.

Darling sat at his desk, watching the door close, then looked down at the pictures before him. He spread them out and examined each one. Then he thought he was going to be sick and he reached for the wastepaper basket. He fought the nausea down and stacked the photographs up again.

Goddamn Ramsey MacDonald. Whenever you needed him . . . that tinny goddamn tape recording . . .

that metallic, echoing, brainless phone-answering robot . . . that . . .

Darling stopped in the middle of his mental reading-out of MacDonald. He reached for the phone but was interrupted.

The office door flew open and Ronald Gilpert came through as if he had been tethered outside and had finally broken free from his leash. He seemed to push a mass of air into the room ahead of him.

"Luke," he said. "I see. I see."

Darling quickly scooped up the photos, shielding them from Gilpert's view, and put them in an envelope in the top left drawer of his desk. Then he looked at the young lawyer who was shifting his weight from left foot to right foot and back to left again, like a first-grader with a bladder problem.

"Sit down, Ronny, for a minute." Darling stepped outside his office to Miss McGirr's desk.

"McGirr, who do you have in personnel?"

"What do you mean, Luke?"

"McGirr, please. There's nothing or nobody in this department you don't know. Do you have somebody in personnel?"

"I have a cousin."

"That'll do. McGirr, I want anything you can get me on Agent Calvin Dempsey. Background, assignment, anything."

"Right away."

Darling returned to the seat behind his desk and

said to Gilpert, "All right, Ronny, what do you see?"

His voice was hard and Gilpert searched the older man's face before answering.

"We blew them," he finally said.

"Blew what?"

"Every one of those four cases. Albend didn't win them. The government blew each one. There was always a critical mistake. Sometimes more than one. Filing the wrong charges. Witnesses who were perjured. Indicting everybody in a conspiracy so nobody was left to testify. Losing evidence." The words tumbled out of him, one after another, a torrent of words. "Luke, damnit, don't you see? It's as if we wanted to lose these cases intentionally and somebody found a way to do it."

Darling did not answer; he only nodded.

"Luke," said Gilpert again, annoyed because Darling was not sharing his excitement. "Luke, I think the government threw these cases. Lost them intentionally. Don't you understand?"

"It all fits," said Darling.

"What all fits?"

Instead of answering, Darling looked down at the envelope of photos in the partially opened desk drawer. He opened his side drawer and took out the thick file of reports.

As Gilpert watched, Darling opened the folder to the first sheet of paper. All Gilpert could see was a few typewritten lines that had lines drawn through them. There was a word handwritten in red at the bottom of the page but he had not learned to read upside down.

Darling took a felt-tipped pen from the holder on his desk and with a careful, even stroke, drew a circle around the word. It was the word Attorney General Walthrop had written: *Conspiracy*.

He snapped the folder shut. "You've done a good job, Ronny," he said, looking up with a small smile. "Thank you." He extended his hand for Gilpert to return to him the summary that Darling had given him the afternoon before.

"That's all?" asked Gilpert.

"Yes. Thank you. That's all," Darling answered in a dull monotone, taking the report from Gilpert and placing it on his desk.

"What are you going to do about it?"

"It'll go into my report," said Darling. "Thank you."

"Not just like that," Gilpert said.

"Just like that. You're excused." Darling looked down at the envelope of photos in the open desk drawer. *Just like that. A career could be ruined, Ronny. A marriage. A life. No. More than just one life. Not just his but Kathy's. Tommy's. Billy's. Mottodocio is already dead. No amount of revenge will bring him back.*

"Just like that," he repeated.

"Damnit, Luke, not just like that." Gilpert rose

to his feet and leaned across the desk, his face moving close to Darling's. "We were supposed to find out why we were losing. I think we did. Now you're not going to sweep it under some rug. Do you hear me? You're not, Luke. You can't."

"Did you hear *me*, Gilpert? You're excused."

Gilpert stared at Darling, then wheeled and headed for the door, foot-stomping angry. Darling looked at his back. Gilpert was thin and tall; his square bony shoulders, up around his ears, almost screamed outrage. Darling had been like that once, able to feel outrage. Able to be infuriated because somebody was doing something to America, because somebody was tampering with justice. How long ago had that been when he had been able to feel like that? How long? It couldn't have been more than a hundred years ago.

Gilpert's hand was on the doorknob.

And Lucius Darling yelled at him.

"Goddamnit," Darling shouted. "Get back here."

Gilpert turned. For the first time, he did not seem frightened by Darling's bellow. The look on his face was almost one of relief and satisfaction.

As the young lawyer walked back to the desk, Darling reached into a center drawer and turned the electronic dial that turned up the television volume, tuning it past the merely annoying to the brutally loud. Gilpert looked around at the noise as if it were an intruder, but Darling said, "Come over here," and led Gilpert to a window, looking out over 10th Street. He pressed the button on his window air conditioner. The long unused machine wheezed slowly into operation, chugged its way up to "supercool," and ground it out from there.

"Ronny. Ever since you talked to the *Washington Post*..."

Gilpert blushed.

"...stop worrying. Ever since then, everybody around here is sure you're on my shit list."

"But—"

"Shhhh. Listen to me. It's important that they go on thinking that. So much so that I'm going to fire you this afternoon."

"Fire me?"

"Ronny, this may be the most important thing you'll ever do in your life. I'm going to give you an envelope this afternoon. I don't want you to open it. But if something happens to me, *then* open it."

"I don't understand."

"You're not supposed to. Ronny, believe me." Darling clapped his big hand on the younger man's bony shoulder. "If everything goes all right, I'll rescind the firing. Chalk it up to my stress at working too hard. But if not, well, you'll know the reason why. Ronny, this is important... life and death important... and nobody can know that I'm entrusting anything to you."

Gilpert looked out the window, over the body of the air conditioner. "It has something to do with this report, doesn't it? The way we lost these cases?"

"Yes. And I apologize now for any embarrassment I cause you this afternoon. If you ever have to open that envelope, you'll understand why."

"Your word's good enough for me, Luke."

"I hoped it would be. Stay at your desk so I can find you this afternoon."

Gilpert nodded. Darling saw him out, then turned off the air conditioner and turned down the television volume. If his office were bugged, as well it might be, it was the best he could do.

His phone rang.

"Yes, McGirr."

"Dempsey, Calvin. Native of Fargo, South Dakota. Went to Annapolis. Served in the Marines in Korea. In the bureau since..."

"Never mind, McGirr. That's enough."

Darling hung up the phone. It was enough. It had all come clear now.

He picked up the telephone again, dialed nine and then Ramsey MacDonald's number.

It answered again on the first ring.

"This is Colonel MacDonald on tape. Neither Karen nor I is available right now to answer the phone. At the signal, please leave your name and number and we will call you back as soon as possible."

The voice. Tinny. Metallic. Almost echoing.
And familiar.

Beeeeep!

Slowly, Darling said, "Ram, this is Luke. I want to talk to you about Jericho Day."

He hung up the telephone, then took a large yellow pad from his desk. He inserted a sheet of carbon between the first and second pages and at the top, carefully printed with a ballpoint pen, pressing hard: JERICHO DAY—A GOVERNMENT CONSPIRACY.

The telephone buzzed. Without looking, he punched the last button and picked it up.

"What line is he on, McGirr?"

"Three."

Darling felt for the third button and pressed it. "Yes, Ram," he said.

"I think you should see the whole film, Luke."

"I think I should too."

"Come over to my house right now?" MacDonald said.

"I'll be there in two hours."

"Don't do anything foolish, Luke."

"I never do, Ram. Two hours."

Darling hung up. He wrote on his yellow lined pad for the next hour and finally stopped, sorted the sheets into originals and carbons, then taped them together at the top in two batches. He signed each sheet of both batches.

He sealed the carbons in an envelope and, with

tape, stuck them to the bottom side of his top right desk drawer. He folded the other pile of papers around the envelope of photos. He put them into a large manila envelope, which he licked to seal, then pressed down the two metal locking tabs. He signed his name three times across the envelope's flap and back, then put tape strips over the signatures so that the envelope could not be opened without destroying his signature.

He put the slim envelope into a legal accordion-style folder, then reached for the phone and called McGirr.

"Take this down and type it immediately."

"Okay."

" 'To Ronald Gilpert. For inefficiency and rank insubordination, you are discharged from government service, effective immediately.' Date it today and type my name."

"But, Luke—"

"Type it, damnit," Darling interrupted. "I want that read in exactly sixty seconds."

He sealed the legal accordion folder with package tape and then tied its strings tightly around it. From the coat rack, he took his top coat and put it on. At the door, he thought to turn off the television set but decided the hell with it.

Outside, he stomped toward Miss McGirr's desk.

"Is it done?"

"Right here. But—"

"Give me it." Darling grabbed a pen from an expensive onyx set on Miss McGirr's desk and scrawled "Lucius Darling" over the typed name at the bottom. "Do whatever you do with the other copies. I'll deliver this one personally."

He snatched up the blue sheet of paper and walked through the connecting office that led to the offices which housed his tiny task force. Gilpert was at his desk. Across the hall in another open-fronted cubicle was Willoughby. Rothblatt was separated from Gilpert by a partition, open at the top.

Darling stomped into Gilpert's cubicle. "Goddamnit, Gilpert, I'm fed up to here with your screwing up. You're fired."

Gilpert looked up and seemed almost to forget himself in the fluster caused by Darling's anger.

"But—"

"No buts. Here's your goddamn notice. Don't even pack. Just get out of here. They'll mail you your junk." Darling turned to walk away. He stopped and turned back. "Here's your report. It's as worthless as everything else you've done around here. Take it with you. Maybe you can paper your walls with it."

He tossed the folder onto Gilpert's desk and turned quickly away, but outside the cubicle, he stopped and spoke loudly.

"I know you're all listening. Well, I want you to know that I could even put up with a bigmouth leaking stuff to the press. But I can't put up with stupidity and incompetence to go along with disloyalty. Any of you who want to keep working in Justice better remember that."

Darling walked off, heavy-footed, down the corridor back toward McGirr's office. Without a word, he passed her desk and went out into the hall. He felt sorry for Gilpert and someday, with luck, he would apologize in a proper fashion. But America right now was more important than Gilpert's feelings.

He walked to a nearby garage where a car that was permanently assigned to his office was parked.

Five minutes later, he was driving out into the Maryland countryside, toward Ramsey MacDonald's home.

CHAPTER ***** 23

The Near Future

WHEN HIS TELEGRAM TO THE ATTORNEY general demanding the file on Lucius Darling had failed to get an immediate response, Lonzo Gates had called a clipping service he occasionally used and asked them to dig out everything they could on Darling and his Justice Department study of radical trials.

They had warned it might take weeks; he had told them he had only days and offered to pay them more than their usual fee, but here it was Tuesday and he had gotten nothing from them.

And the phone rang again.

Even as he said hello, even before the caller spoke, Gates knew who it was. Yes, it was...

"...Joshua at the magazine."

"Yes, Joshua."

"It's deadline time. Is your Jericho piece done yet?"

"Not quite," Gates said.

"Ummmm. That's bad. Very bad," the editor said.

"Look. I'm just waiting for some stuff from the Justice Department. It's coming under the Freedom of Information Act. I expected to have it by today. But it's got to be here this week. I'll have the Jericho Day piece for you for next issue. For sure."

"Is that a promise?" Joshua said after a long, threatening pause.

"Yes. You have my word."

"All right. I'm going to put a piece in this issue promoting your Jericho story. A big conspiracy, you say?"

"Yes. The biggest," Gates said as he poured himself another drink.

"Okay," Joshua said. "But Friday for sure."

"You'll have it," Gates said.

Joshua hung up and Gates went back to watching the soap opera on television. Screw *Mossback*, screw Joshua, and screw that whole gang of three-piece-suited clones that hung around the place. They were going to fire him anyway, but he would beat them out of one more week's pay and then...

And then what?

The more he thought about it, the more relaxed he became. He had a few bucks in the bank. He could write a column for someone else. Maybe even a book. There had been a lot of interest over the years in a book of his firsthand reminiscences. Why couldn't he write a book? Tom Wolfe had written a lot of books, and he was certainly a hell of a lot better writer than Tom Wolfe ever was. And he dressed better too.

He tried to think of a title for the book. After another drink, he had one: *Life on the Line*. By Lonzo Gates. The father of modern American journalism tells you how it was.

It sounded beautiful. He'd get a publisher who would send him out on a six-month national tour. The best hotels. Wine, women, and song. He would do radio shows, TV interviews. He would tell the truth about that lesbian bitch he married. He would be shocking and outrageous and totally charming and when he was done, *Mossback* and those pin-striped munchkins would come crawling back looking for him to write for them again.

Well, not a chance. He was done with ingrates.

He must have dozed off because the sound of the doorbell startled him.

It was a delivery boy who held a large manila envelope.

"You Gates?"

"Yeah."

"From the clipper service."

"Clipping service, you mean."

"Whatever. Sign here."

He pushed a coffee-stained receipt pad to Gates, who scrawled his signature and took the manila envelope. The young man stood there examining Gates's signature until Gates realized that the man was waiting for a tip.

"Sorry. I'm a little short today."

The delivery boy nodded and looked past Gates into the littered apartment. "Yeah. I can tell you had to lay off your cleaning lady."

"Hey, pal, get paid by whoever hired you, huh?" Gates said as he slammed the door.

Behind him, he heard the deliverer kick it once, hard, but Gates ignored it and took the envelope over to his old metal desk. The envelope was disappointingly thin. When he opened it, only a half-dozen Xeroxes of newspaper clippings spilled onto the table.

He looked at the first one and sat back heavily in the chair.

"Holy shit," he said aloud. "Holy shit."

CHAPTER ***** 24

The Mid-1970s

Friday, October 28: The Twelfth Day

COL. RAMSEY A. MACDONALD, USMC, MET
Darling at the door of his sprawling, split-level home.
He was dressed in a long-sleeved sports shirt tailored
through the chest and waist and light tan doubleknit
slacks that flared slightly at the cuff. He wore highly
polished brown loafers.

He smiled when he saw Darling.

"Hello, Luke."

"Jericho Day," said Darling.

"It's going to be that way?" When there was no
answer, he said, "Come on in."

MacDonald turned and left Darling to follow
him downstairs to a door which he opened with a
key and which entered into a large study. The walls
were lined with books, the same red, white, and blue
color scheme as Bea Whittaker's bookshelves. At the

end of the room was a small movie screen, extending silvery-white upwards from a blue metal cylinder that was both carrying case and base. At the other end of the room was a small projector. It was turned off.

Darling stood in the doorway. MacDonald went behind his desk at the far side of the room and sat down. He looked like a young doctor, catching up on correspondence after office hours. Darling looked around.

"It's all right, Luke. Karen's away. Visiting relatives."

"Jericho Day," Darling said.

"Was that you last night at the base?" asked MacDonald.

Darling nodded.

"I thought so. You hurt a good man. He might not see again."

"Fuck him," Darling said. "Jericho Day."

"What do you think you know, Luke?"

"I know this. That Dempsey served with you in Korea. That somehow the two of you—him in the FBI and you working out of the White House—managed to fix it so the government blew the cases against the radicals."

MacDonald smiled. "Now why would we want to do that?"

"That's what I didn't understand either," said Darling. "It kept coming at me. We're losing these cases intentionally. But I couldn't figure why. Of course, I didn't know you were in it. I figured Dempsey, but I didn't know what. It was just too complicated. People tailing me. The film. A training film, isn't it?"

"Partly," MacDonald said.

"And Americans in Readiness. I couldn't figure them out. Mottodocio said they were getting funds from some private foundation and I couldn't figure out why anybody would want to fund air raid wardens."

MacDonald laughed and began to fill a pipe from a wood and glass humidor on his desk. Darling still stood in the doorway.

"But they're not air raid wardens, are they? They're just supposed to be ready at a moment's notice to identify your targets. All the radicals you sprung. But what was the idea, Ram? Why not just let them go to jail?"

MacDonald sucked deeply on his pipe. "Even with luck, the government wasn't sending them to jail," he said. He blew his smoke toward the ceiling. "Remember the riots in the sixties? Remember how they stopped?"

He was satisfied the pipe was lit and he put it into an ashtray.

"And don't give me that soft-witted bilge that they stopped because we started to do something about conditions in the slums. Crap. They stopped because the cops started shooting back. All of a sudden, the rules of the game were changed. It just wasn't so much fun anymore to go around pegging bottles and bullets and bags filled with human shit at cops because the cops started to shoot back and to bust heads. Exit rioting from the American scene."

"Social comment from Ramsey MacDonald," Darling said sarcastically. "So what?"

"So this. It's fashionable today to be a radical. They call it radical chic. The government tolerates it, the press praises it, the kids get sucked up in it. The Communists drew up the program and now, forty years later, we're finally seeing it start to play out. America's going down the tubes." He picked up the pipe again.

"And?"

"And we're going to take the fun out of being a radical. They're trying to shoot down America. We're going to shoot back." MacDonald bit hard into the mouthpiece.

Darling shook his head.

"Too many of them, Ram. You'll be killing for the next nine years."

MacDonald returned the shake of the head. "They didn't have to shoot every rioter to stop rioting. You don't have to shoot every radical to stop radicalism. Luke, would you believe it? One hundred and sixty-three people. If they go, the radical movement stops."

"Never," Darling said.

"Goddamnit, Luke, you saw it yourself at the arts center the other night. Those weren't radicals. They were silly twits who like to play at it, who like to yell 'tear down America' because America never seems to run out of cheeks to turn. The day they find out that the game's over and America's not going to be torn down, that's the day they all go into something new. Like protecting the fucking seal or something. Radicalism will be out. Out. Dead and buried. It only takes a hundred and sixty-three."

"Where'd you get the hit men?"

"Hit men? This isn't the Mafia, Luke. This isn't some kind of guinea gang shootout. Call them patriots."

"Call them killers. Where'd you get them?"

"I wasn't advisor to the officers association all these years for nothing, Luke. They're ex-Marines ... mostly men I served with. Some I went to the academy with. Others I got to know. People like me ... like you ... disgusted with the country going under." He puffed the pipe again and leaned back in the chair. "Oh, there were problems. We trained them down at Bryant for the elimination of spies closeup. They thought initially it was for Russians. That's the way we could weed out anybody who couldn't hack it. Later on, the ones who stayed didn't really care about Russians or not Russians."

"That's what you think," said Darling. "Do you

really think they'll kill Americans?"

"I thought Mottodocio would have told you that. They're pros. A pro doesn't care who."

The name brought another question to Darling's mind. "Mottodocio. Was that you?"

MacDonald shook his head. "They caught him on the base. Olsen put him off the road. He's the one you blinded. At least you evened that score for yourself, Luke." He saw Darling's disbelieving look and said, "Not a copout, Luke. If they had called me for instructions, I would have told them to do just what they did. If intent means anything to you, Mr. Lawyer, I'd have had the intent."

"And then you told your men to close down the base?" Darling said.

"As soon as they could."

"I hope it screwed up your plans."

"It did," MacDonald said.

"It was a shit thing to do with Bea Whittaker. The photographs."

"Hey, Luscious Baby, that was your dick in her, not mine. Anyway, that was Dempsey's end of the operation. All those people, Americans in Readiness, he got them from FBI files and interviews. You know how the bureau is. It's got thousands of people all over the country who feed them information just so they can feel important. Well, these people think they're doing that, working for the FBI."

"And they identify the target and your killer knocks it off."

"That's about it. Luke, we're not talking about Americans and we're not talking about thousands of people. One hundred and sixty-three people. That's shit, Luke. A drop in the bucket. How many people are going to die at how many more Clark States or Wounded Elks or Panther shootouts because these goddamn radical bastards are allowed to run free and poison our world?"

"I was young then, but I think they talked like that once before. In Hitler's Germany," Darling said.

MacDonald shrugged. "When'd you guess me?"

"I didn't guess. Dempsey kind of tipped it. He was just too cocky. And then your voice on your phone recorder. I knew then who narrated the film; it had that same echo sound to it. And then I remembered something...how you showed up after each little crisis. You were out of my life for a couple of years and then, just when I got this job, you butted back into it. Old apple-eating Ramsey MacDonald who was such a whiz at calculus, well, I just didn't believe you were so damned innocent about radicals. And suddenly it all came together. When I was on your base down there, I saw it, but I didn't understand it until the next day. A school for assassins. And then I realized what I'd been afraid to think before...we lost those cases intentionally."

"We blew them to create the right public climate

for Jericho Day," MacDonald said.

"One day?" Darling asked.

"You've forgotten your Bible, Luke. When Joshua took down the walls of Jericho, he didn't take it down one stone at a time. If he had, the people inside would have repaired them one stone at a time. He took it all down at once. We're taking down this entire radical movement at once. One day. Jericho Day."

"Ram, you know you'll never get away with it. America'll hunt you down."

"I told you that you should watch the end of the film." MacDonald hit a switch and the room turned dark. From behind his desk, he pressed a button and the movie projector lit up and began to whir.

Darling stood in the doorway as the picture flickered onto the screen. The sound went from a stop, through a rising curve of noise, until it was again Ramsey MacDonald's voice, tinny, metallic, echoing.

It started up where the film had ended for Darling the first time he had seen it.

"Poison," said MacDonald's voice over the face of the pug-nosed actress who had been agitating for prison riots. "And the courts never took care of it and the police were afraid, so could you blame me? With all the yelling you're probably hearing right now, think of who is a prisoner and who isn't. What are they yelling about? Who is your real enemy?"

The picture of the pug-nosed actress faded. Onto the screen, first at long focus so that it looked like just a dot, then with the camera zooming in on him until his face and medaled chest covered the entire screen, was Ramsey MacDonald, wearing Marine dress blues.

The echo chamber was gone from his voice now on the film as he said:

"I am Colonel Ramsey MacDonald and I am responsible for today's events. For Jericho Day.

"This has not been an easy thing for me to do. I grew up, as you, loving America. I fought for it in wartime and stood for it in peacetime. I have a wife and a family and a career. But all the while, while I enjoyed my family, while I loved my work, I saw all around me the signs of an America that was coming apart. And I saw that this coming-apart was not the sign of age or of ill-use or of not being fit anymore, but that it was the work of a small handful to whom America's dream of a people living in freedom and justice was hateful.

"I will not say that these people were Communists. There have been too many false prophets crying 'Communist, Communist,' and all together they have weakened the anti-Communist cause. So I will not say they were Communists.

"But I will say that they could not have followed the Communist program for the destruction of

America any more carefully than if they were paid agents of the Kremlin.

"Like you, I saw them and was sickened. But like you, I sat back and thought, well, sooner or later, America will stop them. Sooner or later, America will come to its senses and hush the voices of these purveyors of hate and anarchy.

"And I waited. And America waited. And nothing happened. The voices grew louder and stronger. More listened, because they took the silence of the rest of us as agreement with what these animals were saying.

"And our children died on campuses. And our policemen were degraded. And our elderly were mugged and raped and tortured. And America sank slowly down, deeper, into a hole from which it could never climb. And so I created Jericho Day.

"It was my idea totally. No one else involved had any idea of what they were doing. No political figures supported me; no agents of the law. There is a file in my office which will prove this and I would prove it too, were I to be here to speak out.

"However, I will not be. I know that what I have done is technically unlawful and like a good officer in combat—which I was—I have decided to mete out my own punishment. When you see this, I will be dead. But I hope America will live."

The camera began to pan back farther and farther, zooming down until the colonel disappeared again into a little dot of blackness against the bright white screen. And then, over the dot, just before it vanished, came MacDonald's voice again, tinny and echo-chambered.

"God bless America."

MacDonald hit a switch. The projector stopped. He hit another and the room lights came back on.

"Well, Luke, what do you think?"

"It'll knock 'em dead in Podunk. Tintype tyrants always do. It would've been even better if you promised to get the trains running on time. That worked for Mussolini."

"Luke, you don't believe that. You know me too well." He stood up behind his desk. "You've got to forget about all this for your report at Justice. Turn in some crap and go home to Troy. A few more weeks is all I need."

"I think you're crazy, Colonel."

"You might not get out of here alive, Luke," said MacDonald.

"You know me too, Ram. Do you ever remember me being careless? Do you think I came here without being backed up somehow?"

"I tried to tout you off it, Luke. I even tipped the press, hoping Walthrop would drop the project."

"I was in, Ram. I was given a job. I do my jobs."

"Then I tried to get you to join us. That night at the arts center."

"I know. But killing civilians was never my idea of justice."

"Luke, you've got to keep quiet about this."

"Goodbye, Ram. God have mercy on your soul." Darling turned from the doorway and began to walk away. Behind him, he heard MacDonald shout:

"With us or with America's enemies!"

"Goodbye, Ram," Darling called and went up the stairs. He looked his car over carefully before starting it up and driving back to Washington.

It was late afternoon when he got to his office. Miss McGirr was at her desk, but she did not speak to him. He chucked her under the chin as he walked by.

"Cheer up, McGirr. Things are getting better."

The television was still flickering light across his office as he went in and sat behind his desk. With the key on his ring, he unlocked the side desk drawer and removed the thick folder of reports from his assistants. He pulled out the top drawer and peeled off the envelope he had taped to the bottom of it.

There was no longer any question of what to do. He would take his secret Jericho Day report and the task force report to Walthrop. He would tell him what they contained and he would recommend the immediate arrest of Colonel MacDonald and FBI Agent Calvin Dempsey.

He had been given a job; he had carried it out. Even Kathy would understand. And if those photographs ever came into her hands, she would still understand.

He opened the envelope and as he spread the report out in front of him, he glanced up at the TV screen. The word "BULLETIN" caught his eye.

He fumbled in the center drawer for the electronic control and turned up the volume. A still picture came onto the screen showing people lying in the street.

The announcer's voice:

"Four students and one policeman were killed today in Jersey City, New Jersey, as student rioters at St. Luke's College charged a police barricade that had been raised outside the school's library.

"Students hurled bottles at police and when both sides began scuffling, shots were fired. Students broke and fled. Four of them lay mortally wounded. One policeman was killed instantly by a bullet in his head."

The film cut to shots of the students fighting with police. Then a face filled the screen. A face Darling recognized.

The announcer's voice reported: "A student leader had this to say . . ."

Darling knew the face as it began to speak. It was Blalock, who had run the meeting two nights before to protest against Darling and his Justice Department study. Now he was saying:

"We students were only trying to reaffirm the

right of free speech on this campus. The racist and fascist police department saw fit to answer our requests with gunshots. But this is only a first step. The struggle for academic freedom will continue at this school. If tomorrow more die, even more will step forward to grab their banners and raise them overhead. We will not stop until we win."

The announcer's voice again:

"In Washington to address a student meeting, noted defense attorney Harold Albend had this comment: 'The corruption and inefficiency of the Jersey City police department is well known. It is a stench in the nostrils of any American who cares for justice. I am leaving immediately for Jersey City to offer my services to those students who have been arrested unlawfully in this battle for academic freedom.'"

The announcer: "We return now to our program in progress."

Darling turned down the volume. Five more dead. And just the start. How many copycat killings around the country? How many more campuses would Blalock be free to visit, pretending to be a student while he fomented violence? How many more speaking engagements would Harold Albend have to cancel to go defend the poor children who had been lured into their illegal acts by his words and those of his camp followers?

Ten years from now, would young Thomas Darling be on one of those campuses? Would William

Darling be standing across a barricade, looking at police guns, shouting meaningless slogans, waiting for someone to start the charge?

Lucius Darling, assistant attorney general of the United States of America, stared at the silent television set for long minutes. Then he looked down again at the report on his desk.

He had a few things to do.

He buzzed Miss McGirr on the intercom. "Get me a flight to Troy. The sooner, the better. And don't be mad at me anymore. Gilpert'll be all right."

He pressed another phone button, dialed nine and got an outside line. From a file card inside his appointment book, he got the telephone number of Ronald Gilpert and dialed it.

Gilpert answered it like a man sitting by the telephone.

"Ronny, this is Luke."

"Yes, sir."

"Do you still have that envelope?"

"Yes, sir. Right here."

"Do you have a fireplace in your apartment?"

"Uh, yes."

"Fire going?"

"Yes."

"Put the envelope in the fire. Right now. I'll wait."

Darling heard the phone being set down. He

heard rummaging around the room and then Gilpert was back on the line.

"I did, sir."

"Did you look at it?"

"No. I followed orders," Gilpert said.

"Good for you. Report back to work on Monday. I am rescinding your dismissal which was never processed anyway, and in fact am writing a letter of commendation to the attorney general on your behalf."

"I take it, Luke, that everything is turning out all right."

"Fine, Ronny, fine."

Darling hung up, feeling good for the first time in ten days.

McGirr called and told him he had been booked on a 6:45 P.M. flight from Dulles.

"Thanks, McGirr. By the way, rescind Gilpert's firing and write a memo to Walthrop praising him for outstanding work."

"Yes, sir," she said, then added hesitantly, "Good for you, Luke."

With a smile on his face, Darling got another outside line and called his home number in Troy.

"Hello."

"Kathy. I'm all done here. Everything's wrapped up."

"Good. When are you coming home?"

"My plane comes in at ten-thirty tonight in Vandalia. I'll meet you at the airport cocktail lounge."

"I may assault you right there," she said.

"It's not assault if the victim consents," he said. "I love you."

"I love you too, lawyer," she echoed and hung up.

McGirr brought in the rescission order and the commendation for Gilpert and Darling signed them both with a quick flourish of his pen.

"Take the rest of the day off, McGirr," he said.

"Big of you. Ten minutes till quitting time."

"It's not always I get ready to leave government service. Go now, will you?"

After McGirr left, Darling looked again at the handwritten report entitled JERICHO DAY: A GOVERNMENT CONSPIRACY.

He locked his office door, then returned to his desk. Using his butane cigarette lighter, he ignited the first of the yellow pages. He dropped the flaming sheet into the wastepaper basket. Slowly, one at a time, he dropped in all the rest of the report he had written that afternoon, the report he had given to Gilpert, the report outlining what he had known and suspected of the Jericho Day plot.

He opened the file folder of the reports his assistants had prepared for him. As he pulled out the first page, his initial memo to the attorney general, he smiled at the circle he had made around the word "conspiracy" and dropped it, too, into the fire.

He watched until all the papers had burned out, then turned back to his desk and drafted a note:

"McGirr. Have Gilpert write a summary of all this documentation for Walthrop. Have him draw these conclusions. It is government ineptitude that has blown these cases for us, ineptitude so enormous that sometimes it seems the government has tried to lose the cases. But simply that. Ineptitude. No plots. No conspiracies. Tell Gilpert to recommend a training program, not only for our attorneys, but for FBI agents who will be involved in such cases. Unless our men are better trained, they're going to keep losing to second-rate lawyers like Harold Albend. Sign the report for me, and I'll talk to you next week. Luke."

He put the note neatly atop the folder in the center of his desk blotter.

Only one more thing to do—pick up the telephone and call Ramsey MacDonald. Ram would be shocked at the idea of Lucius Darling admitting that someone else was right. But MacDonald was . . . this time. A hundred and sixty-three lives now; to save thousands later; to save maybe a nation; to save maybe Thomas Darling and William Darling.

He dialed nine and then MacDonald's number.

The phone rang once and was answered:

"This is Colonel Ramsey MacDonald on tape." The voice was slow, heavy, pauses between phrases. "I am . . . out of town . . . for the day."

"Shit," said Darling, holding the phone to his ear, wondering if there were any other place he could reach MacDonald. He could think of none so he hung up.

Later, over his second martini on the plane to Vandalia Airport, Darling realized that he should have left MacDonald a taped message. He should have done that. Darling could have waited for the beep and said something like, "Okay, Ram, you win. Luke." That would have given MacDonald a kick.

Strange. There had been no beep. Nor had MacDonald asked for messages.

Darling was still puzzling over this at 10:15 P.M., when his plane touched down at Vandalia. He stepped down from the plane onto the tarmac outside the airport terminal.

He looked toward the terminal. Coming through the door from the passenger's waiting room was a familiar face, but it wasn't Kathy's.

Lucius Darling saw Bea Whittaker's pretty but cheap face approach him. She was happy, still thinking she was practicing locating important people in case of Communist emergencies. This face she knew very well. She smiled as she came toward him.

Darling decided. If he had to, he would tell her he was not mad at her for tricking him into those pictures. She had been used too, he realized.

He saw her smile. She reached out for him and touched his shoulder with two fingers.

He tried to smile back.

But there was no time. At that moment, the top of his head was blown off by a young, freckled, red-headed man in a checked shirt who had sidled up to him with a .45-caliber automatic in his hand and fired at Darling from one inch away.

CHAPTER ★★★★★ 25

The Near Future

"MR. GATES, ARE YOU ALONE?"

"Who wants to know?"

The man in the hallway outside Lonzo Gates's apartment flashed an official card inside a leather billfold. Gates looked at it, then up at the man's long weathered face, his neatly parted thinning hair. The man said nothing.

"All right, I'm alone. What can I do for you?"

"Someone wishes to talk to you," the man said stiffly. With an amount of force that was firm without being assaulting, the man escorted Gates back into his own apartment. Before Gates could protest, another man came in through the door and closed it behind him. Gates immediately recognized the young, almost-boyish face of the attorney general of the United States.

He nodded to Gates, did not offer to shake hands, and said simply: "I want to tell you about Jericho Day." He was holding a copy of the latest issue of

Mossback, opened to a page which promoted contents of the next issue. One item read: "Next issue, Lonzo Gates tears the cover from Jericho Day, a government conspiracy." Gates had seen it for the first time that afternoon.

The attorney general omitted some names along the way, but still the telling took almost two hours. The story ended with Lucius Darling dead on the tarmac outside the Vandalia Airport terminal.

Gates had not said a word during the entire recitation. He had questions—questions by the score, by the hundreds—but he caught the sense that the attorney general just wanted to tell the story in his own time, in his own way. The big man with the federal ID stood the entire while, leaning against the front wall of the apartment, looking as if he had heard it all before.

Finally, the attorney general stopped. During his two-hour talk, he had not stopped to smoke a cigarette or to ask for coffee or a drink. Gates had kept filling his glass from the bottle of Southern Comfort on the dirty, burn-marred coffee table between the two men. It took him a moment to realize that the story was over and the attorney general was done.

Then Gates asked, "Is that it?"

The other man nodded.

"But what happened? Why didn't they carry off Jericho Day?"

"Because the young attorney who worked for Lucius Darling did not follow instructions," the attorney general said.

The Mid-1970s

Friday, October 28: The Twelfth Day

It was almost midnight when the telephone rang in the apartment of Ronald Gilpert. The young attorney had not been asleep; instead, he had been staring at the fireplace where a fire of artificial logs crackled noisily but threw off little usable heat. The apartment was chilly. The brown cardboard folder that Lucius Darling had given him that day lay across his lap, still unopened.

At the last minute, while talking to Darling on the telephone, Gilpert had been unable to just toss the envelope into the fire. Something, some instinct, some hunch had stopped him. But a warring conviction, a loyalty to a man he had come to trust, had prevented him from opening the envelope.

So he had sat for hours with the envelope on his lap, and he had finally decided to follow Darling's instructions and to burn it. Then the telephone rang.

It was Max Rothblatt.

"Ronny, have you heard?"

"Heard what?"

Warren Murphy

"Oh, shit. I'm sorry," Rothblatt said. "Terrible news. Luke Darling is dead."

Gilpert could not speak for long seconds.

"Ronny. Are you all right? Are you there?"

"I'm here," Gilpert finally said. "How'd it happen?"

"He was shot. Murdered."

Again, the silence came. Without his knowing why, the tears began to run down Ronald Gilpert's boyish face. Then he asked, "Where? Who did it?"

"His airport in Ohio. I just heard it from McGirr. The cops aren't talking, but it looks like some husband of some girlfriend of Darling's... something like that. A messy love thing, but the killer got away so nobody knows for sure."

"I don't believe it," Gilpert said slowly.

"What do you mean?" Rothblatt said.

"Luke wouldn't be involved like that," Gilpert answered.

Rothblatt said, "I thought you didn't like him. After what happened today."

"You thought wrong," Gilpert said.

"Are you going to be all right?"

"Yes. I'm fine."

Gilpert hung up the telephone and carried the folder to the kitchen table, where he sat down and opened it under the bright overhead light. There were six sheets of yellow lined paper inside, stapled together, filled with Darling's small crabbed handwriting.

Gilpert read the title:

JERICHO DAY—A GOVERNMENT CONSPIRACY

He nodded his head.

A small white envelope slipped from the center of the stack of pages. It was sealed, and Gilpert opened it with a kitchen knife. The first glance at the photos made him sit back in his chair; he felt his breath sucking from his lungs.

Then he glanced quickly through the photographs of Lucius Darling with Bea Whittaker and put the photos back into the envelope and pushed it across the table, as far away from him as he could. Then he smoothed out the pile of yellow pages and began to read.

When Ramsey MacDonald let himself into his dark house at 3:00 A.M., he immediately felt—without knowing why—that there was someone inside. But before he could get to his study, where he kept a revolver for self-defense, he felt the muzzle of a pistol press into the back of his neck.

"You bastard. You killed Luke."

Maybe it was something in the sound of the voice; maybe it was the slight tremble that he heard, but MacDonald said casually, "Mind if I face my accuser?'' and reached out and flipped on the light switch that flooded the entrance hall with light.

He knew then that the man would not shoot, and he turned and saw a young earnest man, holding a gun at him, tears streaming down his face.

"Who are you?" MacDonald asked. If he had to, he decided, he could get the gun away from this kid without being shot. If he had to.

"I'm Ronald Gilpert. I work ... worked for Luke. And you killed him. And I'm going to kill you."

MacDonald shook his head and smiled sadly. "A lot of people killed Lucius Darling," he said. "And I don't think you'll kill me. Not without hearing me out."

He saw the pistol waver slowly in the young man's hands, its tip lowered. It took only a simple move, learned years before in Marine boot camp, to disarm young Gilpert. MacDonald examined the gun for a moment, before looking at Gilpert.

"And now we'll talk," MacDonald said.

The Near Future

There was a lot more to the story, the attorney general of the United States told Lonzo Gates. But basically, he said, it boiled down to the reality that the Marine officer convinced the young attorney that Lucius Darling had actually been killed by the same forces that had terrorized America.

If there had been no terrorism, no radical dissenters, no America-haters, Lucius Darling would have been alive still. The Marine might have been the instrument of his death, but the root cause was the dangerous radicals still roaming free.

And then the attorney general stopped talking again, and after a while Gates asked him: "And this lawyer believed that hogwash?"

The attorney general nodded. "Now I've told you all that I know. You tell me what you know."

Gates grinned sourly as he drank from his nearly-full glass of liqueur.

"Until you came here, I didn't know anything. I hadn't even know that Darling was dead until I got some clippings last week from my clipping service. But I didn't have anything."

"What about this piece in *Mossback*?" the attorney general said, holding up the current issue.

"If what we say is private..." Gates said, "not to leave this room?"

The attorney general nodded.

"I figured the magazine was going to can me, so I was stringing them along. I didn't have any story to write. Hell, until you came here, I still hadn't."

"How did you find out about Jericho Day in the

first place?'' the attorney general asked.

"Some guy called my radio program and dropped the name to me in a phone call. But I never knew who it was and never heard from him again." The attorney general looked at the lawman standing by the door but Gates did not notice. The reporter whistled softly under his breath. "Wheew. This is the damnedest story in all history. Darling turns out to be a hero. But what happened to all the people? The Marine. The young lawyer. Jericho Day got canceled? How was that?"

"Sort of," the attorney general said as he rose and walked to the apartment window and looked down into the street five stories below.

"What do you mean, 'sort of'?" When there was no answer, Gates said, "Well, try this. Who was that guy who called my radio program in the first place?"

The attorney general whirled back. "Just somebody who found out something that wasn't healthy for him and managed to make the call before he was found out."

He stared at Gates for a moment, until the reporter nodded.

"Something's confusing me," Gates said. "Why are you telling me all this now?"

"Because the president of the United States thought you ought to know."

"The president?" Gates repeated, unable to hide

his shock or confusion. He shrugged his shoulders. "The president? Why?"

"Because he thought it was important for you to know why you were going to die," the attorney general said. He began to walk toward the door.

Maybe he didn't hear him right, Gates thought. What was he talking about? He tried to get to his feet, but there was that other guy in the room... what was his name?... Dempsey. That was it, an FBI agent named Dempsey, and he would have a few words to say to the FBI brass about Agent Dempsey. But now there was an automatic in Dempsey's hand and it had a long thing... what did they call that? ... a silencer on the end of it. And then the gun was aimed at him and Gates heard a little splat.

And then he saw or heard nothing more.

Dempsey did not bother to inspect the body or check his handiwork. Dead was dead. But he went quickly through the shabby efficiency apartment, scooping up all the papers he could find strewn about, and dumping them into a plastic shopping bag he took from his back trousers pocket.

"We'd better get out of here," he finally said.

"Yes," agreed Ronald Gilpert, attorney general of the United States. "Timing is everything now."

They were across the Hudson River, driving south in their unmarked car on the New Jersey Turnpike, when Dempsey stopped at a rest area and Gilpert went to use a roadside telephone.

A stuffy voice answered, "The White House."

"Attorney General Gilpert. Let me speak to the president, please."

Gilpert heard the phone being placed down and then the soft murmur of voices. The phone was picked up again and the familiar voice said, "Yes, Ronny."

"Gates is done. But he didn't know anything."

"Good," the president said.

Gilpert glanced at his watch. "Do you know what time it is, sir?" he said.

After a moment's hesitation, the president said, "It's just after midnight."

"Jericho Day," said Ronald Gilpert.

"And God bless America," said Ramsey Mac-Donald, president of the United States.

▪ HarperPaperbacks *By Mail*

Craig Thomas, internationally celebrated author, has written these four best selling thrillers you're sure to enjoy. Each has all the intricacy and suspense that are the hallmark of a great thriller. Don't miss any of these exciting novels.

Buy All 4 and $ave.
When you buy all four the postage and handling is *FREE*. You'll get these novels delivered right to door with absolutely no charge for postage, shipping and handling.

EMERALD DECISION
A sizzling serpentine thriller—Thomas at the top of his form.